Deception By Blood
Book: I

Written by: S.N. Miner

Deception By Blood Book: 1
Deceptionbyblood.com
Copyright ©2016 S.N.Miner

Cover Design by Ronda Clarke

Published by the author, S.N.M Publishing.

All rights reserved. No part of this book may be used or reproduced without written consent of the publisher.

Original Concept: 2001
Final Cut: 2016

ISBN 978-0-9973208-0-0

"Never Escaping
The Burden Of Time"

{I}: The Resurrection

Hooves trampled the ground. The horses left clouds of dust in their wake; dirt divots were tossed behind them. The day grew dim, light fading out through the gaps in the tree limbs. The sun was disappearing behind the mountain that carved out the horizon ahead.

Arrays of shadows were cast over the three traveling horses and riders. The people wore hooded cloaks, hiding their faces. The smaller person in the lead grasped the reins and held on as the horse dodged a large rock.

They traveled at the horses' full potential, as if in pursuit of the sun escaping into darkness. As they drew closer, it became apparent that there was a large cave opening at the base of the chiseled mountain.

The broad shouldered, heavyset man riding just behind the lead rider shouted, "That must be the entrance to the cave!" His husky voice cut across the wind. The other two riders exchanged glances.

Shortly, the horses slowed to the mountain in front of them.

The head rider quickly dismounted and ran up to the cavern edge. The cloak's hood dropped, revealing the long dark ponytail of a young woman with lovely features. She had high cheekbones, a small round nose, full lips, a small chin, and shapely eyebrows. Though she was a petite woman, she walked upright with bold confidence. A smile came across her lush lips as she turned to the others. Her dark green eyes reflected in the dim light as did her soft complexion.

"No door, no gates? Just a cave!" she exclaimed.

Having secured his and her horses' bridles to a tree, the taller, thinner man walked over to her.

"Were you expecting more from this trip?" His voice was casual and he smiled, showing his crowded teeth, and then he removed his hood. He had choppy blonde hair, perhaps cut with a knife that shaped his slender face. His bushy blonde eyebrows came low over his green eyes. He had thin lips and a pointed chin. He also appeared to be a few years older than the woman. His mannerism was less than respectful as he looked down at her.

"Well, it just seems too strange. We're looking for treasure, and it's never this easy to walk into a tomb!" The woman had responded with excitement, as she adjusted her shoulder bag.

The other man that was with them had dark hair with a beard around his middle-aged face. His head was squared, as were his shoulders. He was a few inches shorter than the blonde man, but looked twice as muscular. His eyes were dark, maybe brown. He had walked over to them and replied, "Myiako is always looking for a challenge, ever since she beat that gang to that prized jewel a couple of years ago." He had a tendency to slouch as he walked to show his unconfident demeanor.

"That's not all true," she responded. "You guys get some credit for helping me." Her voice could have had less volume for such an inhabited area.

The young woman, Myiako, smiled at her two colleagues and began to enter the cave. The men followed with caution behind the hasty woman.

The taller man lit an oil lamp with a match to see Myiako walking ahead.

"It looks alright, guys, I don't see any traaaaaaaps!!!" she screamed as she fell down into a hole.

The other two ran over to look down the large hole. Myiako was about ten feet below, lying on a pile of bones and other remains. Her brown pants and white button shirt could be seen under her cloak from the awkward position in which she had fallen.

"AAAAHHHHH!" she screamed after coming face-to-face with a human skull.

"Hey Myi, keep it down, we'll get you out of there."

"Why should I keep it down? I don't think we'll find anything alive around here!" she responded, trying to gain footing on the unstable mound.

"Gross, ewwww…guys hurry up!"

A rope was then lowered to the young woman and she was pulled back to cave level. They helped her stand up.

"So, what are we looking for anyways?" wondered the blonde-haired man, as he watched her brush off her pants and cloak.

"Come on, Slayn, you don't even know where you are?" she responded, making the final adjustments to her clothes.

"No, can't you tell that Torru and I just enjoy following you on these dangerous explorations?" responded Slayn.

"If there are no further comments, let's find the casket," said Myiako.

"Uhh…casket, you say?" asked Torru, who was the heavy set man.

"Yeah, this is the supposed entrance of the Tomb of the Vampire, Draish-Jauri," explained Myiako, as she dug around in her bag for her oil lamp.

"We might need more light," she said.

"Wait!" interrupted Torru, "A vampire's tomb? This sounds real dangerous."

"Come on guys; don't chicken out on me now. I said tomb, not lair. We have faced much worse things than dead vampire bones," she said and lit the lamp with a match.

The glow of another lamp that Myi lit illuminated the path ahead into the desolate cave before them.

"Guess that's our way to go," Myiako told the others.

They began slowly down the cavern path. The light from the entrance slowly diminished, as they were being engulfed by darkness, their only protection being the glowing flames of their lamps.

After walking for a while, Myiako broke the silence.

"At least there are no real traps."

"Hold up…" Torru said, stopping to draw his handgun. "What's that?" He then walked forward a few paces with his other hand out. With a sign of relief, he walked back to the others.

"Just a stupid statue!"

"And a dead end," responded Myiako, as she walked the lamp forward.

"The cave ends?" asked Slayn, looking around at the squared-off corner. "Notice how smooth these walls are here. There has got to be a door around."

The girl moved the lamp around, revealing two more statues, different from the first one.

"Hey, there is something on the wall," said Torru, as he brushed off a carved symbol.

"There is a weird symbol on this wall, too," replied Myiako.

"And yet a third," stated Slayn.

"I believe this is the puzzle you wished for, Myi. Three different statues and three different symbols," concluded Slayn.

"And don't forget, there are also three people here," added Myiako.

"Ya, think this is set up for us?" asked Torru.

"Well, it isn't here for the zombies," she responded with a smile.

"Za–zombies?" mumbled Torru, taking Myiako too seriously.

After examining the statues and symbols for longer than they should have, Slayn got the idea to move the statues in front of the closest cave marking. Nothing happened. Their panting filled the empty space. Scraping life size statues across the floor wasn't a job for the weak.

"Of course it wouldn't be that easy," Myiako said with a sigh.

"Easy for you; since we did all the

push'n," said Torru, leaning against the wall.

"I prefer to supervise," Myi smiled.

"We could keep moving around the heavy statues or find out what these symbols mean," Slayn said pointedly.

"I'm not do'n that," Torru complained.

"Find out what they mean, how?" Myi asked.

"Let me just pull out my encyclopedia Britannica collection and have a look see," Torru said with inappropriate sarcasm.

They again examined the statues. One was an armoured man wielding a sword. Another was a strange woman in a dress sculpted as if it was flowing in motion. The third statue was of a dragon creature.

No one could comprehend what the dotted symbols meant. They represented no form of language known to Myi, Slayn, or Torru.

"What are these stupid wall bumps, anyways?" asked Torru, as he pounded on the wall.

"Cut that out. Beating up the walls will get us nowhere," Slayn told the broad-shouldered man.

Statues, symbols, symbols, statues... the dragon lord statue? The thought tumbled through Myiako's mind. She then asked, "Who is the woman this statue represents?"

There was a pause as Myiako glared at the tall, thin blonde, and then at the built, bearded man.

"I...I believe I've seen her in a few books," responded Torru. "Her picture was...."

"Well, spit it out!" urged Myiako.
Torru looked down. "I think she is the necromancer."

"Necromancer?" Myi questioned. "A beautiful woman in a flowing dress is the divider of the dead and the living?!" replied Myiako, not believing him.

"I think he's right, for once," stated Slayn.

"Well then, if that's the case, Torru must have that encyclopedia hidden somewhere."

"Very funny…" said Torru and sighed.

"We have the dragon lord statue, the necromancer, and a warrior-guy." Myiako said thoughtfully.

There was more silence. They sat now, in the dirt and dim light.

"Any ideas?" Torru broke the silence.

"No, but it's getting late. I bet the moon has risen and all the stars…" Myiako replied, then added absently, "Should be a full moon."

"The stars—that's it! Myiako, once again, you're a sorta genius! And by default, I might add," exclaimed Slayn, jumping up to a symbol on the wall.

"What?" asked the other two, and followed Slayn to see what he was up to.

Slayn connected the dots on the cave wall with his finger. Dust and soot were wiped away, leaving a clean line.

"Don't ya see!" he exclaimed.

Myiako and Torru gave each other confused glances, and then their eyes returned to Slayn, who was smiling.

Another moment passed before Myiako responded, "Oh, I get it. It's a picture of the dragon lord like the star constellation! Good job, Slayn!" She hit him on the back instead of a pat.

"So that must be the necromancy constellation and statue," said Torru.

"Yeah, and this last one is the Mystic Swordsman constellation," replied Myiako, as she began to push a statue. "What an odd puzzle, with three supposedly unrelated idols."

Soon enough they managed to move the life-size statues in front of the corresponding symbols. They then stood back in hopes of a response.

Just as they felt their guess was wrong and their guard lowered, a rumble was felt and the cave began to shake. They huddled together thinking the walls were about to cave in, but instead of collapsing, the back wall slowly opened to a large room.

They warily looked inside to see a dim light shining down on a sarcophagus. And then, the familiar glint of gold caught their eyes.

They entered the room and headed straight for the mass of treasure, scattered around the coffin and pedestal. It looked like they were not the first to discover the spoils of this crypt. Someone had already rummaged through, and it looked as if they were in a hurry.

As for the trio of adventurers, they were in no hurry. They began filling their pockets with jewels and coins.

Myiako suddenly stopped to notice the beam of light shining on the coffin lid. She looked up to the small hole at the very top of the cave that was allowing moonlight to seep inside.

"Um… guys…check this out," she said, not turning away from the light.

They stopped rooting through the treasure momentarily and looked at Myiako, who was pointing at the hole in the ceiling. The moon was slowly making itself visible through the small hole as it rose higher.

"Good, that makes it brighter to see whatever in the heck I'm grabbing," replied

Torru, as he returned to pick a stone out of a carved statue with his pocketknife.

Myiako was now looking down at the sarcophagus, as if she was drawn to it. She began running her hands down the faded markings that decorated the tomb. Her fingertips became dusty, but this did not hinder her actions.

"This place was already cleaned out, long before us," Slayn commented, causing Myiako to turn away.

"It is an ancient tomb, Slayn…" responded Torru. "You think we were the only ones who figured out that statue thing?"

"It's strange; but I can read these strange words on the coffin lid." said Myiako, turning towards them.

She could recognize the writing as vamperic in origin, Mortary un Dra`cul, was the scripture of vampires and the language of the dead. *How did I know this?* She wondered.

"I had no idea that you took an ancient language class, Myi," commented Slayn.

"I didn't know either…" Myiako made a vague response.

"Well, what does it say?" wondered Torru.

Myiako began reading aloud: `Dur kadama al-la rula un-la null ull-ant`en ve av`at un lumi!

"Uh…In human, please—"Torru started, but was interrupted by the loud rumble through the ground and walls.

"I would not read anymore of it, if I were you," said Slayn, his voice was nervous.

Myiako didn't seem like herself and continued to read the dead words.

Slayn and Torru attempted to pull her away, but the now-entranced Myiako knocked them back as if she had the power of three men. They tried again, but their efforts were fleeting.

The two fell to the ground and stared at her in shock.

She stood facing the tomb, eyes glazed over. She lifted her arms out to her sides as she shouted, "Tea-al-la-rul! Arise my warrior, Draish Jau-Ri!"

With her eerie words echoing amongst the stone walls; she began to change appearance…

A breeze from nowhere fluttered her hair out, causing it to lighten in colour and even curl. Her shirt, pants, and cloak faded into a white and green gown, which was much longer than she was tall. A new air had surrounded her being; this wasn't Myiako, though the woman looked much like her.

"She's become that necromancer woman!" exclaimed Torru in fear. "Wh-

what's happening?"

Indeed, she did resemble that statue — same hair, same dress.

The sarcophagus lid started to open, slid off by an unseen force, and then came crashing to the ground.

The changed woman held her hands to the sky, causing bones to move from the coffin. The remains began to rise up. A fully intact skeleton seemed to look at them with the dark pits of the eye sockets and four fangs bared among the stained teeth. It levitated higher as the woman stepped back.

A field of glowing energy surrounded the blood-stained bones and it started gaining substance. Muscle tissue bound the bones; tendons took their places and pale flesh covered. Before them formed a lifeless body of a young-looking man with shoulder length, platinum-coloured hair. His body was almost flawless with a tight muscle structure, yet his chest was riddled with scars.

"Supeious-guruns-ohm- chronos un lumi-cruoris ilu dayan veo!" The possessed woman spoke loudly in Mortary then to speak in human tongue, "Now come to life, once again, and vast in the blood of the ages!"

There was a chained necklace that had been around the skeletons' neck, the stone on it shined a bright green. The strange man's eyes blinked open as he squinted for the light of the necklace stone. His neck was limp until he lifted his head. His hair moved from his eyes. His pale gray-blue eyes met with those of the woman. Within that instance of eye connection, the woman fainted to the ground. The flowing dress then melted back into Myiako's mundane clothing. There was a blinding flash of light and the re-formed man was nowhere to be seen. Slayn and Torru cautiously got back on their feet and went to check on Myiako.

"What the bloody hell was that?!" yelled Torru, now at Myi's side.

"Myiako…are you alright?" he asked, as they picked her up and walked a safe distance from the stone tomb.

"Wh–what happened?" asked Myiako, after regaining consciousness. Her hair was back to its black luster and she blinked her dark green eyes.

"Maybe you can tell us," responded Slayn, as he helped her to sit up.

In spite of the current events, they turned to look at the coffin. They were startled to see a hand grab the side, then the creature in the coffin lifted himself to sit upright and stared blankly into the darkness.

Myiako grabbed the lamp from the

ground and held it out to get a better look at the strange figure. "Um…hello?" she said warily.

The three friends stood up and held each other's arms for encouragement.

"Are you…alive?" Myi asked a question that seemed to have an obvious answer.

The handsome man with white hair looked at her and slightly opened his lush, pale lips. He cleared his throat, and then said, "Thank you…thank you for reviving me…I had to get out of there to see you again." His voice was strangely comforting, and his accent gave them the notion that he wasn't a native. In fact, they couldn't place his dialect for it was almost lacking accent.

"What?" Myiako blurted.

"You are Zaira, are you not?" he said, now beginning to show emotion.

"No, I'm not this Zaira person; my name is Myiako Lynn Oaiku," she told him.

He then smiled enough to reveal his upper fanged teeth and now gained slight colour on his once grayed skin.

"Of course you are…" His smile faded as he lowered his head.

"Alright, someone's got to tell me what in the world is go'n on here," demanded Torru.

Myiako, who was stepping forward,

looked back to Torru.

"I think, somehow, I resurrected this vampire, Draish Jauri," she told him in a hushed voice.

"Uhh…yeah, that's what I thought. So, why are we sticking around here!" Torru exclaimed, as he began stepping away.

The newly re-born vampire looked back to them almost expressionless. They felt an unearthly presence.

Torru backed off further, stating, "I–I'm not staying to be his first meal. Let's get outta here!"

The other two stood in shock and made no response.

Torru's fear of the undead took hold and he ran from sight, back the way they had entered. His footsteps echoed for a short time. Though it was cowardice to run from your companions, he somehow already knew what vampires were capable of…

Myiako and Slayn stood in wonderment and confusion, staring at the platinum haired man until Myiako broke the discerning silence between the three.

"Are ya go'na kill us or something?"

She was elbowed by Slayn, whom gave her a contrary look.

The vampire remained devoid of emotion and replied, "Now, why should thy

kill the one who revived my mortal body…
unless death is something that you wish
upon." His teeth were stained with the ferric
remains of blood.

"No. Not at all, it's just you're a vampire
and…" said Myiako.

"Harm you, I can never. You have my
word," responded the vampire called Draish.
It looked as if he wanted to smile at her. His
voice was quiet and soothing.

Myiako and Slayn seemed to loosen up
and they slowly approached him.

Slayn took off his cloak to show his
leather vest with a necktie and black pants. He
handed the cloak to the vampire. Draish then
covered himself, stood in the coffin, and then
slowly stepped out.

The two moved back, not to crowd
him, and looked at him with astonishment. He
stood slightly taller than Slayn, even barefoot.

*A mysterious, but beautiful man; back
from a distant past to live again,* Myiako thought,
not realizing the dumbfounded look she
possessed.

"Is there something wrong?" Draish
asked, maybe wondering why eyes were stuck
to him.

A pause, then a response in unison,
"Nothing."

Draish looked around. "Where is this,

when is this?" he muttered, seeming confused.

"We're inside the Cantu Mountains… in your tomb," replied Myi, not being one to hesitate.

"Yes, the mountains…but this is my tomb?" The creature responded, then began to pace around. He acted somewhat youthful in his responses despite how old he must have been.

"What's wrong?" asked Slayn. "This is your tomb, right?"

"My burial was great…covered with the treasures of a king…protected by an ancient magik…" Draish told them in disbelief, "and this is all the great vampire has left…being not one for human desires is still irritated at the disrespect to one's burial ground." The sounds of conflict now rumbled in his voice. He seemed to be more or less talking to himself.

They would wonder how he would have known of how his burial was decorated, but his pure existence was an anomaly within itself. Myiako and Slayn felt remorse; for that very reason of robbery that they had come here, but that still didn't tell them how he would have knowledge of where he was buried.

"You must understand that it has been centuries since you died, and grave thieves already took what they wanted," explained Myiako, not quite sure of it all.

"What? I was actually left here for centuries!" Draish's tone rose, then he paused. "Was the door seal still active?" he asked, once again in his subdued voice.

"Yes, if by door seal you mean the weird puzzle to enter," responded Myiako.

"I see…" he said quietly, his lips turning into a smile.

"Do you know just how you resurrected me?' he asked Myi, his pale eyes digging into her like a knife.

"Not really…" She answered, feeling the strange sensation in her flesh as she had experienced in the moments before she had gone into a trance. "I just remember looking at that sarcophagus, and as I started to read the writing, everything went blank, as if someone else had taken my body."

Draish walked over to Myiako until he stood in front of her. She was able to take a better look at him and was captivated by his soft-looking, pale completion. He had dark furry eyebrows and sideburns just in front of his slightly pointed ears, which went well to frame his slender nose. She was reminded of a wolf for some reason as she looked at him. Then she realized that she stared for long enough. She was forbearing to blush.

"You really don't know about your true ancestry, do you?" the vampire asked her. He turned from her, having the same response to what she had felt of not being able to face each other directly for long.

He began to piece things together and told them, after clearing his throat, "In my human life, around the year 1348, that's when I met her…being blood to the Lady Necromancy; she gave me this eternal decision to be a pure vampire…not an just an undead cretin. Who could resist such a power and lust for revenge? Not the man that I was…so naive. That is how I came to the choices that I never thought to regret…"

His memory was actually intact after all these years, such remembrance would drive a mortal insane, but that he was not (perhaps insane, but not a mortal…).

"Great story, but what does this have to do with Myiako?" replied Slayn, with a bold disrespect.

"Being a mere human, you must be blind to see that the fates have chosen this lady to be my necromancer, this century, this time," Draish quickly responded.

"I have power over a vampire?" Myiako smiled. "But you lived in the ages long ago, how could I have power over you?"

"I suppose you can state it like that... but who do you think has the real power?" replied Draish softly, taking her hand. "Pleased to meet you, Myiako Oai-ku."

He had pronounced her name a little differently than she did and his tone drastically changed. The attractive man then leaned slightly to kiss her hand. His lips were cold as a reptile's and she flinched.

"First, you're saying that there is a necromancer and she gave you a vampire life? Wouldn't that mean you're not..." Slayn started.

"Go on and say it; I'm not what one would call a human that became a vampire, but an exception to the undead rule."

Draish averted his pale eyes from Myiako's hand to look at Slayn. "I was a human who died and was resurrected as a vampire; I have no master because I am one."

"I think I'm beginning to understand all this for some weird reason," muttered Slayn.

Draish withdrew from their attention and went back to pacing around the scattered remains of his once vast fortune. The look on his face showed deep thought and as if thinking was painful.

A few moments later, he interrupted the silence,

"They even stole my armour…the unfortunate dishonour to fealty…" he then knelt to toil for gold on the floor by his feet. "It means nothing to me now…" he whispered.

"Don't worry; I have some extra clothes out on the horse," replied Slayn. "We don't wear armour anymore."

"Is that so?" His look was curious. "Very well then, I guess I am coming with you," concluded Draish, looking up to them.

"If that's what you want," agreed Myiako.

"I have nowhere else to go…all my loved ones have long past," the vampire said vaguely.

Slayn lowered an eyebrow. "A vampire had loved ones; that's a new one."

"That's not so hard to believe!" blurted Myiako. "He's got no one left; it's a new century, ya know."

"What year would this be, exactly?" asked Draish, now standing again. They noticed how his temperament would change quickly.

Myi looked at Slayn, and then responsed, "It's the 21st century…1901…to be exact."

Draish looked shocked and said, "The

many years have left me weakened."

Then, looking down, his hair rushed to cover his face. "I was revived last in the 1500s by another that I care not to mention, and then died about 100 years later...she didn't revive me as she sent me back to life the first time."

He paused and tried to maintain an even tone. "A long time since my ressurector came; 200 years or so...which is good in a sense, meaning that I have not been needed —" Draish rambled on, being ever stuck in the past that is the future.

"Needed?" wondered Myiako.

"This has all been really fascinating, but..." Slayn interjected, picking up the oil lamp, "We should probably get him back to the house before sunrise. It's a quarter of a day's travel, and —"

"Sunrise..." whispered Draish.

Myiako walked back over to the handsome man and took *his* hand.

"It'll be alright, and no one has to know you're a vampire," she said. "In fact, few still believe in such mythical creatures."

Draish's jaw dropped. "Mythical creatures...are what we are referred to?"

"Well, there are not many vampires around; I was beginning to think that going to discover a vampire's tomb was all lies...but..." Myi explained.

The platinum haired man sighed. "Many years have passed...'til la victor un gurun..." he muttered in human to Mortary un Dra'cul.

Myi had spoken in that language only moments earlier, but understood nothing of it now. Snatching up her bag from the ground, she hurled it over her shoulder and asked Draish, "Are you ready to go?"

"Yes, indeed, I must see this new world of yours," he unsurely responded.

"By the way..." said Myiako, "Can I keep this bracelet?" She held out the piece of jewelry.

"Of course, my dear...you are also welcome to keep those gold pieces in your pockets...and he can have this gold medallion that was stuffed in this cloak pocket. None of my past life means anything now..." said Draish with a smile, as he then pulled the chained medallion from the cloak he was wearing.

Slayn looked embarrassed and took the gold piece from Draish's extended hand. They had never been caught by the person that they were robbing from because they had all been dead — really dead. Slayn felt uneasy.

They turned to the stone doorway opening, leading to the cave with the three statues. After going inside the statue room, the wall closed behind them. They turned to watch it shut with a rumble, reverberating in the walls.

"What do these statues mean, anyway?" wondered Myiako.

"Perhaps you will find thy answers you seek at a later time," responded Draish, who then gave a half smile.

Find the answers you seek? He sure is a strange one, thought Myi.

They continued their walk down the cave corridor. When they reached the large entry room, Myiako made sure to avoid the bone pit that she had been greeted with.

Slayn was the first to step foot outside to see that Torru had been awaiting their arrival. He sat on the ground near the horses, but quickly got up to greet his friend.

"Is everything alright? Where is Myi?" Torru hastily asked him.

He then saw Myiako come from the shadows of the cave.

"You are such a wimp, Torru," she told him with a friendly smile.

Torru gasped when he noticed that there was a third person with them.

"H...he is with you," whispered Torru.

The vampire stood in the cave darkness, hesitant to step outside, but soon enough he moved out into the dim moonlight.

"It...he is the legendary vampire, reborn?" questioned Torru in tones of fear and astonishment.

"That's right; and he is coming with us," said Myiako smiling, either trusting or knowing.

"What!" exclaimed Torru. "Ya know he's gonna have to eat sooner or later. You two are lucky still to be alive this long…"

"I'm sure I can control my bloodlust," replied Draish with a smirk of self-confidence.

"Come on, Torru; we need to get back before dawn," Myiako said, as she walked to her horse.

Slayn walked to his horse and dug around in a saddlebag. He then pulled out black leather pants and a white, long-sleeved shirt to give to Draish, who was still just wearing the cape.

"Here you are," Slayn handed the clothing to the vampire. "Sorry, might be a tight fit."

Draish thankfully took the clothes, and without a care, he dropped the cloak.

Myiako had turned away, blushing at the sight of his shapely physique, and focused her eyes on the brown horse behind her; as if the colour of the horse was enough to get her mind on a different subject.

The white-haired man struggled with the clothes to fit his muscular body; ripping parts in the legs and arms. He managed to fit the borrowed clothes due to the fact that Slayn was a tall man, too.

"Thank you," Draish said to Slayn, who was still standing next to him with his back turned. Draish regained eye contact with Myi, who was yards away. She pretended she wasn't watching him get dressed.

"You can ride with me," said Myiako, as her hair fluttered back while she mounted the horse.

After picking up the cloak, Draish put it back around him and walked over to her while the other two got on their horses.

"Our latest home is about a six hour ride, in this new settlement," said Slayn.

Torru looked at Slayn and shook his head "no" in disbelief.

"Come on," said Myi to Draish, "Get on behind me."

"Behind you, but you're a woman?"

Her eyes shot daggers at him. "What does that have to do with anything?"

"A lady never leads," he responded.

Draish looked at the large horse, and then grabbed onto the saddle behind Myiako. After he secured his weight on the mount, he didn't know where he could put his hands until he found a place on the saddle behind him. Without further hesitation, they and the horses took off.

They ran through the night, under the now setting moon. Not much was said between them, even though there was so much to talk about.

"How ya do'n, Myi?" Torru slowed his horse to match her speed.

"Everything's fine…why?" she responded, turning to him.

"It's just that you're usually so talkative, and now you haven't said anything for a while," said Torru, trying to avoid looking at Draish.

"I'm talking now, aren't I?" she replied.

Torru just rolled his eyes and regained speed to ride next to Slayn.

"Just leave Myiako alone, she has been through a lot today…and she is …I mean, we're both kind of mad at you for darting out on us in the tomb," Slayn said to his friend.

"Um….Slayn, come on, a skeleton rises from a crypt and becomes a vampire guy, who none-the-less is traveling with us. Bandits and scalawags, I've seem then all, but this is way outta my hands," responded Torru with wide eyes.

"Yes, that is messed up…but if you had

bothered to stay, you would have found out that Myiako and *that guy* are magically linked; and somehow, I know she was destined to do this," said Slayn with sincerity.

"How do you know so much? Besides we're just ordinary people, right?"

"That, I do not know," answered Slayn.

Shortly thereafter, they reached a stream that needed to be crossed. They dismounted so that the horses could rest and drink.

"I needed to stretch my legs," said Myiako. "How much further you guys think?"

"Roughly three hours, if the horses can keep their speed," responded Slayn, as he knelt down to cup water in his hands to splash on his face.

"So, what are we going to do? Just go home and act as if everything's the same?" Torru said, looking agitated.

"I don't see why not," said Myiako, smiling. She was being too casual for Torru's comfort.

"This wasn't one of our usual evacuations, Myi," Torru commented, as he nervously shifted his weight back and forth. "So easy for you to bring your treasure home..." he peered at Draish, who was looking at his reflection in the water.

Myiako crossed her arms. "That's not what this is about…he's not my treasure."

"Easy for you to say…" said Slayn with a sigh.

Draish turned to them, rubbing his chin. "Would you feel the same about me if I was a woman?" he said then, smiling.

"A female vampire might be easier on the eyes," Slayn responded with a smile, water still dripping from his face.

"A vampire's a vampire, they all have the same motives," remarked Torru. "I really don't care if there is some legend preceding this one…he shouldn't be."

"Your words are harsh, but thy mind is weak," said Draish, almost becoming defensive.

Torru's expression angered, as if he was being provoked for a fight.

"Look, Torru. It's not his fault that we broke into his burial place and all this happened," Myiako stated, defending the circumstances as well.

"But why bring him with us?" Torru questioned, talking as though the vampire wasn't there.

"Because I am responsible for him," she said. "Therefore, he's with me." She looked back to Draish.

"I thought you said that he wasn't your treasure," said Slayn, laughing at

Myiako.

"Does this not bother you at all?" Slayn looked to Draish.

"I am in debt to her..." responded Draish. His voice was low.

"Why is that? If you're immortal, I don't see how death could be such a bad thing," Slayn replied. "If anything wouldn't you be mad about seeing this world again?"

Draish sighed and brushed back his hair. "If you only knew what happens after you die."

They all looked at him as if they were about to get some deep insight on his thoughts.

Torru became curious, saying, "Feel free to tell us..."

"I cannot," Draish responded solemnly.

"How is it that you were dead and still have memories of what happened before?" asked Slayn.

Myiako followed with another question. "Where was your mind in death?"

Draish became uneasy. "I cannot bring up such things with the likes of mortals."

"You're a tough one to crack," Slayn commented.

"Are you really what we know as a vampire?" Myiako interrogated. "You say it's been hundreds of years, but you still haven't fed on blood."

Draish just looked down.

She went on. "You were re-born, yet you still have scars, aren't you suppose to heal? I have seen your reflection, too."

"I can sustain without sustenance. As for my scars..." he paused, "they were inflicted on my mortal body. Know that some wounds will never heal."

It was obvious they were bringing up bad memories, causing him to be uneasy. "I have a reflection because I have a soul..." he added.

"Show us something that only a vampire could do," Slayn demanded and saw Torru shaking his head 'no' again.

"You do not think that becoming living from bones was enough?" Draish responded, becoming exhausted with their mistrust. He looked to Slayn. "I could drink your blood."

"So could a human..." commented Torru.

"Why are you questioning one's power?" Draish asked of them.

"Well..." started Myiako, "any vampires that we heard about have killed many people without all the banter. Why do you still give me the impression that you have humanity?"

"Perhaps it was just the way that I was

made."

They couldn't tell if he was bluffing or not, but he liked to avoid personal questions.

"A shame that you do not think that any vampire could be civil with humans. We are supposed to take pride in our upbringing."

"Sorry to say that it's not like it was 300 years ago," said Slayn as he walked to his horse. "We should get going."

"We should," Myiako agreed.

"Wait…" Draish said. "All the questions you have for me, what of you?"

"There's not much to say," responded Myi.

"What kind of person are you?" His pale eyes caught her attention.

She didn't know what to say. "Umm…a boring one until today." She held the reins of her horse.

"Are you treacherous, disloyal, or whatever word is used in this time to describe one who betrays?"

That was the most serious that Myiako had heard his voice as of yet.

She gave him a 'where did that come from' look. "I don't think so. You can ask my friends if you don't believe me." She looked nervous.

Draish looked down. "Before we go any further…we should make a truce."

She looked confused.

He went on, "If you don't hurt me, I will not hurt you."

Myiako exchanged glances with the others then looked back to Draish, who wasn't looking at her.

"Shouldn't I have been the one to ask you that?"

"Yes...I suppose, but if you only knew what was done to me."

Myiako didn't respond and just jumped onto her mount.

Draish looked up to her. "What do you say?" He still wanted her word and almost seemed desperate.

"Why would I want to hurt you?" She looked to him. "How could I?"

{II}: Blood For Life

They looked ahead to see the dark outline of a village. The houses seemed small and poorly constructed, as if they'd been erected within a few days, with unsteady foundations and thatched roofs. The homes couldn't have been well planned out; especially if someone was to spill their oil lamp. A few structures had architecture, with one tall one in the back of the village. The faint glows of candles were seen through some windows; not many were awake these early morning hours...

As they were almost to the gates, Draish decided to break his silence with some words with Myiako. He leaned to her ear and spoke softly. "Do you believe in destiny?" His whisper gave her chills.

She turned to him with a raised brow. "Hey, somehow, I'm the necromancer for a vampire, so my willingness is to believe anything at this point," she responded, still with an optimistic smile.

"That's not quite the answer I was going for," Draish told her, sitting back again.

"I hope we get through the town alright; don't want to cause any suspicions on who you are," Myiako said to the man behind her. "I mean these people know what kind of work we're into and having another person coming back with us might seem odd."

He didn't quite know what to make of that, so he said the first thing in mind.

"Well, you could tell people that I'm your estranged husband, who has been comatose for hundreds of years and has finally woke up to be with you." Draish smiled.

She seemed surprised.

"Making jokes, are we?" responded Myiako. "Besides you're too strange-looking to pass as a commoner."

"Ummm…thanks…" Draish sighed.

Myiako turned around to him and grinned.

"Come on, ya know what I mean," she said and blushed.

The clip-clop of hooves echoed down the graveled streets, as they rode slowly along until stopping in front of a cabin-styled house, one of the few actual houses in the town.

"This is our stop," replied Slayn, as he dismounted.

Draish jumped off the horse before Myiako then turned to help her down.

Slayn and Torru started to take the reins off of the horses while Draish watched

Myiako open the gate to the fenced-in yard where the horses stayed.

"I say we should get some sleep," stated Myiako, as she pushed open the door to their house.

They all entered the front room; yet Torru was hesitant to do so.

"How would ya sleep soundly with a vampire around!" he exclaimed.

"I'm right here. I can hear you…" said Draish, peering at Torru.

"Give him a chance, Torru, if he wanted to harm us, I'm sure a good reason would suffice….so don't give him a reason," said Slayn, annoyed with Torru's cowardice.

"Ya don't give a vampire a chance to harm you is the thing," Torru argued.

"Troubles with my kind in the past?" asked Draish.

Torru exchanged a quick glance with Draish and walked away. He took off and threw his cloak down to show the brown slacks and suspenders over a white button up shirt that was tight over his gut. "Am I the only sane person here?"

"Just make yourself comfortable. I think it's better that we discuss what to do after a few hours of sleep," Myiako said, ignoring Torru and looking at Draish.

"What is there to discuss? Have not we already done so?" Draish asked, knowing the apparent answer.

"What are we to do with you?" she responded, smiling.

"I'd like to know a thing about you… What's your daily life like?" asked Draish.

She hesitated to speak.

"We go looking for treasures of lost civilizations, for profit and knowledge," Myiako told him.

Slayn walked by them and added, "That is just a fancy way of saying that we're thieves."

He walked on into another room. "If it wasn't obvious," he continued out of sight.

Myiako looked embarrassed and soon noticed she was alone with Draish. She looked around nervously.

"You may sleep, if that is what you wish," the white-haired man replied softly to ease her mind.

"Is there anything that you need?" she asked him.

After a moment, he responded in the same soft voice, "Actually, could you close all these window shutters. I can sense the daylight rising and…and it will pierce its' way into my skin any moment now."

"Ahh…oh…okay," she mumbled on her

way to a window. There were four windows there in the main room. After shutting the final shutter, she stretched out her arms and yawned.

"Thank you, my dear, you've been more help to me tonight than anyone in centuries," he said, with a short laugh, and then went on, "Don't worry; I'll be here when you wake."

"How can we trust you?" she asked.

"Look at me...how can you not?" He made uneasy words seem like they were the truth.

Myiako yawned again. "Alright...I'll see ya later...make yourself at home."

She walked into the adjacent room and covertly glanced back before shutting the door.

Draish took a moment to look around this modernized house, and then he found a seat on a sofa chair. After allowing his weight to sink into the puffy seat, he put his arms on the rests and relaxed, sinking further down. He sat in silence for a few moments before being disturbed.

"Heh...Heh," Torru chuckled as he entered the room. "Never seen a chair like that before." He noticed how comfortable Draish looked.

"Never have I felt a chair so soft,"

Draish responded, turning his head to Torru. "Exception being a throne..."

Torru took a seat in a wooden chair that he had pulled away from the table to stare at the vampire.

Draish slightly tilted his head and said, "You probably should think again before you do something rash." He gave the first unnerving look Torru had seen from him.

Torru changed his body language and sat at the chair's edge.

"Look, enough mess'n around. Ya know I don't like ya and if ya do anything to hurt us...I swear I'll..." Torru then stood up and pulled out his handgun from his right pocket. "I'll shoot you!"

Draish looked amused and stood back up with curiosity to face him. "You will what? What is that? Am I supposed to be threatened?" He was intrigued, but he also felt the man's intent to harm him.

Torru stood nervously, the gun shaking unsteadily in his hand while sweat dripped down his face.

The vampire stepped closer to the armed man, and then grabbed the gun barrel and pulled it from Torru's grasp before he was able to react. He dangled the gun in front of his face holding onto the barrel with the handle pointed down.

"Now this strikes me as odd. What is it called?" asked Draish.

"A–a gun," stuttered Torru, with fear.

"A gun, a weapon is it not?" replied Draish.

Torru nodded "yes" and backed away.

Draish lay the gun down on the nearby table. "Relax..." he whispered to Torru, with a smug look.

Torru's body tightened and his brow line narrowed. "You relax, demon, when you return to your grave!" Torru raged and ran over to the nearest window, throwing open the shutter.

The bright morning sunlight came pouring inside; chasing away the hiding shadows.

Draish drew back in pain, the light beams attacking him like flames. The smell of burning flesh filled the room, while Torru watched, frozen in place. The suffering man fell to the ground, gasping in agony as if he was drowning.

Myiako came rushing from her room, and Slayn looked from his open door. The air smelled of burning flesh.

"What in the hell are you doing?! Close the damn window; you're killing him, Torru!" Myi yelled.

Running to the window and pushing Torru out of the way, she slammed shut the wooden blinds.

Slayn began to argue with Torru as Myiako knelt down next to Draish, who was passed out on the floor, arms covering his face.

"Draish? Are you alive? Say something!" Myiako exclaimed as she put her hand on his smoldering shoulder. "Please say something!"

"...define alive..." he managed to say. His head moved and his body jerked as he gasped for air.

"What?" responded Myiako. She then leaned closer to him.

"...I need blood..." he mumbled.

Myiako rolled him over to his back and was startled at the sight of his boiled skin. Torru and Slayn were then looking down on him as well.

Draish looked at Myiako with watery, bloodshot eyes and whispered, "Please forgive me...cruorem-rau-la-ull..."

Myiako became confused, but then quickly began backing away, "Huh? What the..."

The vampire began to get back up righting himself by will and in one swift swooping motion, he grabbed Torru; clenching his arms to his sides from behind. With an inhuman growl, Draish sunk his four fangs into the throbbing neck veins.

Torru screamed from the pain of the bite.

Draish tried to pull himself away, but couldn't resist his temptation for the taste of human blood. The other two tried to pull him from Torru, but were just knocked back by a shockwave of light expelled from Draish.

Finally, he raised his head and Torru dropped to the ground.

The white-haired vampire stood looking down on Torru's dying body, with no expression on his sun-scared face. He just wiped his chin clean of dripping blood with the back of his hand, and licked his lips.

Myiako ran to Torru's side to check his condition.

"Why?" she yelled at Draish, no longer concerned with *his* condition.

Slayn began to pace around nervously.

Draish knelt down on the other side of Torru to face Myiako. "I had to…once one is injured there is little free will," he said quietly.

"Will he survive?" she asked in barely a whisper.

"Only for a few days…unless…" he responded, and then stopped.

"A FEW days! Unless what?" she demanded.

"No? You cannot!" broke in Slayn.

Draish looked at Slayn in surprise.

"Then he shall die a mortal," Draish replied, standing up. His skin was now completely healed, leaving no scars on his once again symmetrical face.

"Tell me!" Myiako demanded from Draish as she stood up to face him.

"He could become an undead with *my* blood," he told her with sincerity.

"That is NOT a good thing to consider… he could become a mindless zombie or something…there has got to be another way," Slayn exclaimed, trying to avoid the worse outcome.

"You can only prevent, not cure, an illness such as this," Draish said, with a soft smile then a chuckle, but not of joy.

"You're mad!" blurted Myiako, staring at Draish in anguish over her dying friend.

"After living and passing throughout six hundred years, one goes far beyond the extent of madness," Draish responded with an uneasy expression. When he gazed back down to Torru, he looked saddened.

"They should have listened to you…" he said to Torru, then turned to look at Torru's two friends. "I'm sorry…but he shunned me with light…how dare he!"

They couldn't tell if he was trying to be

humorous or serious because his use of words was outdated.

Myi and Slayn looked down at Torru in silence.

"I can feel his life energy…" stated Draish. "Shall he live or shall he die?" He then held his wrist over Torru's head.

"No…don't do it!" Slayn exclaimed. "Let's see if we can find a doctor or something!"

Myiako put her hand calmly on Slayn's shoulder and told him, "We can't tell a doctor that our friend has a vampire bite. This way at least he can live as an undead."

"If you can call this living…" Draish said to himself now showing bitterness of his ways.

Myiako took a moment to think. *Maybe we can find a doctor that knows what to do.*

"Come on," she said shortly. "Let's get him to bed. I think I know of a doctor."

Draish gently lifted Torru, who was unconscious, and Slayn and Myi led him to the bedroom.

"Who is this Doctor you speak of…one who helps the sick, right?" Draish asked them from the front room.

"Yeah, but this doctor specializes in monsters." Myiako responded to him without turning to look. "I thought he was running a

 DECEPTION BY BLOOD

scam, until now."

"Monsters…thanks, I adore being slandered as such."

"At least he's breathing," Slayn said, looking to Myiako then Draish.

Draish stood at the doorway, watching them care for the man he had unintentionally wounded. A few moments later, Myiako walked to where Draish was impatiently standing.

"You know…I…I had to…" the handsome man said quietly to reiterate to her.

"Shhhh…" Myiako hushed his words. "I know…" She seemed to understand his erratic behavior. She couldn't be upset with him after looking into those eyes.

Draish slowly walked over to the chair and sat down, while Myiako followed. She repositioned a chair in front of him and sat down.

"So if it comes down to it…"she started, looking into his pale eyes, she hesitated, "He still can live?"

"Only if that's what he wants…to live…but not quite," he responded then put his hand on his forehead and looked down. He covered his eyes with his hand as matted locks of white hair fell forward.

"You should probably get some sleep

yourself, my dear; beauty doesn't last without rest," he suggested to her without any eye contact.

Myiako sat looking at Draish, and then got up and left the room without another word. She went to check on Torru, who seem to be dreaming. Slayn wiped the sweat from Torru's brow with a damp cloth, and then looked to Myi.

"He could be helped, right now," she told him.

"Becoming an undead is not being helped, it can't be predicted that he's going to have human memory or that he'll want to kill us," stated Slayn. "It would be more help just to put a bullet in him now!"

From the other room, Draish heard Slayn's criticism and grew upset. He was seated in the darkest part of the room to contemplate. It seemed only natural at this point to be reborn, but to mortals it was very aberrant.

Myiako came from Torru's room and went to hers after glancing at the vampire. Then Slayn came out and looked at Draish.

"Can I get your promise that you won't do that ever again?" Slayn asked.

Draish looked up to respond. "I cannot give you my word on that."

"Is there no honour amongst your kind?"

"There is, but mind you I have fed on countless humans."

The skinny man went on to the front door, giving the vampire a harsh look. "I advise you to stay put. It is menacingly bright outside. I'm going to look for help for my friend. You better not mess with Myi," Slayn told Draish. He then reached for the doorknob. "Cover your eyes," he warned, before opening the door to the morning.

Light flowed inside from the opened door and Draish drew back, bringing his knees to his chest where sat. The light didn't hit him long enough to do anymore damage.

Slayn had left the house, shoving the heavy door quickly behind him.

Draish let out the breath he was holding and relaxed in the chair.

"There is no help for him except the blood of the dead..." he said to himself through blood-stained teeth.

{III}: Forbidden Love

There was a pleasant breeze flowing though her blonde hair. The wind pushed through the tall meadow grass and a familiar woman found herself in a beautiful field, which was painted with the colours of flowers. Snow-capped mountains covered the horizon on one side and a grey stone castle stood out amongst the trees on the other.

A castle? The woman resembling Myiako became confused, even more so when she noticed the clothes she wore. She had on a long skirt and under it a petticoat. She wore a corset top covered with a kirtle, which was purple and white.

*This just has to be a dream or a memory of another life…such a beautiful land and all the flowers…*she thought, then ran over to a patch of sunflowers. *Real enough to smell.*

She looked to the distance to someone approaching on horseback. She looked up and squinted at the bright sunlight. The horse was wearing a robe saddle, but she couldn't yet make out the face of the man who was riding.

He wore broad shouldered armour

with a cape that almost hung to the ground.

The horse and rider neared her.

She saw his somewhat long white hair, and then, to her astonishment, saw the handsome face of Draish Jau-Ri.

He looked down to her and smiled, revealing his perfectly normal and sparkling teeth. "Good day, isn't it my lady? What brings ye so far from the castle?" he asked her in a pleasant voice.

Myiako still stood standing in disbelief of where she was or who, and why is the man she had met as a vampire out during daylight?

"You look a bit flushed, are you alright?" he added, interrupting her thoughts.

"I…I am fine," she finally responded, as she looked at his black and silver armour that was molded to his body. "I think my corset is too tight."

"Would the lady like a ride back then?" he asked, extending his gauntlet-protected arm with a friendly smile.

"Yes, I would," she unsurely responded, while taking his armoured hand. She was then lifted onto the back of the saddle.

For a moment, she almost sat straddled, but remembered she wore a dress so she sat to the side as one would in her position.

The knight Draish pulled on the reins and the horse started to walk at a normal pace as it gnashed its teeth on the bit. Almost loosing balance, she quickly wrapped her arms around his leather-clad body.

They were headed slowly into the woods, toward the castle. The leafy canopy blocked out some light and the horse pushed on through some tree limbs.

Myiako looked down to see where a clanking noise was coming from and saw a large sword hanging down from the gold and blue horse robe.

It looks as if Draish is a knight and he is taking me back to the castle; I must be royalty too, she thought.

"How come ye are out here by yourself?" he asked, breaking their silence.

"But I wasn't alone; I was with you," she answered.

"Well, if that is what you want me to tell *the prince*," he replied, then making the horse stop.

He turned his body to face her. "But we really don't have to tell them anything," he gently told her, "Now do we?"

He looked into her green eyes and leaned forward.

She was caught by surprise when he pressed his lips to hers and opened his mouth for a kiss.

Myiako jerked back and blushed.

"Oh come now, have ye decided to back out of this because of your fiancée?" he asked as he ran his fingers threw her blonde hair.

Who the heck am I? she thought. *No, what kind of weird dream is this?*

"Zaira…" he said to her, "you were anything but coy with me the other day, when we, ummm…"

She realized she had been staring off.

"I…it is not you, it's just I haven't felt like myself today…is all," she said.

"Maybe I can make you feel better." He smiled again. "Where would *you* like to go?"

"Where should I be?" she wondered, looking into the distance.

"In the village…I suppose," he replied, giving her a confused look.

Then from within the surrounding branches, rustling noises could be heard. Their horse reared up to the sight of a large black wolf approaching. Before she fell off, Draish grabbed Myiako and jumped off with her clinging to him. He motioned for her to stay put before he retrieved his sword.

The aggressive wolf lunged forth and the blade blocked the fangs. The steel did not cut the giant wolf but just made it angrier that its attack had been deflected. Draish dodged back and swung his sword in desperation.

The wolf creature growled and spoke, "Enough of thissss!" It then morphed into a man's form.

Draish stood dumbfounded, almost shaking in his armour, while Myiako watched with consternation.

The wolf was now a large man with long dark hair and a pale complexion to his handsome middle-aged face. He had a long slender nose and sunken-in dark eyes. He wore unique black plate mail armour that had a matching loin tunic with spiked shoulder pauldrons over a red and black silk cape. He stood on two legs even taller than Draish.

"What do you want? What the hell are you?" demanded Draish as he took control of the heavy broad sword.

The man said nothing, simply raising his arm, and then motioning downward, causing Draish to be driven to the ground with by an unseen magic force. Draish tried to regain ground by pushing up with his arms, but the spell had frozen him in place.

"I suggest that you stay out of this!" The dark haired man said with a growl, exposing his fanged teeth.

Myiako screamed; only to be grabbed by the attacker. She did all she could to free herself from the man's arms.

"I was vaiting..." the man said to her, "I was vaiting for you to be away from the castle today." His accent was unique.

"Let me go!!" she screamed.

"I have been vaiting for you, my dear. It is time to come home to me."

The dark-haired man opened his mouth, causing his large, drooling fangs to extend.

"No! You bastard! Let her go!" pleaded Draish, being helpless to do anything.

He watched the vampire bite down on the undisturbed flesh of her neck. She screamed again, this time though it was muffled by blood.

"You god-damned demon!" yelled Draish, still struggling to move. "How are you even existing in daylight? I will kill you for what you've done! Bound by honour, I will have your head!"

The vampire put down the woman and gave Draish a bloody smile with a twisted laugh. "You sure talk a lot. A shame you can't fight back...I'll return for you next, boy," the creature told him.

Once Draish was able to move freely again, the dark beast had already vanished into the trees. He ran to Zaira's body and knelt down. He then took her in his arms. Being filled with melancholy, he tried talking to her one last time.

"This isn't right, why does it have to be you?" he cried over her body, her dress now covered in her blood.

"I don't understand why? Zaira, wake up…Zaira…" he quietly said, shaking her gently.

"Wake up!"

Myiako jolted herself up right in her bed and found Slayn looking at her.

"Gee…I finally got you awake. You've been sleeping for a while now," the skinny man told her.

"I had the most vivid dream…" she told him, but then was quickly sucked into reality. "How's Torru holding up?"

"He's alive…if that's what you wanted to know, but I could not find Doctor Helsing. He has already boarded a train to another country," Slayn said to her.

"What should we do, now? Wasn't he the only doctor that aided in these matters?" she asked as she got up from the bed.

Slayn looked away to the door and said, "It looks as if our new friend or shall I say fiend, took off before I woke up." He referred to Draish.

"He's out around people!" exclaimed Myi.

"Yes, and let's hope he decided to keep his bloodlust at bay," replied Slayn as they exited the bedroom.

Myiako grabbed a button up shirt and put it on over her tank top. "I'm gonna go find him," she said. "You stay with Torru…has he said anything yet?"

"Nothing but nonsense and rambling; it doesn't look good for our friend, Myi," Slayn said grimly.

"Ya know…Draish only did that because Torru made the first attack. I know he wishes to protect, not harm." She looked at Slayn.

"You're surely gullible if you think you can trust a vampire, even if you happened to resurrect him." He gave her a scolding glance and walked into Torru's room.

Myiako grabbed her coat off the rack and opened the front door.

The night air was cool and unsettling against her neck so she lifted the cloak hood over her head. She shut the door and walked into the early night and down the torch lit street of this small boomtown.

Back in the house, Slayn sat in a chair next to Torru's bed. He wiped a damp cloth across the wounded man's forehead. Torru's eyes fluttered, and then opened.

"Torru…" said Slayn. He squinted with watery eyes to make out his friend. "What's go'n on….?" Torru asked in a weak voice.

Slayn looked at the floor and responded, "You're infected…from a vampire bite…"

"W–will I live?" he whispered.

Slayn tried to avoid eye contact. "I…I want to live, ya know that, Slayn," Torru said, then tried to sit up.

"Please, save your strength," said Slayn, as he urged Torru back down.

Myiako looked above at the waning moon, and then averted her attention to others walking around at night.

Still must be before mid-night, she thought. She then found the stone path to the town square, where she saw that several stores were still open.

After I find Draish, I should get some food for us, she thought, looking at the fresh market vegetables. She was so sure that she should find him nearby for some unknown reason.

She took the dirt path between two houses to the trees that outlined the town. She passed by the tree grove and it reminded her of that dream. She then wearily put her hand in her pocket, around the knife there, as if it would be any defense against any vampire.

Myi slowly walked through the trees, using only the diamond canopy of the night sky to see. The shadow of the distant mountain range could be made out, but other than that the vast field was dark and empty. While looking up, she noticed eyes on her. She focused her eyes to see the white-haired man sitting up on a nearby tree limb.

He looked down to her. "Looks like you found me."

"How could I miss that silver hair of yours, glistening in the moonlight," she said.

"The moon tells the truth, as do I…but what about you?" he said, looking down to her.

"I'll try to put the pieces together." Myi's voice faltered.

"I did not want to leave you, but I know where I'm not wanted," he replied with a soft tone.

"I'm sure they'll forgive you after this ordeal is over," she said. "Why don't you come down and walk with me?"

A smile came across his lips and he said, "Step back." He made himself fall from the high tree perch and landed like a cat on the ground, right before Myiako. After standing, he stretched his arms, his shirt lifting to expose his abs.

"Where shall we go?" he asked.

She hesitated, and then removed her cloak hood, her bangs falling forward.

"Um…I have something to talk about." she told him.

"Alright then, go on," he responded, stepping closer to her. She noticed then his eyes slightly altered colours, from pale blue shades to tints of grey due to his ever-changing temperaments.

"I had a strange dream about…well, about us, together. And she or me, well, she was killed," recounted Myiako.

Draish put his hand gently on her shoulder. "I don't know if that was a dream… The soul has the power to pass on memories, my lady." He looked into her lovely green eyes. "She was taken from me…a life so simple to diminish such as my own." He then looked down and his usual self-righteous posture dwindled.

"It's alright," she assured him. "Forget the past. You're here in the present, with me. The new millennium is upon us, so let's do what we gotta to make a happy future." Her voice was surprisingly cheerful.

Draish gave her a nice smile, but thought: *Forget the past? Can I forget?*

{IV}: Nécessité de une Vampiré

The door was pushed open and Myiako entered her house. Draish followed her in, holding a bag.

Slayn was sitting in the lamp lit room, reading. "I see you found the bloodsucker," he said, as he put down the book.

Myiako shook her head as she took off her coat.

Draish sat the bag on the table next to Slayn and said, "Surely one should know, that I have many talents."

"I hope it's not a severed head…" Slayn was skeptical of their jovialness.

"No silly, he bought us dinner," replied Myiako.

Slayn exchanged glances with her, then commented, "I'm not gonna find a dismembered body part in here, you sure?"

Draish smiled and opened the bag that contained a loaf of bread, a fresh fish with potatoes, two bottles of wine, and two bottles of whiskey.

Slayn's expression changed to see real food.

"Are you cooking it, too?" he joked.

"I don't think that I should cook it on account that I do not eat such things," responded Draish. "Besides, I have not cooked food in 600 years…"

"Oh yeah, you just like eating our friends raw." Slayn looked un-amused.

Draish took a bottle of whiskey in his hand. "I still enjoy other libations."

He smiled at Slayn.

"Does that even affect you?" asked Slayn.

"Yes, and if it's through the blood of someone who is drunk, it can be quite a delight."

Slayn took a glass from the table and said, "If you can't beat 'em, join 'em. Hit me!" He then took the glass next to the bottle.

Draish looked confused. "Now, why would I strike you?"

"No, dumb-ass, it's a figure of speech." Slayn laughed. "That means: pour me the drink."

Draish overlooked the insult, *dumb-ass* for his lack of understanding and tilted the bottle to the glass and poured a lot more than Slayn needed.

Slayn stood up and held his glass out. "Let's toast to Torru…for good luck."

Myiako walked over to them and popped the cork on the wine bottle. They exchanged looks, and then touched glasses to bottles for a toast.

"To long life and health, may we all survive by the grace of the gods," Slayn said calmly.

Myiako and Slayn took a sip of their drinks while Draish took the bottle to drink from. The other two looked at him and shared a laugh as he removed the bottle from his lips and exhaled.

"That had to burn, this is some strong stuff!" exclaimed Slayn, watching in disbelief. "Shit, did you leave your nobility in the grave?" He smiled.

Draish cleared his thoughts. "Now, that is no way to speak in front of a lady. My drinking habits are beside the point of cognitive faculties."

"Well, that's only if you consider Myi a 'lady'," Slayn teased Myiako, who then stuck her tongue out at him.

"I have a feeling that you humans are as mysterious as I am."

Slayn made his way over to the room corner to fire up a stove. The flames illuminated the dimly lit room.

Myiako started slicing the fish while Draish sat and watched.

Draish finished the entire bottle and

clanked it down. Myiako glanced toward him.

"I...I used to be wealthy, feared, and respected...and now I am nothing," he complained.

"You're still feared, that's for damn sure. You're a vampire...a living relic," Slayn said, taking a drink of the same glass as before.

"You can't say you're nothing..." Myiako stopped what she was doing and looked at Draish. "You may be a vampire, but your heart beats warm."

Draish acknowledged her with a quick grin, and then slumped back into the chair. "If that is what you wish to believe..."

Myiako picked up the de-scaled fish meat and threw it on the grill of the potbellied-stove, along side with the tubers. She then quickly closed the door so that smoke wouldn't fill the room.

Draish watched her in wonderment.

"Such a strange fire box...such strange new things these towns...much different than the times I lived before," he mumbled, obviously intoxicated.

Myiako sat down beside him and took a sip of her wine.

"That's right; there are technologies now that a person with your mind state would think are magic," she said, quickly changing the subject.

"Should we see if Torru will eat?" she wondered.

"That kind of hunger is already gone, but a drink is always good," responded Draish, looking at her from a slouching posture.

She thought about it, and then walked into Torru's room with a cup of water. Moments later, she came back, saddened, and rejoined them.

Slayn stood by the stove to watch the food cook, and then turned away momentarily.

"How come the necklace that Myi wears has no effect on you?" he asked.

The white-haired man looked at Myi, and then responded, "Indeed, it is a cross, but I personally have nothing against religion. I'm really not a demon, you *will* realize," he paused. "I am of an ancient race, far greater than humans." It was clear Draish was becoming irritated with Slayn's narrow-mindedness.

"Don't ya get all upset now," Slayn said with sarcasm.

Draish's voice was lowered, again. "It's just all the lies that have been said about us."

"Well, maybe we should clear up the stereotypes then," replied Slayn. "Do you sleep in a coffin, daily?"

"I suppose anyone could. A vampire's

main priority is to seal out light," said Draish.

"What about water? Can you touch it?" asked Myiako, getting into the conversation.

"Well, I can touch it… but not lower vampires. Most water supplies are so impure… You probably mean, ummm, holy water," he responded.

"What do you mean by lower vampires?" asked Slayn, as he took the food off of the stove.

"What I mean is that they are not as old as I, and of course, they would have less powers and immunities," Draish answered him, and then he grabbed the second bottle of alcohol. "I cannot stand natural light, but I've seen one do so." He looked at Myiako before opening his second bottle.

"So one day the sunlight won't affect you?"

"Perhaps…" he took a drink.

"You sure can drink, just like a pirate!" exclaimed Slayn, who was now sitting at the table with the cooked fish.

"My body is very different from yours," replied Draish, and then burped. "Pardon me!"

"Not so different…" said Myiako with a smile.

The two began eating while the vampire drank more liquor.

After a few silent moments, Slayn asked, "What about garlic? Can it harm you?"

"Now how could I be harmed by it?" Draish smiled. "It just makes the blood taste bad."

"Really," mumbled Slayn, as he grabbed a garlic clove from out of a bowl on the table. He then used it to season the fish.

Draish grinned to sense Slayn's fear. "So, you really haven't seen anyone like me before?" he asked, scratching his head.

Myiako looked up from eating and swallowed. "In several places, we have heard of them living, but were never 'fortunate' enough to encounter a vampire until…you know."

Draish sighed, sat back and looked down. He then pulled a necklace from under his shirt. It was a green stone on a long chain. He then noticed Myiako looking at him.

"That seems familiar…" she replied.

"It…it was hers," he vaguely responded, putting it back under his shirt.

Myiako became quiet again to finish her food and take a gulp of wine.

Slayn interrupted the odd silence.

"Let's play some cards to buy us time," he said, taking a deck off of the side table.

"I do remember a card game in the mid-

1500s, but these cards look very different," Draish replied, as he pulled the heavy chair easily to the table.

"Let's teach him royal poker," said Myiako smiling.

Slayn shuffled the deck and passed out the cards.

Draish held them in front of him with a peculiar look on his pale face.

"Um…why is this king stabbing himself in the head?" he described the picture on the card.

Myiako chuckled. "That's just how they were made, and for some games it's used."

Slayn and Myi began to explain the rules of poker with their new 'friend'.

"So, that is the jist of it," Myiako concluded after a while.

"I find those conditions satisfactory enough. I'll make the first move," Draish told them. "Let me trade these two." He put down two cards, which Slayn replaced.

They waited for Draish to make his move and call it.

"Let's see…I have this queen of diamonds…" he lay down the card, followed by a jack of hearts and a red ten, as well as a red ace. "And my suicidal king would make it a royal party."

The two saw his perfect hand,

disbelieving that his physic powers weren't being put to use.

"How did ya–that would be royal straight!" exclaimed Myiako.

"I'm sorry, but a hand like that proves you are evil," commented Slayn.

"Ummm…no, I am medieval."

They all laughed.

They continued to drink and play cards as if nothing was out of the ordinary; despite the fact their friend was near death in the other room…

After a few hours of this, Draish fell asleep over the table with a half-drunk bottle still gripped in his hand.

Myiako walked by Slayn, who was fast asleep on the couch, and stepped over to Draish.

After gently taking the bottle from him, she closed it and placed it on the table. She stared at him for a moment, sleeping quietly, and then bent down and kissed his cheek.

"Sleep well, my knight of darkness. May our dreams tell us the truth," she quietly said, then left to go into her room to sleep as well.

{V}: Fear Of The Truth

The white-haired knight wept over the motionless body of his love. Not holding back, his tears streamed like a fountain. Then wiping away tears, he stood up with her body in his arms. He felt that he had failed her, why couldn't he protect the one he loved, was that too much to ask?

"I promise you, Zaira…that vampire-creature will face my sword," he quietly said, walking toward his horse.

After laying her over the horse's back, he took the green stone necklace from around her blood-covered neck. He touched her soft face one last time and put the necklace into his pocket. He grimly mounted the robed horse and headed slowly through the woods toward the castle. He had cried over her death more than he would ever admit. He would have to wipe the tears away and act strong before he encountered his compatriots.

Perhaps The Next Day…

The royal council; priest, guards, and noblemen were positioned around a glass casket that contained Zaira's body. A young, lanky man, who wore a crown, approached the coffin. Tears fell onto the glass and he took a deep breath to say, "Les ceremony de la mortuary le fin." He turned around, blinking away tears. "You may all leave."

The people began exiting the large castle room in a predestined fashion behind the congregation.

The crowned prince changed his sad expression to say, "Sir Jauri…"

Draish turned to him. *They will never pronounce my name correctly…*

"I wish you to be in my chambers in a quarter's time," the prince told him.

Draish then slowly walked out next to another knight.

"We know you did all one could to protect her," the man assured him.

"We believe your story…" another one of the armoured men told him.

"Guess it wasn't enough…" he responded.

The human Draish paced the hallway, armour clanking. What was to become of him without her? What did the prince want of him? Surely it was not that he was to think that he committed this travesty.

Fifteen minutes later, the knight, Draish, found himself entering the prince's wing of the castle. The double doors were much taller than anyone needed in order to pass through and the walls were elegantly decorated.

When he had reached the throne room, he stopped. At the end of the red carpet was the chair where Prince Andolein was seated. He was a young king, dark hair slicked back and of an olive complexion.

Draish bowed down to him, respectfully.

"Come closer to my throne," ordered the prince with an unsettling glare on his mildly attractive face.

Draish began to show regular human signs of fear and nervousness as he walked toward the prince.

"What do you have to say for yourself?" Prince Andolein suddenly exclaimed, grabbing the sides of his throne chair.

"Believe me sir," started Draish, "I was no match for a vampire who could walk during—"

"I know that you would have done *anything* to save her...but, THAT IS NOT WHAT I AM TALKING ABOUT!" shouted Andolein, who stood up in anger.

He raised his arm to silently order his guards, the two large men standing on either side of the doors, to shut them. Once that task was done, they walked up to flank Draish.

"*What's going on?*" he wondered, looking at the guards.

"This is such a tragedy because you were such a great warrior, Draish Jauri," Andolein said slowly walking toward him, his voice lowered again.

The white-haired man stepped back, but was grabbed by the arms. The large guards made sure that he was going nowhere.

"It's Jau-Ri..." he grunted.

"Really, well, I guess this won't be too hard to do considering that *you* had your way with the woman to be my queen!" The prince's voice grew with anger and intense hatred for what he had found out.

Draish was shocked and began struggling to free himself, but it was no use, having only human strength...

Andolein positioned his rings on his fingers and made a fist. He punched Draish in the side to the face and the stones in the rings cut him.

"What are you talking about!?" asked Draish after recoiling from the blow.

Andolein gave him a disgusted look. "Ha...You think I'm an imbecile! Those late-nights she had left her room, to come back hours later. Those times I saw the way you looked at her! I figured it out when a little bird told me something—yesterday," stated the prince, losing his patience. "Remember that time she was kidnapped?"

He brought back his arm and punched Draish again, this time in the stomach. The white-haired man fell forward and the guards kept him from falling. He coughed to spit out blood. For a skinny man, the prince could pack a punch.

"You know what I heard!" raged Andolein. "My sources told me that they saw you with my Zaira, in the stables of all places… engaging in…in intercourse!" He gave Draish another abdomen punch. Gasping, his head hung low, as the guards still held his arms.

"You're a fool if you want me to beg…" Draish panted. "You can't prove a damn thing……you need me for your military."

"You are not all what you think… Do you try to tell me that there was another silver-haired man with my fiancé!" the prince said with a sneer. He then swung his leg, and brought his booted foot up, kicking Draish on the head. This time the two men holding him let him fall to the ground. Draish grunted, but never called out in pain.

Andolein looked down, smiling now, a look of vehemence. Then he motioned to the guards again. They picked Draish up and drug him to the wall that happened to have chains and shackles secured to it.

"You have really pissed me off, Jauri! You could have had any other woman except MINE! What were you thinking?! Now I will be delayed of becoming king!" exclaimed the prince as he walked over to his desk. He dug around in a drawer until pulling something out of one.

Andolein nodded his head to the guards.

The guards stripped Draish of his top armour and shirt, and then locked his hands in the wall shackles. It looked as if his servants were used to doing this. Who knew what other men had been tortured at the prince's wrath.

It was now apparent that Andolein was holding a double-tailed whip. The leather was grasped in his hands.

"Now you must repent for you sins; what you did to me, traitor!" he said walking over to the wall where Draish was secured.

"If she never went out with you…this wouldn't have to be…" Andolein raised his arm.

One slash cuts though his chest; Draish clenched his teeth in pain. Another slash of the whip and another; he lets the scream come out this time.

"I am your leader and you defiled my wife!" exclaimed Andolein, pausing to strike.

Draish weakly looked to him. "D…Did you ever…" he started to say, "Did you ever ask her how she felt!" he managed a stronger voice.

The prince came at him with the whip again. "That means nothing now! She was mine, damn you!" Andolein stated with another strike, there was no stopping him; the look in his eyes proved ruthlessness.

Draish's muscular chest was covered with swollen welts and another series of lashings caused the wounds to bleed.

He gasped and let out another scream. "This is no way to avenge her death!"

"Well, it is satisfactory enough for me!" The prince told him with a grimacing smile across his young face.

At this point, Draish was too tormented to even hold his weight; he had to lift his head to look at the greedy prince. He realized then Andolein wasn't standing in front of him anymore. The prince was calmly putting the whip back in his desk drawer and he took a seat. Sweat dripped from the prince, resting from the work out.

"You scream like a bitch…some great warrior."

"You…wouldn't have done that…if I wasn't chained up…" Draish mumbled, as blood ran down his chin.

"HA, too late for you now, you are pathetic," Andolein growled. "I've had whores last longer than you!" He then got back up and walked over to him.

"…you…will…" the white-haired man mumbled.

Speak up!" demanded Prince Andolein.

Draish's brow line narrowed and his blue eyes turned cold. "You will get yours when I come for you!" he growled.

"A little late for threats, don't you think?" Andolein responded, then reaching under his robes, he stated, "You are a dead man, Draish Jauri!" He unsheathed a blade. "Such a waste, you know…you were always so attractive."

The restrained man tensed up as the prince approached him with a large dagger in hand.

"You sadistic usurper…I cannot forgive you, she never loved you…" Draish glared at him.

"You are really not good at talking yourself out of things…so, where shall I start?" Andolein said with a menacing look, glancing at his two guards that were still standing around. They stepped away.

He scraped the knife against Draish's face, gliding it down his neck and stopping at his chest to stab it in just far enough to conceal the tip in his skin. Andolein was enjoying himself, playing along with his distorted view on what had really happened between Zaira and Draish. He cared not if she ever loved him; but to prove a point across his courts, he would show no mercy.

"Does that feel good…to know that you killed her and now I kill you?"

Draish growled in pain and hatred at his torturer while the prince responded with an insane smile. The knife was then pulled down, ripping into more flesh.

Draish yelled in agony, "Death…won't even save you from me!!"

Andolein pulled the dagger out and stuck it in between the man's rib cage and cut down a few inches into his stomach. A blood-curdling scream caused the guards to avert their eyes.

Andolein removed the dagger again, but this time slashed it down on the man's chest. Blood splashed out and hit their faces. The guards turned away to avoid seeing this.

"This is just too much fun, sorry it has to end…"

Draish's blood dripped to the ground, covering his pants and boots.

"Any last words, my beloved knight?"

"Yeah…I'll see you in hell."

The enraged prince gave one last blow and shoved the knife into Draish's gut; the handle quickly was soaked with the red liquid and covered his hand as well. These were his last mortal wounds that would haunt him for eternity.

Everything went blurry for Draish; he was then unchained and fell hard to the floor.

The voices echoed around him, blood rushed from his body, his heart gave out, and the world faded to black. He found himself in an indescribable void of nothing, not feeling the pain of death anymore. He remained in this timeless void for seconds, or hours, or days.

"Come to me," spoke a heavenly voice from the darkness.

He then saw her walking toward him in the black abyss. She was wearing a long light-coloured gown that flowed behind her.

Draish stood in wonderment and noticed he was wearing nice, new armour with a long cape.

"Where am I?" He tried to speak, but was muted.

"Come to me," the woman said again.

"Who are you?" Silent words he spoke.

"The gatekeeper…of the real and the spirit worlds. The divider of the righteous and the damned. But, my dear, you get a third choice and a second chance."

The woman's silhouette was enchanting.

"Unjust execution leads to the wandering souls...I can't die and nor will you," she explained, her glowing hair blowing in no wind.

He tried to see her face, but she was merely light.

"So...I'm *really* dead?" He seemed surprised. "Death was so easy."

"Yes, it is living that is the hard part," she told him.

"What do mean by a third choice?"

"It is beyond life and death, but both at once," she said. "I offer the pleasures of life, but the painlessness of death. To get the revenge we seek, you could go back to the world as an undead master, as a...vampire," she said, her voice quiet and soothing.

"Understand though, that in itself, is the price to pay," she added.

His eyes could only remain on her and he gained confidence.

"That won't bring her back," he told her.

"Maybe so, but you can live as a supreme being. You, Draish Jau-Ri, are chosen as the pure vampire."

"What does that include…what does that mean?" he asked, looking unsure.

"You will be sent back by the will of the gods, and at your full potential you could be a demi-god…you must see, you really have no choice here, and you are wasting valuable time on Gaia. You must understand that the pass of time holds irrelevance, because the time you spent here is many months on earth and things might be different," she replied. "Let us go now in time to seek your revenge for your love."

Draish didn't quite know what to make of it all. He was never a religious man, nor had he ever thought too hard on what followed after life. Yet, he did know enough to trust her, and his instincts.

"I will go back for Zaira's sake — revenge shall be mine!" Draish said, stepping toward her. He then realized that this woman might not have been Zaira, but her predecessor.

"Very well, a new vampire of light shall be born," she said, and then to raised her arms. "By thy Lady Necromancy and thy powers of light…Pryvante` de lumi un guruns!" An overwhelming light was emitted by the gatekeeper and magic was set in motion.

⊰◆⊱

Draish opened his eyes to a shadow-filled room of Myiako's house, lying face down on the hardwood floor. His memories quickly fading as he returned to reality. He suddenly pushed himself up after hearing a moan from the other room.

Torru suddenly yelled from the other room, "It's getting so dark… please help me!"

Draish stood up and put a hand to his head, then saw Myiako run into the front room where he was.

"Oh…you're awake," she said to Draish, seemingly startled to see him standing after almost two bottles of alcohol the previous night.

Draish peered at her and said, "He must be reaching the void already…not much time left…"

"What can we do, Draish?" she asked with growing concern.

"I had told you the only thing I could do for him….Sorry, my lady," he responded.

"Let me talk to Slayn," she told him. "Stay right here." Myiako then turned back into the bed room.

Slayn stood at Torru's bedside as Myiako entered. Torru continued to moan as Myiako talked to Slayn.

"I know you don't want this to

continue," she said.

"I think it really should be Torru's decision," Slayn responded, looking down at their bearded friend, who was now awake.

"Torru…can you hear me?" asked Slayn.

"Of course I can! Help me! Don't just stand there—" Torru muttered through gritted teeth.

Myiako took his sweaty palm and asked, "Do wish to keep living if the only way is to turn you into an undead?"

"What!? I'm gonna die!" Torru exclaimed, seeming to realize his condition.

"Not if you get changed into an undead," repeated Myiako.

"What, an undead?!" Torru grasped Myiako's hand and looked at them both. "I'll do to live…for life…"

{VI}: The Mystic Swordsman

He didn't hesitate…

"We should hurry up and get this over. Close the window shutters and I'll get Draish," Myi told Slayn.

Slayn remained still as Myiako left the room. He then looked down to Torru and said, "Don't worry, Torru, I got to go now, but you'll find me soon enough."

"What are ya say'n?" whispered Torru.

Slayn closed the window on one side of the room and crawled out the other.

"W—where are you going?" The man lying in the bed questioned his friend again.

"Goodbye…" This was Slayn's only response as he shut the window from the outside.

Torru was even more confused than before as he watched Myiako and Draish enter his room.

"Where did Slayn go?" Myiako asked.

Torru hesitated, nearly too weak to answer.

"He climbed out the window and left… shows what little faith he has in my life," he told them.

"He must not want to see you go through this," Draish commented, looking down at Torru.

Torru quickly forced himself up when he saw the vampire nearing him.

"This is your fault, ya know!" Torru snapped at Draish.

Draish smiled. "At least you have enough life left in you to argue…this might not be so difficult," he told him. "It won't be too easy on you either."

"What are you saying?" asked Myiako.

"He's sayin' that I should have put a bullet into him when I had the chance." Torru broke in, holding back his aching pains.

Draish shook his head but remained smiling inappropriately.

"You guys need to get over this human-vampire dispute already! The only way to move forward is to work together," said Myiako, bringing a woman's sensibility between their harsh glances toward one another.

"You are going to become a vampire, Torru, if you want to live."

"Torru doesn't hate me entirely because I happen to be a vampire. It is because I show a great fondness towards you…" said Draish, averting his eyes to Myi.

Torru looked displeased and sicker than before. "Get outta my head, you fiend…just do what ya gotta do, I'm already infected…"

"I don't think it's the right time to bring up such a topic…my friend is dying…" Myiako told Draish, her eyes narrowed almost to a squint.

"Oh, I think it's the perfect time," Draish responded with a cocky attitude. "This is all about our feelings for you. How naive are you, Myiako?"

She continued an annoyed glance at him and responded, "Sorry, I don't have your vampire mind tricks. How am I supposed to know how people feel?"

Torru broke in. "Hurry the hell up! I'll tell you how I feel. I feel like I'm in hell! Now do what ya gotta do!" He mustered the strength to yell at them as he was struck with a searing pain.

"Are you sure you want to drink the blood of the undead to restore your life?" the platinum haired man asked Torru, for the last time.

"I'm sure as heck not dyin' now! If I died…I couldn't kick your ass!" exclaimed Torru, making his decision.

The vampire walked closer to the man propped up on the bed, and then held out his own arm and put his wrist to his mouth. He then closed his grey eyes and chanted in half Mortary: "Seca` ve guruns…I invoke the inner spirits…to manifest the gift of the cursed!"

Draish then stabbed his top fang into his own vein and blood slowly began dripping out. He held his arm over Torru.

"Drink to the gods! Octisous la dante un lumi!" He finished the chant.

Torru was hesitant to take the bleeding wrist, but finally grabbed the arm to his mouth to drink. He quickly pulled away with disgust.

Draish grunted in anger, or maybe pain, while Myiako watched from what she thought was a safe distance.

"Drink, I say!" demanded Draish, as his blood continued dripping.

The man with the beard took his hand again, and this time continued to take blood from the vampire's wrist, indulging with each swallow.

After a minute, Draish pulled his arm free and cringed in pain.

Torru fell forward, putting his hands to his blood-stained face and suddenly let out a scream that soon diminished to a moan.

Draish stepped backwards, grabbing his wrist, and stood next to Myiako.

Torru's body began to seize, and then he was gagging. Myiako lunged forward to help him, but was grabbed by Draish.

"What's the big idea?" she snapped at Draish, struggling to break free of his grasp.

"This is normal…at least, I think," Draish told her.

Myiako stopped struggling when she saw a light began to glow around Torru.

"What!?" she gasped.

"That cannot be…" quietly commented Draish.

"What's wrong?" wondered Myiako, stepping back.

"It's different!" vaguely responded the vampire.

"What is? Did you say the wrong spell?" demanded Myiako.

Torru started to heal and regain colour. Then his clothing began magically changing into armour. Soon enough, Torru was wearing full plate mail, shining dark blue with a silver lining, as well as being equipped with a helmet and sword. Then he went still and simply lay on the bed like some Olympian statue.

Draish sighed in awe, his eyes wide, "By ye gods…" he said. "He is the Mystic Swordsman of this age!" he exclaimed. "This is not to my understanding…a true miracle."

The armoured Torru now stood up next to the bed and looked around with astonishment and delight to stand again. The light faded around him as the other two stood staring at him with open mouths.

"I have no clue what just happened," said Torru. "But I feel great!" His voice was more energetic than normal.

"Looks as if your blood did more than expected," commented Myiako to Draish.

"How can this be…already the time has come?" wondered the platinum-haired vampire to himself. He knew that he had to prepare for the unwanted already, in this life.

Torru was happy, but confused. "I am alive and normal…well, this armour is kinda strange…but I'm a human, I'm sure of it!"

Draish stepped forward. "You were bound by destiny just like Myiako is bound to the necromancer. You are fated to be the Mystic Swordsman," he said to Torru. "What of Slayn…?" Draish looked to the closed window.

"Keep your distance, vampire," cautioned Torru. "I still remember what was done." He then drew his sword from his back harness.

Draish stopped stepping forward and growled, "You don't seem to recall that you indeed befouled me with sunlight for me to do such a thing!"

Myiako became fed up with their

continuing feud and yelled, "Would you two cut this shit out!"

They were quick to silence their bickering to stare at the angered woman.

"Alright Torru, let's make a truce—" Draish began to say.

"—No bargaining with you, demon!" exclaimed Torru, and then came at Draish with his sword.

The white-haired man dodged the attack to go behind Torru and elbow him in the back of the head. Torru's helmet clanked into his skull causing his ears to ring.

After regaining balance, Torru shook his head and retaliated with another lunge at Draish. The vampire grabbed Torru's arm and twisted it just enough to make the sword drop.

A punch with a metal glove then caught Draish off guard, slamming into his jaw.

Myiako watched, furious, and exclaimed, "If you two don't stop; I'll just have to kill you myself!!!"

She then pulled Torru back with an abnormal strength.

After she made Torru calm down, his armour and helmet started fading before their eyes until he just wore a shirt and pants again. The sword on the ground still remained though and didn't vanish. He looked dumbfounded from uncontrollably losing his power.

"The moment has passed, I see," said Draish, rubbing his bruised jaw and glaring at Torru.

"What…that's it?" asked Torru.

"That power of yours is new…" said Draish. "I'll be glad to tell you more if you try to stop killing me."

Torru responded with an angry sigh.

Draish went on to say, "Kill me not, but rather idolize me, if anything, for I renewed your ancient life."

"Maybe we should make a pact…I *am* still living," Torru eventually agreed.

Draish was happy to extend his hand to Torru for a shake. Torru hesitated to look at the vampires' wrist where he cut himself, but it was already healed. Torru looked to Myiako, who nodded, and finally shook hands with Draish.

"So, what is my new power all about?" the bearded man then asked.

"To defeat them…" Draish vaguely responded.

"We should find out where Slayn went. He'd be happy to see you're not a ghoul or something," suggested Myiako.

"But first, I want to learn about how to get that armour again," commented Torru.

"You'll find use for it when the time is right…the ancient powers feed off your emotions to protect innocence…" Draish told him.

"Well, let's see how my newfound ability works in tracking down our friend," said Torru and smiled.

Draish became uneasy and replied, "Um…it is daylight, so I have no choice but to stay behind."

"Ha…some powers you got." Torru laughed at Draish.

Myiako then elbowed him to catch his eyes with an annoyed look. She then smiled at Draish, and she and Torru left the room.

Draish stepped forward to hear the clank of metal at his feet. The Mystic Sword lay on the floor and he had pushed it with his foot.

Torru and Myi had turned back to Draish.

"The sword?" wondered Torru.

Draish then maneuvered the blade over his foot and kicked it up to catch it. "It is the key to your power and forever yours," he told Torru.

"I think you know more than you're letting on," Myiako confessed to Draish with a discerning look.

"I get that same impression with you, my dear. And you should also know that I am capable of more than I lead thee to believe," Draish smiled. "I have to keep an air of mystery."

He then handed the sword to Torru. "Take it with you always," he told him.

Myi went to get her cloak coat from the chair in the main room.

Torru went to join her, looking the sword over as he did so. It had a large handle, covered with gold and silver inlay, and a broad, double-edged blade. He had to get his cape to conceal such a large weapon.

Draish looked at them, almost saddened by their leaving. He leaned against the doorframe, covered in the shadows he had learned to trust in. He didn't want her to go anywhere without him, but her words rang like law to him.

"We will be back soon." Myiako smiled at Draish. "I think I know where Slayn ran off to."

"Yeah, and don't you do anything I wouldn't do," replied Torru, as he hid the sword in his cloak.

Myiako and Torru walked to the front door, and when it was opened, Draish drew back into the room until the light was shut out again.

The white-haired vampire walked over to his favorite chair and took a seat. "Oh — what they don't know could fill a series of books," he said to himself in the darkness of the shadows, as thoughts sped through his mind before he finally nodded off to sleep. He found that he was tired often since his long sleep...

Meanwhile...

Myiako and Torru mounted their horses, noticing Slayn had taken his.

"If we can't find him by nightfall, I think we should come back and get Draish," said Myiako.

"What makes you so certain that he will stick around?"

"Because he won't leave me."

"Myi, you are just way too trusting..."

It actually didn't take Torru long to agree and he followed Myiako through the gates. He wanted to show off his new look to his friend, plus show that he didn't die after all.

The sky was filled with white clouds and the air was frigid. They had at least six hours of daylight left before being blinded by the night. The riders were soon out of town and were traveling at a decent speed down a gravel path. After a grove of trees, the town grew distant and the road ahead was barren.

"He told me that we'd know where he went," Torru said about Slayn.

Myiako looked at him. "He must have gone to those weird caves where we tried to take that treasure chest before. But I really wonder why he'd go so far without us."

She loosed her grip on the reins.

Torru smiled at Myi. "He is a grown man, I think he can fend for himself, ya know."

"Yeah, but not if he encountered an evil vampire or something," Myiako said, unsurely.

"Did you see any vamps prior to Draish around here before?"

"No, and that is why I'm worried that they're around here now…because of the resurrection," replied Myiako, becoming tense again.

"…great…" Torru responded, unenthusiastically.

They came upon the mountain range east of the one before and were greeted by a cold wind as the mountain cast shadows upon them. They slowed their horses to follow the narrow path through the valley.

As they went further between the mountains, rocks crumbled from the ledge above them. They looked up, but saw nothing.

We're not alone, thought Myiako, as her tension grew.

More rocks then fell behind them. They stopped to listen.

"What was that?" Torru wondered, knowing she knew of it no more than he.

This time it was a cracking of rocks that made them look all over with nervousness. Torru took out his sword for self-contentment.

Right before their eyes, something started emerging from the rocky mountainside.

"What the…" said Torru, as he watched the figure take shape from the living rock.

It soon became apparent that a woman's face was forming, and then her shapely body was formed.

The two held on to their startled horses and looked at the rock woman with eyes wide.

The strange form motioned her rock chiseled arms, causing the area to rumble around them. Rocks from the high ledges began hitting them.

The horses reared up and bolted. Myiako and Torru were forced to cling on as they barreled down the valley path.

The rock woman eagerly kept pace with the horses, taking on the camouflage of the passing rocks and dirt. A twisted smile came across her narrow face as she chased the two farther though the gaping valley.

"You humans cannot run from me!" the rock woman's strange voice cut into their ears, as she lifted an arm to throw a couple of large rocks at them. They hit both riders squarely, knocking them off their horses.

After a moment of recovery, Myiako and Torru stood face to face with the rock woman. They were covered with the dust of the escaping horses that were retreating the way they had come.

The chiseled woman had risen from the ground and extended her stone claws toward them.

"Shit...what now!" exclaimed Torru, as he guarded Myiako, his head bleeding.

Myiako stepped aside and pulled a handgun from her boot. She aimed it at the woman creature and hollered, "What do you want with us, creep!"

The stone woman smiled. "It is not a question of what I want with you, but my master's choice."

Her smile faded for her oncoming assault. She didn't hesitate to shoot rocks spikes at them; they were formed from her body and flew at Myi and Torru.

Myiako maneuvered a drop and roll to dodge while Torru deflected the rock spears with his sword. Myiako huddled down and cocked her gun. She aimed at the woman and unloaded, chipping away part of the rock that was her body and continuing to pump bullets into her until the revolver turned to the empty clicks of no ammunition.

The rock woman fell into a pile of rumble only to re-materialize in the rocks behind Myiako. Before Myi could react, she was smacked on the back of her head.

Seeing his friend fall to the ground, Torru yelled, "Noooo!"

He ran at the woman with the sword held high, yelling in rage. Doing this caused his aura to come out in a bright light and dramatically change him into the Mystic Swordsman.

"WHAT!?" exclaimed the rock creature, surprised to see the armour form on the man.

The sword came forward, just missing the woman, who vanished into the wall. His sword became stuck, embedded into the mountain from the force of his strike. He was distracted with his struggle to loosen the sword and was attacked.

The rock woman lifted her stone arm and bashed Torru in his helmet-protected head. The force was so intense it knocked him out cold, and he fell beside Myiako.

The rock woman looked down on the two of them and laughed. Her insane laughter echoed throughout the valley causing the high perching birds to flee.

{VII}: The King
And The Countess

Draish found himself in a tight-fitting space. As he struggled to move around, he tried to free himself. He shifted his weight and fell onto the dirt. He lay there for a minute, and then was able to get his knees. After looking around in the dark cave, he realized he was in the castle's catacombs.

He rubbed his face in disbelief of the perfect sight he had in the utter darkness. His mouth felt different to him, dry and gritty. He scraped his tongue along his new pointed teeth, which took up more space in his mouth. He touched his elongated teeth to reassure that he wasn't dreaming, poking his finger on a tooth that easily cut him.

He wearily got to his feet to see that he still wore the tattered remains of his former knight armour.

"Is this it?" he wondered out loud. He looked over his chest to the faded whiplashes and the large scar where he'd received the wound to end his mortal life.

The flames of a torch focused his attention, reflecting in his pale grey vampire eyes and revealing the pointed ears that stuck though his white hair and furry side burns. His physique wasn't as it had been when he had been reborn from resurrection of bone; instead he looked worn and thin.

Someone approached holding a torch and he backed into the shadows. It looked like a guard making his nightly patrol of the dungeons.

The armoured guard walked right passed Draish, not even noticing him watching from the darkness.

The white-haired man felt a new sensation course though his body. His mouth opened and he started drooling. The sound of his breath caused the guard to turn and look toward Draish, who had left the shadows and was right behind the man, ready to attack.

Draish could see the blood pulsating though the human and didn't procrastinate at pulling the open-faced helmet from the guards' head. The man turned around in confusion and flailed around with the torch in his hand. Draish was ready to knock him down and grabbed the torch to throw it of reach.

The man fell back and whispered in a fear-filled voice, "What in god's name are you?"

"Nothing in god's name..." responded

Draish quietly.

Then grabbing the man and ripping off his gorget, he brought his fangs down on the man's neck. A scream echoed within the empty corridor of the catacombs. The vampire covered the man's mouth and twisted his neck to silence him. He lifted his bloody mouth from the man's wounded neck and tossed the body aside. He licked his lips to savor this new flavor of power. Killing wasn't a new ordeal to him; therefore, he wasn't second guessing what he was to do.

Draish then looked saddened, not from killing, but from remembering something. He dug around in his pants pockets and his expression changed when he found he still had Zaira's necklace. He attempted to polish the stone on his blood-covered loin tunic, and then put it around his neck to hang over his scar-covered chest.

He finally looked down, sympathetically, at the body. Then he knelt down after an idea crossed his mind. *I can't go around looking like the corpse that I am,* he thought, as he began taking the armour from the dead man. He clamped on the chest plate, poleyns, cuirass, and elbow shields. Then he lifted the plated shoulder guards to rest on his shoulders as the cape unfurled behind him. He was happy to rip off his blood-stained tunic to replace it with the guard's clean one.

"Nice fit...thanks..." he said, looking down at his victim.

Draish stood up again, holding the helmet. He rubbed the wet blood from his chin and walked over to stomp out the discarded torch flames.

Someone else approached and a voice was heard to say, "What was that!?"

Another armoured man was coming his way. Draish slammed the sallet down over his matted hair and met the man entering the cave.

"I thought I heard a scream...is everything alright over here?" the approaching guard asked of the vampire, who was dressed as he was.

"I do not know what you're talking about, Sir...everything's fine over here," said Draish, mimicking the dead man's voice.

The guard suspiciously stared at Draish, and then finally turned to walk away.

Letting out a breath, he wondered aloud, "What's with all the security?" as he scanned all the armoured men patrolling around the castle.

He stood at the cave entrance, staring off into a somewhat familiar village, with the castle as a backdrop. The tunnels of the catacombs started in the depths of the castle and circled under the village.

As he looked around with his new eyes, he noticed someone looking back. He averted his eyes to gaze at the full moon through the helmet visor. He was a vampire, new to darkness…the velvet curtain of despair that was the night…

Draish casually walked around to gather information from the village surroundings. From the royal crest that adorned the flags and armour, he knew that his foe still had legions here. It was the crest of the hawk, representing the wrenched Prince Andolein and his predecessors.

"Yes…" his voice was deep and quiet, "That is why I am here…to get revenge on this human, and then to find the one who killed *her*." Thoughts of vengeance caused his body to tense up. He continued walking through the night and looking at the quiet houses, peeking into the windows of the commoners as they slept.

His corrupt thoughts were soon interrupted when a knight called to him to ask, "What are you doing!? Get back to your post!"

Draish turned and started walking toward the knight that had shouted at him.

"Go back…I say!" The man responded

upon seeing the other quicken his pace toward him. The knight began to scold Draish as he stopped in front of him, "Would you stop messing around and go patrol the west…"

Draish swept off his helmet then, causing his platinum-white hair to fall over his pale eyes.

The knight recoiled and drew his sword on the strange man.

Draish disappeared, only to re-appear behind the unsuspecting man, who still peered ahead, searching for him. The vampire used his god-like speed to grab the man's head. The sword forte was heaved back, but only caught Draish's cape. Draish brought his fist down on the man's elbow causing him to lose grip on the sword, which went clanking to the ground. He then lifted the knight off of his feet with his clawed fingers around the man's neck. As soon as he uncovered the man's mouth to do so, the knight started screaming.

"Shut up!" growled Draish, who then effortlessly snapped the man's neck.

By this time, other guards had noticed the security breech and gathered around the creature that they knew was a vampire. They watched Draish drink from the man he was holding before making their attack. He could feel his muscles grow as he regained his health.

Lifting his head, he tossed the corpse

aside to face these new competitors.

This is fun.

"My god…it's another one," said one man that held a halberd.

"Where do you bloodsuckers keep coming from?" snarled another knight.

Draish grabbed the sword that had been dropped and replied, "Where do you think we come from…but the grave, of course."

He held the large sword out with one arm, knowing that is was meant for a human to wield with two—but human he no longer was.

"I…I can smell something…" Draish said, looking at the men.

"What's this one's problem?" muttered a knight, wondering why this vampire was hesitating to fight.

Draish was quick to smile again. "Oh, I know…I can smell your fear!"

His voice was no longer calm as he stepped closer to them.

"Die, Devil spawn!" one of the men yelled, the first to attack.

He lunged at Draish and their swords clashed. The vampire pushed the man aside and blocked the axe that came at him. He grabbed the wooden handle and lifted the man holding the axe. He then threw the knight down and out of his way.

"So, who will be next to face me?"

Draish wore a confident smile, realizing he had much more strength than any man had ever encountered.

The four knights that remained on their feet came charging at Draish, who simply extended his arm as though trying and halt them, but, to his surprise, a powerful wave force shot from his palm. The men were forced to the ground and struggled to get up with their weapons and useless shields.

Draish looked at his hand in confusion, not being accustomed to having such powers and not yet being able to maintain control of them.

"Ha…ha, even I remember it is unwise to challenge a vampire at night, and under a full moon, no less." He laughed before the knights came at him again.

Their medieval weapons flailed about uselessly, as one after another, the supernaturally strong man knocked them down.

Draish swung the sword in his possession and it sliced through one man. Without hesitation, he heaved the blade forward, and another knight was stuck in the gut. Blood poured out as he pulled the sword from the body and swung it over his back to guard the oncoming attack from behind. The sword protected his back and he turned and was able to kick the man to the ground.

He was charged from the other side and this time a knight managed to stab the vampire in the side of his chest, just between where the front and back of his armour latched.

Draish pulled his body from the sword and touched his virtually painless wound. He looked up and gave the scared man a menacing smile.

Draish could run much faster than human eyes could see, and he tackled the man to the ground in rage. While on top of the knight, he knocked his helmet off and started pummeling his face with clenched fingers. Left and right to the side of the man's face. The other two remaining guards managed to pull Draish off their ally, but were hit with his rampaging fist.

The vampire regained his sword and ran it though the man on the ground. He looked to the two men who had pulled him from their ally, but they were ready to retreat and began to run.

The man with the axe stood his ground though, looking at Draish in pure fear.

"Wish to try me a second time?" the white-haired man asked, making his wound heal itself.

The wounded knight stumbled off,

followed by the one wielding the axe.

The vampire, Draish, found himself awkwardly alone in the darkness of the moonlight. After using a body on the ground to clean the blade, he sheathed the sword and brushed his hands together as a job completed.

"That was even easier than usual," he said as he headed for the castle.

This all comes so naturally to me…

He stumbled over a body and kicked another as he left the bloody scene. "What a waste of good blood…" he said with a smirk.

As he walked on through the village, other guards scrambled to hide from the approaching vampire.

There was a tall stairwell with wide steps that eventually led to the castle's wooden doors. He stopped when he saw three figures on horseback appear at the top of the stairs.

Draish instinctually sniffed the air and recognized a devastatingly familiar scent.

"Seems like we meet again, Andolein!" he called to the crowned man.

"Do I know you, peasant?" wondered Andolein, and then descending the stairs on horseback one step at a time.

The two royal guards stayed right beside him.

As the man drew closer, Draish knew

for sure that this was Andolein, though now grey with age.

"Who are you to address the King by his first name!?" demanded Andolein.

"Dost thou not recognize me?" Draish said with sneering fangs.

The horses reached the bottom of the broad stairway and the men paused to look at the vampire.

"You are not one of the Countess' minions," started the king, "but you do look familiar, vampire" he added, drawing a thin sword.

"I have been waiting a time in limbo, just to kill you…" replied Draish quietly, as he drew the blood-stained sword from his side.

"That white hair…why…why it cannot be you," the king stuttered, losing his confidence. "But I had killed you over twenty years ago and stuck your corpse in the caves for the rats!"

Though his tone was strong, he was obviously scared. He then nervously motioned for his guards to stand closer.

"You seem slow in your old age," Draish told Andolein. "I can't believe that you didn't recognize a former captain of the Calvary. Now, you must know me as the Vampire, Draish Jau-Ri!" His voice deepened with anticipation.

Andolein stared at the vampire as if he had seen a ghost; as well he did.

"I am dominating ruler of this kingdom! You still have no right to dishonour me, alive or dead," the crowned man shouted, growing intense with anger.

"All who do not bow before me shall be ordered to death! I am sure you know of this, Jauri!" Andolein arrogantly pointed his sword at Draish.

"My name is pronounced Jau-Ri, you impudent fool."

"OH, pardon me. Mind you last time we met you were screaming like a bitch."

"You liked that didn't you...but will soon you will see that I am anything but a bitch...You—you never gave me a chance, and you are still hiding behind your guards," growled Draish, lifting his head with equal arrogance.

"Seize this traitor!" the king shouted to his guards.

The two guards on horseback attempted to throw a long chain around Draish, but were knocked off their saddles instead. He used their chain to his advantage and pulled on the links that had been wrapped around his arm to bring one of the men to him. The platinum-haired man then reached his arm back and flexed his muscles. His veins could be seen starting to protrude where his arm gauntlets didn't cover. The vampire cracked his knuckles and his claws tore through the leather gloves he was wearing. With claws out, he jammed his hand into the man's gut, breaking through his armour and reaching the soft gel of his insides.

He pulled his blood-covered hand out of the screaming man, clenching something in his fingers. The guards' liver had been ripped open and he fell to his face.

Draish took a bite from the bloody mass in his hand and threw it down. He shook off the liquid dripping from his hand, and then slowly licked a finger. The vampire peered at the other guard, who was already retreating on horseback.

"Coward!" the king called to him, dismounting his horse.

Draish stared at him, grinning, and laughed in a way that it sent chills down a human's spine.

The king in his fancy robe, still was able to stand ground, with his sword gripped tightly, before the vampire.

Draish's smile faded and he vanished, to then appear behind Andolein.

The king had been ready for the attack and swords struck together. There was a flash of sparks as the friction built up between the blades. The vampire started forcing the man back as the swords were locked together.

"You should have run away while you had the chance…" stated Draish, his voice lowered again. He then gave a shove forward and the man fell back.

"Why should I run from a creature as weak as you!" snapped the king, as he got back to his feet.

"So, what makes you sure that I am as incompetent as the average vampire?" Draish wondered, furrowing his dark eyebrows. He then held the sword back up waiting an attack.

"I have encountered far greater ones than you!" The king grew angry and held his thin blade out in a fencing stance.

The swords clashed from side to side and the king's feet shuffled frantically under him. Draish kept calm while he swung the large sword.

Their weapons deadlocked again, as they tested each other's strength. Andolein was soon thrown to his back. Draish heaved the sword down, but the king was able to roll away before being run through.

Andolein retaliated to throw a small, shiny dagger that stuck into Draish's thigh.

The vampire was forced to shift his weight on to the other leg as he grabbed the embedded dagger. As he pulled it out, the metal burned his hand and he growled, "What is this?" This stab wound did not heal itself; instead, the hole looked cauterized, as if he was stuck with a hot fire poker.

The king was able to catch him off guard with another tactical strategy and grabbed the pouch that had been tied to his belt. The satchel was thrown and as it smacked Draish's face, water broke out.

The clear liquid boiled his skin and his face began to smolder. He frantically buried his face in his hands.

Andolein lifted his leg and kicked Draish in the stomach. His boot dented his armour and the vampire fell back.

"You whelp! You have every single vulnerability that a vampire could have!" the king shouted. "I know everything there is to know about your kind." He now stood over Draish.

A twisted look of hate came across Andolein's aging face as he brought his sword down on the vampire's chest. It only took him a second to realize that no one was in the chest plate armour he had just stuck his sword into. With growing confusion, he pulled out the sword and poked around in the attached cape.

The white-haired vampire was behind Andolein again. He was now topless, with his muscles flexed. He squeezed his arms around the man's arms and body, to restrain him as Draish's gauntlet-covered forearms dug into him.

The king dropped his sword from the grasping pressure and his face started turning blue.

"What...are you..." Andolein struggled to say as the grip tightened. He looked at Draish's water scarred face. Draish exchanged the glance with glowing eyes.

The vampire looked different from his handsome, pale-eyed self; the scars on his face were apparently done by water due to the wave-like burning pattern. He opened his mouth enraged to inhale.

The king watched the vampires' fangs elongate, and he flinched to a rumbling growl. He struggled to free himself, but was virtually powerless against this creature who owned the night.

The fangs came down on Andolein, but he was saved when Draish stopped after seeing two puncture wounds already on his neck.

"What the hell?" wondered Draish, as he noticeably loosened his grip.

The king took this opportunity to get away from the vampire and retrieve his sword.

Draish stood still with bewilderment.

He lost his concentration, causing his eyes to fade to pale blue and his muscles subside as he calmed down.

"Are you starting to figure it out?" the king said with a laugh. "Now, why would a human take on a vampire at night!?" he exclaimed. "Why would he, Jauri?"

The platinum-haired vampire then slowly bent down to retrieve his sword, and he replied, "A human would be so naïve, but a human you are not, nor a vampire!" And he raised his sword.

"I am sure that you are that bastard prince who put my mortal body to death… so that is why I must kill you with no holds barred," the vampire told the king.

"If you dare to kill me, you will face a far greater threat!" Andolein said with nervousness.

"Well, well. It seems that these days, even the king has someone to answer to. You frighten me so…"

Draish gave a quick grin, and then went flying at Andolein.

The clank of metal shatters the air and sparks flew. The King Andolein seemed more powerful than before, pushing his sword toward Draish for a longer time. He was pushed to the ground again, but this time by a magic force exerted from the vampire, not from the sword.

Andolein remained on the ground while Draish came at him with the sword, but before the charging vampire could come any closer, a black wall of energy pushed him away.

The king realized what had happened and started laughing. Another person's laughter then joined his.

"Ha, Ha, Ha, Ha, Ha!" A mysterious woman's voice echoed in the air.

Draish looked passed Andolein to try to find where the woman was hiding. He saw no one standing in the dark. He watched Andolein stand, as to greet the woman appearing beside him.

She was of great elegance and beauty, with fiery orange hair bound in her tiara crown. She looked young, but fumed of wisdom, with her high cheekbones and ruby lips. She wore an exquisitely decorated dress that was red and black.

Draish stared at her in awe and lowered his sword. "Who are you?" He found his attention fixated on her ample bosom.

"I am the Queen Scarlet, and formerly a countess of this kingdom." Her burgundy eyes caught his attention. Draish couldn't help but to stare into them, feeling her power manifesting inside.

"Stop that gawking at my wife! Have you never seen a lady vampire before?!" exclaimed Andolein, who was standing next to her.

The countess stepped forward and said, "Watching you fight made me believe that you're exceptional compared to the other night creatures. Who sent you?" she demanded of Draish. "Who gave you your un-life?" she demanded.

Draish lifted his sword and strongly said, "I was given the dark gifts by the necromancer herself. I am to answer to no one."

He swung the blade downward, cutting though the air. "I have no dealings with you, my lady." He looked from Scarlet to Andolein then back to Scarlet.

"Really? Your powers are from the Lady Necron," she responded, walking toward Draish.

As she came closer, Draish found he was unable to move, being captivated by her radiant beauty.

"Any grudge with my King is a dispute with me," she said with complete eye contact.

She kept moving in on Draish until she was uncomfortably close. Draish raised an eyebrow, unaware of what she was planning. He held the sword at his side, but still gripped it tightly.

"I could spare your life if you become a royal guard for us," Scarlet tried a one-sided compromise with the white-haired vampire.

"If I live a hundred lives, I'd never serve such pond scum again!" Draish growled, and caught the countess off guard to run his sword in her body. She screamed as he pushed further on the sword handle, driving it through her body until she fell to the ground. He shoved the blade into the dirt beneath her.

Andolein yelled, "Scarlet!!!" and backed away.

She gave an angered scream though the gargled blood and made herself transform, using the vamperic ability to turn into a bat. The black bat had her orange hair and it shrieked before flying toward the castle.

"Ha, Ha!" Draish laughed. "Was that pathetic display all your precious queen had to offer!"

He smiled at Andolein. "She bailed out on you now! You know she is just using you for your blood." Draish continued his laughter.

"Shut up! You know nothing of this!" shouted the king, who then was shrouded with a dark light. He had somehow disappeared and left.

Draish let out a sigh of relief, and dropped the sword.

"I have a lot left to learn," he said to himself, and then picked up the cracked chest armour and cape.

The young vampire was new to his combined powers of the light and the dark, but already was getting accustomed to the overwhelming blood lust that caused malicious intent to rise inside of him. He now awaited his destiny as an honourable ruler to this disease-ridden land…

{VIII}: The Wolf And The Rock

Draish's head jerked from sleep at a knock at the door. It was dark outside, now, but the house remained empty. Another knock sounded, and he got up slowly, shaking off past memories.

"Hello? It's your neighbor…" called a man's voice from outside.

The door slowly opened to show no one standing inside.

"Um…hello? I just wanted to tell you your horses are out." The villager walked inside the house. "Hello?"

The door slammed suddenly behind him and the man jumped. Draish dropped down from his ceiling-hiding place, in front of the unsuspecting man.

"Who are you? Where are Torru and the others?" asked the man, as he stepped back from the white-haired man.

Draish didn't wish to engage in conversation and instead grabbed the man. A hand covered the scream as he bit down on the flesh of the man's neck. The vampire drank to his heart's content and then dragged the body to the back of the house. He came back to the front room ten minutes later with an energetic smile and new black boots on his formerly bare feet.

After wiping the excess blood from his face, he put on one of Slayn's cloaks and opened the front door. He looked around, and then stepped outside and shut the door. No one seemed to be within the vicinity; except the horses that were saddled and walking around the house. They had found their way back home. Draish took hold of the reins and pulled the two horses back into the fenced area.

He held his hand out for the horse to sniff and he rubbed its soft snout. He was able to see what the horse had seen, merely by petting it. He saw flashes of the rock minion that had attacked Myi and Torru in the valley and quickly drew his hand away. That was information enough to tell him what he was to do.

Draish looked around and saw no one watching him, and then looked up to the waning moon. He began concentrating to form energy around him as his clothes started to change into thick fur. His face elongated into a snout and he became a wolf. The only thing that withstood the transformation was the green stone necklace that hung on the white wolf's furry mane.

Before the horses had time to react to seeing a man change into a dog, the wolf ran off into the night. He didn't stop running until he reached the tree line at the outskirts of town. The wolf put his nose to the air, and then sniffed the ground. He took a few steps forward, and then quickened his pace, tracking the scent.

The silver wolf that was Draish followed the hoof prints out of town and toward the mountains. He soon reached the narrow valley and continued to follow his nose though the high cliffs.

By this time, Draish knew he was being trailed, catching sight of a shadow that wasn't his. The wolf stopped and peered into the empty valley, his panting echoing within in the rocky corridor. He held his breath a moment and perked his ears up to listen. Nothing…

He continued on, but was then stopped in his paw tracks when by a deep laugh.

"Ha, Ha, Ha! Valk into my trap, little doggy," a deep, unnerving voice said, echoing through the mountain walls.

"What do you want!" barked Draish, who then turned back into a man. The fur melted back into clothing. He stood on two legs and freed an arm from the cloak.

"I know who you are, even though we've never been properly introduced," the man said, his voice causing an immense echo.

"Is that right..." Draish said casually. "Who are you then?"

The dark shadow his eyes were focused on moved closer to him.

"I am the King of Vampires, and if you do not know of me, you are not one of us!" stated the voice that resonated throughout.

"Show yourself!" said Draish, enraged. "I doubt you are who you say!"

"Watch your tongue, boy! Maybe you could ask the Lady Necromancy or the Mystic Swordsman to find out who I am, first hand," the deep voice radiated a strange accent.

"Since when does the king of the undead hide in shadows?" Draish made a cocky remark.

"Such a foolish vampire you are, and always were," replied the shadow's voice as it melted into the mountain.

Draish took a step back when he saw the rock wall start to split. There was now a cave type entrance in the side of the mountain. He peered into the cave and hesitated.

"They are vaiting for you, inside..." the deep voice told him.

The white-haired vampire then found himself walking though the hollow cave, headed in no particular direction. The cave opening began to close with an earth-shaking rumble behind him. He turned around and growled, realizing there was no going back.

"If you can make it though my first test, many more are to come until your fate awaits when we meet—" The unseen man was then cut off.

"Hold your tougue! After I find them, I'll hunt you down myself, and then you can only hope for something as simple as death!" Draish yelled into the darkness.

"My, you are such an anxious young vampire. You may just have what it takes to entertain me briefly," responded the voice, and his ominous presence then left Draish in unnerving silence.

He continued down the cave path, angrily stomping his boots with each step. He gradually quickened his pace. "How long is this wretched tunnel?" His voice bounced off the narrow walls, and then he finally noticed some torch light ahead.

Draish suddenly paused to smell the air. It was faint smell of blood, enough to catch the attention of any bloodsucking parasite.

He started jogging down the path until he stopped when the cave widened to a room where torches hung on sconces, as if awaiting him. It only took him a moment to become familiar with the area. Seemingly knowing where he was, from a distant past, he stood in a forgotten necropolis, a cemetery deep with the mountain range where he had been buried as well.

He looked around frantically for signs of life, digging though the many burial dugouts and coffins, in search of blood. *These old corpses could not contain any…but that smell is starting to drive me mad,* he thought, as he lifted another coffin lid to a smiling skeleton.

"Ha, Ha, Ha!" It was the shrieking voice of the rock minion woman.

He turned to see her body emerge from the wall parallel to him.

"You! Where are they?" Draish ran at her. "Tell me!" His fist just cracked into the wall when she sank back into it.

"So close, but too slow," she replied, her voice then gaining intensity. "I have no choice but to crush you!" With that, the room started to vibrate and rocks were knocked loose.

Draish scurried to remain grounded as he dodged the oncoming avalanche. A boulder came down on him, slamming him to the ground. It only took him a few seconds to push it off and stand back up.

The woman rose up from the dirt in front of him and replied, "It must be true that you're really the one of legend that my master hath spoke of." She put her chiseled hands on her rocky hips.

Draish raised an eyebrow in wonderment of the minion before him. Her sculpted female shape was almost flawless and taking form right in front of him.

"And just who might you be?" he asked her with an annoyed glare.

She smiled; and then surprised him with a sudden attack of a stone spear in the gut.

"I will be your end if you let your guard down again!" she screeched, as she ran her arm-spear though Draish.

He grabbed the rock skewering him with both hands, gagging up blood.

She pushed and ran him toward the wall as his boot heels scraped the ground.

He tightened his grip on her arm-spear and howled though bloody fangs. A magical force was summoned from the vampire that went though the rock woman. It started to crack and crumble her rock body. As the spear within him broke away, the rock wench's cacophony of screams echoed through the cavern.

Draish backed away and fell to all fours with the gushing hole in his body. He watched the woman crumble into pieces, leaving her slender face on top the pile of debris, like a mask lying in sand.

"I will see you again, Draish Jau-Ri!" cackled the woman's face that then sunk into the ground.

Draish held up until she left, and then dropped to his face from the substantial exsanguination. Blood continued to gush from the wound that had a six-inch diameter. The spear had gone right between his rib cage, and left a gaping hole though his clothes and torso. He lay there momentarily, making pathetic sounds of agony until he was able to focus. His pale eyes closed and he gained aptitude to heal. The large wound started restructuring itself, from the inside outward.

After his flesh was healed, he pushed himself from the ground. He looked down and felt his exposed abdomen, thinking of how that used a lot of energy to heal, but also thinking of how pissed off he was at the minion who attacked him. Draish let out a sigh of disgust and leaned over on a nearby coffin.

He rested his arm and put his head down, only to perk back up again.

"That smell!" he exclaimed, knowing to open the coffin. He lifted the wooden lid to reveal Myiako, who was lying unconscious with a line of blood on her pretty face. He stared at her and knew that she wasn't dead, but just out from the bump on her head. He couldn't resist touching the soft nape of her neck, uncontrollably causing his canine teeth to extend. He lowered his neck and bent his head as his open mouth came closer to her neck.

Myiako screamed and jerked away. She looked harshly at him and slapped him across the face. "What in the hell do you think you're doing?!" she screeched. "Were you gonna bite me?!"

Draish gave her a baffled expression and mumbled something.

"Well, at least you found me…" she then said, her lips turning into a smile to see the red hand print on his pale cheek.

There was a pounding coming from the coffin beside them. Myiako climbed out of the casket and put her feet on its bier. She then watched Draish lift the lid of the other coffin.

Torru was quick to sit up, gasping for air. "I'm not dead, I'm not dead," he repeated in utter confusion.

Myiako went to comfort him, placing her hand on his back, and his breathing slowed as he calmed down.

"Oh thank thee gods, you're okay, Myi." Torru got up and looked around in the dark cave. "My sword…I—I lost it!" he then exclaimed.

"I remember seeing it embedded into the side of the mountain…right before…" Draish said quietly, and stopped himself.

Myiako rubbed the back of her head and looked around. Her eyes noticed the wet pool of blood on the ground where Draish had fallen.

"What happened here?" She looked with concern at Draish and noticed the rips in his cloak and shirt. She then stepped closer to the vampire, causing Torru's brow to furrow.

"Don't worry, my dear. I have gotten rid of that rock minion, at least for now," Draish said with a slight grin.

"Good, because that weird woman thing sure is a bitch to knock me in the back of the head," replied Myiako, with noticeable signs of anger.

"At least you're alright," Draish said, looking into her green eyes. She found herself not able to resist and gazed into his eyes as well, as if hypnotized. "Yes, I'm all right…"

"Um…hello? Shouldn't we find a way outta here?" Torru broke in. "There is something out to get us, and it probably already has Slayn." He stood up and looked around.

Draish looked annoyed for Myiako to change her thoughts.

"No sign of him, huh?" she then asked.

"I know that he is not here, because while I was following your scent outside, I came across that of Slayn's. It went onward through the canyon," stated Draish.

"How did you find us?" asked Myiako.

"Mind you, I am a master vampire and my ability reaches into the minds of the living." Draish gave an almost automatic response to her.

Well, at least he's honest, she thought.

"Come on," said Myiako, "I'll know where Slayn is once we get out of this cave."

They all walked into the darkness of the cave corridor, in search of the exit...

{IX}: Three Guardians

After the three of them reached the end of the path, Draish's spell-casting aptitude came of use.

"When I got here," Draish started to tell them, "there was an unnervingly familiar voice and he used a spell to open the mountain."

"So, where's the exit now?" wondered Myiako.

"This time the temporary effects of magic were anything but to our advantage," Draish explained.

"I have no idea how Myi and me got in here, because we were knocked out, ya know," Torru said, trying to make out their faces on the pitch dark.

"That voice you heard must have been that of the rock woman's master. I wonder who he is," said Myiako, as she tied her dark hair back.

"I remember how to use that spell to make a magic door, so stand back," Draish told them, and with growing concentration, he stared at the wall.

The vampire crossed his arms in front of him and before he began to chant, lowered his tone.

"Powers of the ancients heed my call: Nalay-la-begi-gurun; al'ra'tos!"   He slowly moved his arms down. "Dajin' la limite` seca' pose~a!!"

He finished chanting and slowly spread his arms out, which caused the mountain stone to part and the star and moonlight to come rushing in. The rock gap was large enough to walk through, so Myi and Torru hurried outside. Draish then stepped out, and as he did the rocky walls rumbled shut behind him.

"Alright!"   exclaimed Torru   upon seeing his sword impaled in the rock where he'd left it. He regained the Mystic Sword and concealed it in his cloak again.

"Good thing ya put on those extra pounds, I can't even tell you have that huge sword on ya." Myiako gave Torru a friendly smile.

"Tis strange that they didn't take the sword, knowing that it's the beacon to the transformation," Draish commented. "He must be planning something for me," he then said quieter.

"What do you mean? What aren't you telling us?" Torru asked the vampire, showing confined anger.

Draish's pale blue eyes turned gray as he sneered at Torru, "Have you no recollection of the past five hundred years of history? Have you really no knowledge of the immaculate powers that your body hath received?" He was annoyed with naive human minds that were incapable of remembering the past deception.

"My memories are but as vague as a dream, but I recognize you, Draish. Is that because I'm a reincarnation of Zaira?" Myiako asked.

The white-haired man looked down.

"If one fails to learn history, thus it repeats, so I must explain to thee."

Draish began expressing his confined knowledge. "When I was new to the world of darkness...but already accustomed to the feats of deceit, I took my chances with changing a human to become my slave. He was resilient. To my surprise, this human did not turn into an undead creature, but the Mystic Swordsman. A completely different one from you, I might add."

He glanced at Torru but quickly looked back to the pretty woman. He went on. "It was the year 1265, before the Common Era, when I knew to start my allegiance with the righteous."

"So the other guy who was the Swordsman disliked vampires as well, that is not completely different," replied Torru.

"But he was smart enough to

distinguish between friend and foe; and his swordsmanship was excellent," Draish responded. "We fought against the dark legions side by side, that we did."

"So what about you and the guardians, was this series of events set up to continue to protect the innocent?" Myiako asked.

"When the dark lords rise, a light will subside the shadows for equality of good and the evil. One must exist for the other. Daytime exists for the night to shroud. The Mystic Swordsman is sworn guardian of celestial bodies: stars, moons, planets. The Lady Necron or the necromancer is the protector of souls between the planes of space." He then stopped. "These are the elements of life and death."

"Wasn't there a third guardian?" asked Myiako.

"Seems that our search for the final guardian will be made simple, for the Dragon Lord lives deep within someone you know, too." Draish exchanged glances with both of them.

"You don't mean…" started Myiako.

"Slayn is the third guardian!" stated Torru.

"Yes, I know it just sounds too perfect… the chances of you two knowing each other is rare, but now the third," Draish said. "Our battle this century has come quicker than ever. I think they're even becoming weary of this never-ending onslaught."

"I'm glad that my brother, Slayn, decided to live with me after all." said Myiako with a smile.

"What? He's your brother? Guess that explains it," Torru said in surprise, unaware of Miy's and Slayn's relation, even after living with them for two years. "It all makes sense now…"

"I knew that," commented Draish, pleased with his intuition.

"I believe that we're caught up for now and we really should continue looking for Slayn," Myiako suggested, as she looked around in the shadows in hopes of finding the horses.

"The horses are back at your house…" Draish said, and then, becoming anxious, he added, "Um…that is how…I knew something wasn't right with you."

He stuttered at remembering their neighbor, who he had made dinner out of.

"Crap! It'll take all night to walk to the other side of the mountains now," stated Myiako, looking at the valley path ahead.

They reluctantly started walking on the continuing path. After about forty silent minutes, they walked past a small cave indention in the side of the mountain where Myiako wanted to rest.

"You're correct about the time spent walking. Too bad my flight ability is restricted to myself," said Draish. "Do you think I should go back and get the horses for you?" he asked.

Myiako yawned. "That seems to be our best bet…I already need to rest." She started to become drowsy.

"Are you okay, Myi?" wondered Torru, watching her sit down.

"I just feel strange lately," she mumbled.

Torru gave Draish a harsh look, thinking that the vampire was the reason they were in this situation.

Draish knelt down next to Myiako to look her over. Despite all the sleep she'd been getting, her eyes had bags and her cheeks looked flushed. Draish looked concerned and stood back up. "I don't think it wise to leave you here, alone."

"Hey, ya forget'n about me," Torru responded.

"It is in your power to protect her." Draish lightened his mannerism toward Torru. He then looked down to Myi, who was sitting with her legs pressed to her chest.

"Pray thee that *he* hath cast no spells on you…is there nothing more to contribute to my suffering?" Draish raised his voice. "I'll take a short leave, besides if they wanted to kill you, it wouldn't have been set up for me to find you."

"And just who do you keep referring to?" demanded Torru.

"The enemy that I still live to destroy…" vaguely responded Draish, as he started a transformation. The vampire had turned himself into a large bat with a white scraggly mane and flew up into the sky.

"Protect her, this time! Besides I think it's me he's after…" Draish told him through his bat vocals.

Torru watched him fly off in awe, and then looked down to Myiako. She was already asleep on the dirt of the small cave.

"What oddities our future holds…" Torru quietly said, looking at the sleeping beauty.

{X}: Blood Reign

Two figures stood in opposition of each other in a large stone room surrounded by pillars. Parts of the room's structure had been destroyed and debris lay at their feet. The broken remains of once intricate stained-glass windows revealed the dark world outside.

It was as if someone was watching the standoff…

Draish looked formidable, wearing different, fitted-leather armour, painted black, with a royal blue tunic that matched his cape. Shielded plates covered his knees and shins over his leather pants and he had black shiny sabatons. The armour pieces on his arms were cracked and war-scarred, showing a sizable gash on his forearm. Blood dripped with sweat down his angered face. He stood readied, with a slender sword out in front of him.

The 'person' he was engaged in battle with was the Countess Scarlet, in a tight renaissance-styled dress, her orange hair frizzed out from immense power use.

The white-haired vampire stepped forward and intentionally kicked the dismembered body that lay on the ground.

Under the bloody robes was the body of the now late King Andolein. Draish had finally fulfilled part of his personal purpose with little effort; slaughtering the undead king.

Another dream...she thought.

Draish now had to face the underlining consequences of taking on the queen-countess.

"How..." exclaimed Scarlet with anticipating anger, "how in hell did you kill my husband and best minion? This is impossible." Her burgundy eyes turned red.

Draish grinned and responded, "Your best minion...he was just a sadistic little bitch, and you know it."

"I should have done away with you the first time we met...Even the greatest of us make mistakes," Scarlet told him, hesitating for further battle.

"You need to stop putting on this façade, acting as if you're greater than I. You are even more arrogant to believe you're even more powerful than the dark lord, Dra`cul." Draish was content with power.

"How dare you speak any less of the Dark King! I am in his service to kill any threats to his kingdom," she was quick to respond.

"Remember when we met, Scarlet? I was already able to scare you off with the first of my vamperic abilities. Think of the energy that I have harnessed over these many years...I dare you," Draish told her.

"Why is it that you wish to protect the weak humans? This wouldn't be happening right now if you had joined our legion," demanded Scarlet, her eyes darkening again.

"As a human myself, I fought in the name of honour, love, and justice. That is why I was reborn into the darkness to ultimately fight it. The undead blood in my veins still flows of nobility; unlike the accursed life that pulsates though you. 'Tis shame to even call you Countess properly, as you have dishonoured your noble bloodline," Draish said boldly.

"You...with your moral intrigues... You speak of honour and love as if you're still human. Such things don't apply to undeads. You must know that we live far beyond the boundaries of the mortal realm," she told him, and then her voice rising, she continued, "I cannot comprehend this! Why be a servant to the mortal's impudent gods, the dark lords obtain the true power that you will soon face!" She then cracked her knuckles.

"Tell that to your husband..." Draish smiled again. "You'd rather rule in hell than serve in heaven, is that so?"

"This faded reality of humans in which you remain entrapped will be the death of you, blinding you with ignorance can be more devastating than the truth." Her eyes were changed to red again with her words and she readied an attack. She held her palms out and blasted a magical flame wave at him.

He had vanished to avoid it and reappeared in front of her, sword swinging.

She ducked to avoid decapitation and reached out and struck Draish in his gut with her hand. She pulled it from his ripped armour and flesh, and he looked down. Her hand had been formed into steel claws, which would have been capable of piercing though even plate mail.

He jumped back a safe distance while throwing a blue energy bolt at the countess that was projected from his hand. She deflected it with her big metal hand as Draish summoned another bolt from his free hand. The red-haired vampire was able to catch the energy with her normal hand and threw it right back at him. Her throw proved superior to Draish's and caught him off of guard. He was pushed to the ground, onto his back.

It was simple enough to tell that Draish wasn't a challenge for the elder vampire, but his initiative remained dominant to suffice his noble actions. He held his composure despite the injuries and the beads of perspiration (which was strange for one who never seemed to sweat).

"I do give you credit for keeping up, but it's not good enough! For shame, you must die!" Scarlet cackled then appeared over him.

She slowly raised her normal arm, causing the platinum-haired man to lift from the ground but still not on his feet. She motioned him close to her, just by whim.

He struggled to free from her invisible grasp but was too weak.

"I will return again, this I assure, because you're next. And give Dracula my regards for our battle in the future," he bravely told her, with his eyes turning completely white.

"Ha, Ha, Ha! No coming back!" she laughed, belligerently.

The vampire countess motioned him closer with her hand, urging his face close to hers.

"You could have had all the life blood and fortune one could desire. I could have had some enjoyment from you, even." Her tone was disturbingly soft.

She then forced her dark lush lips onto his mouth and engaged the unwilling man to a kiss. He clenched his eyes shut and started to struggle, especially after experiencing her tongue in his mouth. She then pulled her head back.

Draish snorted and spat on her face.

She responded with a growl that echoed off the walls.

"HOW DARE YOU!" she yelled, raising her steel fingered hand. She then rammed a long sharp metal finger into Draish's heart. He gasped with gargled blood that splashed to the ground.

"I do not wish for things as easy to acquire as blood or fortune..." Draish said through bloody fangs, "...but to find happiness, a thing a creature like you couldn't grasp in endless lifetimes..." He strained out the words. It was apparent he was in great pain.

She just responded with a hiss and plunged her claw deeper into his chest.

The red liquid gushed out with each dying pulse. The hole in his chest from earlier made it impossible for him to heal. His last gaze pierced into her mind, ever etched into her memory, which disrupted her laughter. It seemed to disturb her. She dropped her magic grip and her smile faded as she looked down to him. He was apparently dead, with his eyes in the back of his head, lying in a pool of his own blood, but his body started glowing with white energy. Scarlet knew immediately what was happening.

"Damn you, Lady Necron...To bring

him back to life," growled Scarlet. "Never again!" She used her metal claws to cut off his head, doing everything to kill a vampire.

The pure light still shrouded his body.

To the Countess's surprise a voice spoke to her.

"Though one can kill him, he can never be destroyed."

It was Zaira's voice, talking from the spirit realm. And it was the necromancer's power that caused Draish's body and head to vanish with the light.

"Light vampires will return to sanctuary until another year…" Zaira said to Scarlet, who growled with intense hatred.

The echo within the walls reverberated until the castle room faded.

ଓ ◆ ଛ

Myiako awoke, her face covered in tears.

"All that for nothing!" she cried out, startling Torru.

He looked at her with wide eyes, seated nearby, leaning on the mountainous wall.

Myiako sat up and rubbed her eyes that were bloodshot from crying while she dreamt.

"He—he couldn't even get his conclusion in a second life," she said, looking to Torru and sniffling.

He looked back to her, knowing she had been saddened by the overcoming knowledge of the past.

"I know," he assured her. "The Mystic Swordsman couldn't do a damned thing either." His posture relaxed again.

Myiako cleared her throat. "You have memories of a past life as well?" she asked, her eyes now dried.

"Well, no, it's just in the legend of the vampire." He scratched his dirty dark hair and went on. "The humans under the king and countess's reign, revolted first. They were grateful that Draish had killed King Andolein to weaken the Vampire Queen Scarlet," Torru told her. "Well, that's what I read, anyways."

"Was the prince Andolein really *that* horrible to the people?" asked Myiako.

"Who said it ever really happened… history or a story, people have their own interpretations," responded Torru.

"Then, why do I dream about a legend? I remember that she saved his remains with her protection magic and entombed his body for centuries," Myiako said, now fully sitting up.

"Yeah? But what happened to the Countess?"

Their attention was diverted by the

sound of approaching horses. They could see the dark shadow of a man riding a horse with another horse tied behind him. The horses were saddled and bags hung from the sides. Apparently it was Draish, with his face shadowed by his cloak hood. Myiako could see his eyes reflect like a cat's in the moonlight. After nearing them, he dismounted and took down the cape's hood.

"What is ever wrong with you two?" the white-haired man asked them.

Myiako stood and walked to him. "There is so much we don't know, how are we gonna solve something we can't understand?" she asked with growing curiosity.

"We should really talk things over on our way. The moon is setting," Draish replied with anticipation, avoiding eye contact with Myi.

Torru walked to his big black horse, not forgetting his sword. Draish then helped the woman onto her brown horse.

"Aren't you gonna ride?" Myiako asked, looking down from her mount.

"I think it best for me to scout ahead," Draish told her. "This all started too soon."

"No...you have to explain some things to us before we go any further," Myiako demanded from him. "Like what in hell was that rock woman thing...and why is it?"

"If you must know," Draish started, "Vampires can create other vampires, right." He grinned.

"I guess…" responded Myi.

"And you know vampires can create other undeads, ghoul creatures, if you will."

He paused. "These are a vampire's minions…ever servants to their masters and slaves to the dark," explained Draish.

"Why don't they all become the same creatures? What makes the changes different?" questioned Myiako, as she adjusted on the leather saddle.

"That is something that even I cannot tell you. Only the gods are to know, the ancients decide one's fate," he told her, his eyes up to the moon.

"So, that must be how I became the Swordsman…fate from the gods," concluded Torru.

There was a quiet moment for the three to exchange glances.

"Then tell us whose minions we're to watch for," said Myiako.

Draish became impatient. "I'll explain more when we reach the other side of this valley," Draish replied, and then he closed his eyes.

They watched him melt into his wolf

form and howl with his silver mane to the air.

The horses reared up from the sound, causing Torru to almost fall off.

"What the hell?" But before Torru could complain, the wolf-Draish ran off into the twilight.

The two on horseback were not reluctant to follow, and soon were engulfed in dust. The horses galloped down the valley, behind the wolf.

Draish stopped when he reached the end of the canyon to wait for them and to look around. He saw the native ruins that had been intricately carved on the back side of the mountain and noticed that a few of the window holes contained light. He then looked into the field, able to collect more information from the surroundings in his wolf form, as his vamperic senses were increased.

The grassy field was followed by a thick forest. Further in the distance was a silhouette of the castle's towers. Draish remembered the dark stone castle from another lifetime, yet to be mentioned. He took a few steps out on the grass and sniffed around, as a dog would. The wolf then crouched to the ground and his ears went flat, in defense initiative. Draish then turned himself back into a man, still crouched down on all fours and growling.

From the grass shadows the woman rose from the ground, chiseled in the brown rock.

"I truly advise you to leave me alone, minion of stone!" Draish snarled, then standing on two legs.

"Oh, I cannot leave you alone; my master has just begun with you," she told him in her shrill voice.

"I will make gravel of you and face this master of yours," threatened Draish, as he clenched his fist.

"You won't get rid of me so easily this time; you see, I brought some friends." She smiled with her dark rocky lips.

"Believe me…I know. You thought you could actually distract me from the creature behind me!" he exclaimed, then leaping into the air. He jumped off the hidden creature right behind him, and it went flying back. The wolf-like minion was pushed to the ground, its stealth attack failing.

Draish landed lightly and looked up. "And the other one," he said then doing a back flip to dodge another enemy's attack. A winged bat-man creature flew at him, swiping down with long claws. The bat minion was too slow and only caught Draish's cloak, to rip it.

Claws swiped again and this time the

vampire jumped up and landed on the man-bat's back. The creature struggled to get him off and flew high into the air. The rock woman and the wolf demon looked up to their elevated fight.

Draish made reins of the giant bat's coarse fur to hold on. The winged creature trusted his body while his arm wings vigorously flapped just to keep altitude. The white-haired vampire freed a hand to flick his wrist. He had now the ability to alter his hand into steel claws, which were double the size of his normal hand. He brought his hand blade down on the back of the monsters' neck. Blood sprayed out like a geyser, covering Draish. The minion screamed in agony. Draish then used his unnatural strength to pull his steel claws down the creatures' back, slicing it in to two. Within the same maneuver, he jumped off the dying minion. He landed on the ground in a crouch, with his normal hand for balance.

The mangled remains of the bat-beast dropped to the ground, followed by a shower of its blood. Draish's cloak and matted hair were soaked in blood. He wiped the mess from his face, just to smear it with a bloody sleeve.

"Bring it on!" he said with a grimaced smile on his red-stained face.

{XI}: A Dragon Revealed

Myiako and Torru cleared the valley to see Draish facing these opponents.

"Stay back!" warned Draish to them, but was too late.

There was another minion he had overlooked; the smell of the wolf monster overwhelmed this scaly demon. The 10-foot tall black-skinned creature made its way to the approaching riders on four legs. It had a muscular humanoid body with large horns protruding from the sides of its head and back.

Draish attempted to go after the black beast, but was attacked by the rock minion. She changed her arms into long rock spears and swung. Draish blocked with his metal hand and summoned energy with the other. A transparent sphere formed in his palm and he threw it at the rock minion. She tried to deflect the spell, but it surrounded her. His magic easily demobilized her and she yelled from being unable to move.

"Just too weak for me," Draish told the minion, then vanished to help the others.

The big demon grabbed Myiako from the panicking horse. Torru jumped from his mount and came at it with his sword. With each step and the emotion escalating, Torru gained the mystic armour as he could now by will, but must possess the sword as well.

Draish held back his defensive attack to watch Torru's.

The sword went down at the demon, but it moved and clawed at Torru. It then jumped back with Myiako under its large arm. She screamed and kicked uselessly.

The Mystic Swordsman gave another clumsy sword thrust while the demon minion swiped his claws again. Torru was sliced in the shoulder, the claws cutting though his armour. He dropped the sword in pain.

"Hey! Help us! Don't just stand there!" Myiako screamed at Draish upon seeing him watching.

Draish rolled his eyes, and then had to reason with his human side to get incentive to go assist them. He ran a few feet to jump incredibly high into the air.

The creature was still concentrated on Torru and continued to claw at him, while Draish made his attack. He came down on the demon with his metal hand readied. At the right distance he swung and slashed through the flesh of its neck.

Myiako was dropped to the ground. She scrambled away before the beast hit the ground. As the big creature fell, the area rumbled.

Draish shook the wet blood from his metal claws and he changed his hand back to normal. He did this just in time to see the wolf minion charging Myiako. Draish teleported over to her just to be knocked down by the rampaging wolf. It trampled Draish and picked up Myiako with both arms. He knew that they weren't going to hurt her at this time, but take her in front of him, being a sort of mockery.

The white-haired man tackled the wolf-man and Myiako was thrown. Draish used his arms to strangle the creature, and continued to do so until it went to its knees and then passed out.

"Shit!" exclaimed Draish, realizing that his incapacitate spell had worn out, and now the rock minion was attacking Torru.

The stone woman appeared from the ground before Torru. He had regained his sword and struck the rock on her body. Sparks just few off from the steel to stone and Torru was pushed back.

Draish shot an energy bolt from both hands and the white light came in contact with the rock woman. It hit one of her arms and broke the rock spear. The woman minion melted into the ground, but then rose up to capture Myiako.

Draish and Torru tried to attack the rock minion again, but were stopped by a magic field. The wolf creature had regained consciousness and put out this invisible force. They watched it power up to have something rip from its back. The wolf man had grown sizable bat-like wings.

The rock woman jumped onto the wolf's back with Myiako struggling in her non-broken arm. Wings flapped and the creature gained altitude.

Draish lunged at the minions but was forced down by the transparent field. Then the rock woman engulfed him in a blue inferno she cast. Draish's body was compressed with the magic flames. Apparently, she was just holding back what she could do.

Draish growled from his skin scorching and to see the minions fly away with Myiako as their captive. As they flew off toward the forest, he could hear the rock minion's laughter echo off the mountains.

Draish collapsed to the ground as the blue flames subsided from his charred clothes. Torru was yelling obesities into the air after them. After his outburst, he looked down to Draish, who was lying on the ground.

"Not the time to take a break," Torru joked inappropriately.

Draish picked his head up, looking as if a bomb had been dropped on him. He looked at Torru with a sour expression. "See if that one is dead."

He was referring to the black demon that had its throat slashed. Torru looked at it. "It sure as hell looks dead."

"Just run the sword into its heart to make sure," responded Draish, already regaining his strong voice.

Torru put pressure on his shoulder wound and lifted his sword. He approached the bloody demon and raised the sword. Gravity took over and the blade came down, completing the decapitation the vampire had started. He then lifted the sword again to drive it into the creatures' chest. A disturbing noise indicated that the beast was no more.

"Can't say it's alive anymore," Torru said with a disgusted look.

Draish got to his feet. His skin was healed but his pants and shirt were bloody and singed. He had this undead ability to draw blood into his skin so his flesh and hair looked clean again, despite his tattered clothes.

"Why didn't you kill that wolf thing before it grew wings?" accused Torru.

"I couldn't that easily. Some minions are stronger, like that rock bitch that dared to besiege Myiako." Draish growled. "If they harm her, every minion under their master will suffer." His dark eyebrows angled down with anger.

"Well, let's go find her!" exclaimed Torru.

"I cannot do that with the sun about to rise. I must seek cover," Draish responded quietly.

"Alright then, let's go into those ruins," suggested Torru, as he took hold of his horse's reins.

Draish then surprised the other horse by jumping up onto its back.

They galloped over to the strange abandoned village that was sketched out of the mountainside. Torru had tied a cloth scrap around his injured arm and Draish found himself staring at the blood being soaked up from the wound.

"I really hope this is where Slayn is hiding. I couldn't last another unpleasant visit from those minions," rambled Torru as they reached the small entryway. The apparent door was sealed with a round boulder.

"I bet ya this is the way to get in," replied Torru, as he got off his horse.

"Really, you think? Whatever gave it away?" responded Draish with sarcasm as he looked at the perfectly rounded boulder, which was fitted in front of the cave door.

Torru began to push on the rock. "Come help me move this," he asked Draish.

Draish got off the horse and barely had to assist Torru with moving the boulder.

They looked inside the makeshift building of stone and entered.

A torch hung on the tan stone walls, lighting the tapered corridor. The ceiling was almost too low for Draish to walk upright, and the two had a hard time walking side-by-side due to the narrow width.

"I'll take the lead." Draish told Torru as they moved down the diminutive hallway.

"What's up with this tiny hall? These must have been some little people to live in here," complained Torru.

"Right you are. The Cantu Tribe were Halflings, small and strange, but probably extinct or unknown by this century," Draish responded, having ancient knowledge of past lives.

As they maneuvered down the corridor, it became noticeable that the walls were gradually widening. The tapered hallway then opened up to a large coliseum-type room. It was an awkwardly shaped room with a circle of pillars. There was an altar table set in the center with tall torches on either side of it.

There was no one to be seen as they entered the room from the widened hall. Silence was heard until their footsteps echoed off the beryl stone floors.

"I don't see any—" Torru started, but was hushed by the vampire.

"...heart beating faster, is it not?" Draish said in a casual tone, his voice echoing off the walls. He was not talking to the man next to him, but something else. Draish could hear a rapid heartbeat on the opposite side of the room.   Then a familiar scent caught his attention.

"Don't harm me," said Slayn, as he stepped up from behind the altar table with his hands up in surrender. His cloak was torn and his clothes were different. Also, it was obvious he was without food and looked weak.

"Hey, where the hell have ya been!" exclaimed Torru, happy to see his friend.

"Stay back!" Draish warned to Torru. "He is not what he seems."

Torru ignored him and continued to greet Slayn.

"I see that you have the sword," replied Slayn to Torru.

The man with the large sword stopped in his tracks. "What ? Is it that you knew this whole time?!" exclaimed Torru, now bemused with his forgotten past. He drew his sword and stepped back.

"Of course he knew, he is the Dragon Lord," replied Draish. "Now show us your true colours!" he exclaimed, then appeared right beside Torru.

"What is the path thou will take? Have you converged with the darkness, or have you become a righteous guardian?" demanded Draish, and then transforming his hand into the steel claws.

"Mind you to stand down, vampire!" Slayn's voice turned into a powerful growl. "I am on your side, worry not."

"What's go'n on?" wondered Torru, backing away further.

Draish put his arm down and the metal claws subsided into his hand.

"You say you're on my side, but who is to decipher whose side we are on, after all?" Draish quizzed Slayn and gave him a toothy smirk.

"Very well," Slayn responded, then caused a yellow glow to radiate from his body. He took off his cloak and started to unbutton his shirt.

"What's going on!?" Torru was confused.

The white-haired vampire crossed his arms across his chest and watched Slayn's unwitnessed talent with amusement.

Colours began to resonate off of Slayn and his body began to change form. He was fading from human to reptilian in likeness and he grew several feet in height. Golden scales and large muscles ripped through his clothes.

Slayn was now apparently a dragon, not very large, but bigger than any minion. He perched on four legs in front of them. His head stood about eight feet from the ground. He still had Slayn's shaggy blonde hair though and his tattered remnants of shirt and pants. The massive wings expanded and subsided with a glint of gold.

"Ha, ha!" Laughed Draish. "You are the Golden Dragon… magnificent!"

The dragon lowered his scaly head. "I am the incarnation of the gold-scaled dragon of time, and guardian to the order." Slayn's dragon voice, echoed throughout the room.

"So pleased not to see your dark side, Dragon Lord. This situation does tie the loose ends about you..." replied Draish, looking up at the dragon. The golden scales reflected a light that caught Draish's attention.

The sun was rising and this room contained many window holes for the light to seep through. The vampire was quick to vanish into the shadows, leaving Slayn and

Torru to stare at each other.

"Since when have you been a Dragon???" said Torru. He then looked down, not knowing what to say about the refined knowledge his friend, the dragon, contained.

"I guess I have a lot of explaining to do, now," said Slayn, as he gradually changed back into a man. His scales faded to dirty flesh and he quickly grabbed the cloak to cover himself.

After Slayn was himself again, he asked, "Where's Myiako?"

"They took her..." coldly responded Torru, as he went in the direction that Draish had disappeared into.

Slayn had followed him into the back room that was shrouded in blackness.

"I think you'd want to hear what I have to say, Draish," replied Slayn.

They looked around the dark room only to see many shelves of books. They couldn't spot the vampire anywhere.

"Well go on. I am listening." Draish's voice startled them.

Torru and Slayn looked up to see a large bat hanging above them. He would change into animal form to conserve energy. It proved to be more efficient than remaining in his own form since they were smaller.

Torru stepped from under him while

Slayn chuckled.

The bat hung how bats do, upside down with claws gripping, and Draish looked at them though his white mane.

"You'd look just like a giant bat but... that silver head of hair gives it away." said Slayn, laughing.

"Alright, enough screw'n around, just tell us what you know, Sla...I mean Dragon Lord!" demanded Torru, losing the little patience he had with Slayn.

Slayn responded with a sigh, and then sat down on the faded tile floor. He began, "As keeper of irrelevant time, I had it in my power to bring Myiako and Torru into my human life, to purposely unite the earth guardians. This made our friendship a true one, as we are not allied because we have to be, but because we want to be," explained Slayn.

"Not just a strange coincidence, but destiny hath brought us together...yet again," summarized Draish, not losing his deep, calm voice though bat vocals.

"Throughout the ages the guardians were able to maintain the planets' balance... but then the 'Reign of Blood' era began," continued Slayn.

"Reign of Blood?" questioned Torru, who then sat on the floor as well.

"When the vampire king took over,"

replied Draish, "...that is Dracula...he was so arrogant to give a name to his massacre."

"This is when the guardians started turning *evil*," said Slayn. "They would achieve their supernatural powers and destroy, not protect. I left, feeling ashamed of what I knew could happen." He looked at Torru. "After Draish Jauri was awakened, again, I knew the time of reckoning, so to speak, was near."

"What ya mean by time of reckoning?" gulped Torru.

"That's pronounced Jau-Ri..." Draish commented.

Slayn averted his eyes. "The darkness has overcome the constant balance...evil grows and darkness follows, thus the three will assist the Vampire of Light to vanquish the dark," Slayn said, to justify their reason to be. They sat down, unable to see the bat, only hear his responses in a stoic voice.

"Being poetic now? Come on, vampire of light is that not a contradiction, for I am still the undead," broke in Draish, with aggravated bat movement.

"I was quoting from the Draco Tome, not my own words, but past...and you must know that you are contrary, because most vampires don't keep mortals around for anything other than livestock," Slayn replied, looking at the giant bat.

"What can I say? You might think that I actually have a bleeding heart," Draish responded, then leaving his mount to fly to the corner of the room.

"Anyways," started Slayn, "The guardians will keep reuniting for all of time until the dark lord and his minions are destroyed. So, this is where we stand...as guardians of balance and so on." Slayn looked down with a saddened change of expression.

"Is it that I must bring death upon all of the dark ones of Dra`cul or the Count himself?" Draish's voice was awkwardly unstable. "Dra`cul de mortary..." he muttered in the dead language.

"Why is this still going on? Is that vampire, Dracula, really too much for all three of us to handle?" wondered Torru, scratching his beard.

"The sign of the true immortal is to never die. Though we have gotten close... he always escapes...kadama de la sanctant," Draish made an aggravated response.

"Not to mention that Draish seems to get killed by the other vampires, so centuries may pass." Slayn made the risky statement to Draish.

The black bat with white hair formed back into Draish, who was still hanging bat-like from the ceiling. "You think I enjoy lying on the floor bleeding to death, missing limbs, while my executioner lets his minions feast upon my dying body," he said a little too calmly for the other's sake.

"We all have died in many ways," commented Slayn.

"You're wrong!" Draish jumped down and landed firmly on his boots. "Your soul has passed on, while I have resided in the same vessel for over six centuries...despite my time underground."

He pushed back his hair. "This time I feel different, we must work as one to end this. I will not stand the humiliation of being killed by a being lesser than I," Draish went on to say. "While you lie helpless to her every desire in her wicked mind just to have your life and power drained..."

"Ya think that was a little too descriptive there. Even for a vampire you sure act strange," Torru said after he became uneasy, once again, around Draish. He stood up to turn away from the platinum-haired vampire.

Slayn then stood and said, "I believe in time that all things come to an end...no one body can reside here forever...Dracula's reign of blood must end so the undead curse shall be lifted, thus the balance restored."

"Who made you such the connoisseur of vampires? You think that if Dracula is destroyed, the evil is as well?" Draish said to Slayn in a berating tone.

"I didn't say evil, I said undead curse," corrected Slayn.

"Curse you think, or is it a privilege that I get to come back over and over to still claim my revenge." Draish's words were strong but unsure. "Maybe you already know the outcome, and I am to die again." He stepped toward as to intimidate Slayn.

"That talk is bull-shit!" interrupted Torru. "What in hell makes ya think that we lose this century?"

"Because time, history are ever-repeating...because that's the way it's always been," Slayn made a quiet response to Torru's outburst.

"Let's change history and prevail over the dark king, this time!" Intensity grew in Torru's harsh voice.

"I appreciate your enthusiasm, but you think we can do this prevailing over darkness when it is dark outside." Draish changed his attitude as he grew tired from lack of 'donor' blood.

"We have no choice but to wait until nightfall, then head toward the east, the direction of the vampire's castle," replied Slayn.

"So how about until then we find

something to eat..." complained Torru. "I'm so hungry." He pitifully held his stomach.

"Don't worry," assured Slayn, "I had put some food in a room here." He then walked to the room's entryway and turned back. "What are ya waiting for, Torru?" He urged him to follow to exit the room.

"I'm not so sure I can trust you now, what else would a friend hide," Torru told to the skinny man who could transform into a small dragon.

"Would you rather trust him?" Slayn looked to Draish.

Draish raised a furry eyebrow. "What was that?"

"Nothing," responded Torru. "You're right. But ya gotta tell me about my powers," he said, making sort of a deal with Slayn's trust.

"Don't bother ever asking the vampire, but you know that sword holds great powers if you learn how to use it," replied Draish. "I could teach you how to use a blade properly." He gave Torru an eerie smirk.

"Give me a break will ya! I've spent my known life in the 19th century, okay. Sword play isn't a daily task anymore," said Torru in his mundane defense.

"It found its way as a significant factor, did it not?" Draish said then, rubbing his chin as if he had facial hair.

"So then, what is the purpose of the Mystic Swordsman and his sword?" asked Torru.

"Our roles are set," stated Draish. "Slayn, as the Dragon Lord, keeper of time, Myiako is the Lady Necron, divider of worlds, and Torru, you're starring as the Mystic Swordsman, defender of the stars." He finished his casting call.

"Don't you mean he's the defender of the heavens," added Slayn.

"Do I look like one who has ever referred to celestial bodies as heaven.... heaven?" Draish held back an inappropriate laugh.

"Well, let's go eat so he can sleep and I need new clothes again..." Slayn replied, noticing that Draish's skin was as now white as his hair, signifying the weakness of the earlier battle.

They exchanged glances with the starved vampire before leaving the room.

{XII}: When A Dragon Is Least Of Your Worries

Myiako found herself seated in a carriage that jostled from the hasty gallop of the horses that pulled it. Her eyes came focused on the large angular box that sat in front of her. Then she looked down to notice the elegant dress she wore. Myiako would describe it as a Victorian-style dress, but the woman she was found it restricting to movement.

The window shutters of the stage coach were all shut and locked, so she couldn't see the outside scenery as it passed by. She turned around to lift the window latch, and then opened the window. She stuck her head out into the dusk air to see who was steering the horses. The man with the reins wore the familiar mystic armour, but the man was not familiar to her. The stagecoach was made of a metal, not wood, and painted black for the most part.

"Where are you taking me?!" she found herself shouting to the coach driver.

Then an awful noise made her turn the other way. The screeching sound echoed from behind the carriage. They were being chased by a creature that had to be a dragon.

She quickly stuck her head back inside with a shocked and confused expression.

"Close the window!" A familiar vampire voice came from the coffin next to her.

She hesitated, but then finally closed and locked the shutters, and then went closer to the casket. "...Draish? Is that you? Where are we?" she wondered, talking to the box.

There was no response from him, so she sat back down.

"...Did you hit your head?" Draish asked her, unable to receive her thoughts.

"...What?" She wondered why he had asked.

"...Oh, I get it, you are not going to cooperate anymore because I kidnapped you..." His sturdy voice rumbled from within his coffin. "Remember that you resurrected me, I had no part in it, Malphina."

"Mal-phin-a," she repeated under her breath. "You kidnapped me?"

"That is your name, right, that is what you told me?" he asked.

"Why would you need to kidnap me?" she wondered.

Draish pushed aside the casket lid and sat up to look at her. "Are you trying to fool me?" He wanted to know the reaches of her sincerity.

She just shook her head 'yes' but really meant 'no'.

"It is not uncommon during times like these for people disappear all the time. Vampires must kidnap people, because very few come willingly..." he told her casually.

"So why is a dragon, or whatever, chasing us?" Myiako asked.

"Because this time the Dragon Lord has sided with the Countess...you must know by now, my dear." His words almost seemed joyful, as if another challenge for him.

Malphina, or was it Myiako, sat in silence for a while to try to comprehend what was going on. She thought that the Dragon Lord was a good entity, so why was this one after them?

"Did you notice if the sun is set?" he asked her.

She hesitated. "Umm...I guess, almost."

Should she just sit back and play along with the story, not to disrupt the past? Was this just the vivid memory of a long past life, or was this a dream...simply a dream?

His words broke her thoughts, "You have calmed down, but I still cannot get into your thoughts." He then climbed out of the box. He had to lean over in the cabin space.

To her discontentment, he sat down next to her on the carriage couch bench. She was uncomfortable due to his weight sinking in the seat.

He tried not to stare at her. "Just know that I could never really harm you. You are the reason that I am alive...again." His voice was calmer than before.

"I know..." Her voice was unsure, unlike her words.

"I am sorry for my friend being so rough with you...but he says you put up quite the fight." Draish sounded apologetic, but seemed arrogant.

Then a loud explosion was heard, and something came crashing around the carriage. They were shook slightly off balance.

"By all that is holy, help us!" Malphina found herself screaming, as she put her legs up to her chest.

"Don't say such things!" Draish snapped at her.

"Then do something!" she growled back with a harsh look to him.

Outside a dark dragon flew over the carriage. The winged beast shot an inferno from its mouth, but instead of hitting the stagecoach, the flaming masses were being deflected by an invisible shield.

The dragon became flustered and he

glided down to fly parallel to the carriage.

The coach driver steered the horses to the other side of the path and shouted, "Get back you stupid beast!" He then gripped the reins with one hand and drew the Mystic Sword with the other. His gauntlet's glove gripped tightly and he swung the blade when the dragon got too close.

"You could have been on my side, Mystic Swordsman!" the dragon growled. "But instead you protect those I wish to destroy!" he snapped at the armoured man.

"I said, be gone!" the Swordsman shouted back.

The Dragon Lord continued to flap his wings and he arrogantly grinned to show rows of knife-like teeth.

The man pointed his sword's point at the beast and called out the incantation, "Begistalis firas'!" His words caused a blue light to project from his sword toward the dragon. It dodged the attack and drifted to the other side.

"You will be killed human, if you don't come to our side," the dragon growled at the armoured man. "I will destroy time and the dawning light; cast the world into ongoing darkness. It all starts with the death of the bastard vampire, Draish Jau-Ri!" the dark dragon spoke with short fiery breaths.

"Speak all the rubbish and insolence of perpetual darkness that you may," Draish's powerful voice cut through the air.

The vampire was then sitting with his legs crossed in the middle of the carriage roof, relaxing as if he had been there for a while.

"I've heard enough of your mindless remarks, coward!" Draish told him. "A real opponent would not attack my entourage, but would pick the fight with me."

The dragon flapped his wings with agitation. "I am no coward! If you wish I'll start with gnawing on your bones then I'll take the woman." The dragon drifted back.

"Be gone, winged lizard, before you make me angry!" Draish's voice was quite loud considering the rush of the wind.

The dragon gave an annoyed laugh and flew up higher. This time the beast shot the fire ball in front of their path, causing the four horses to rear up, startled by the flames. The carriage flipped on its side due to the impact of the sudden stop.

Draish had jumped up just in time and he grabbed on to the dragon's tail. He was lashed around, but did not lose his grip. The dragon growled in anger and confusion of how the vampire was able to grab him.

The woman in the carriage crawled out

a top side window; her long dress ripped at the bottom. The coffin inside was not strapped down and almost had crushed her when it capsized.

Draish wondered if she was alright and looked down at her. When his attention was averted, the dragon thrashed and he finally lost grasp. Draish was flung away momentarily.

The Dragon Lord dove down to where Malphina was, but before he could get to her, the Swordsman was there to deflect the swipe of the talons.

"Are you alright, Princess Malphina?" The Swordsman peered down to her as his hands were raised wielding the sword.

"Do I look, okay!" she snapped at him.

He ignored her and started to sweat. "Draish…Where are you?" he called out, as he was about to lose the fight with the beast.

Draish was off to their right side concentrating energy. He needed something to scare the dragon away with, for at least a short while. His hands started glowing a bright white light, breaking through the dark of the night. The dragon noticed it just at the moment the energy was released and expelled like lightning bolts from Draish's hands. The creature was struck in the shoulder and pushed back about twenty yards. It growled in pain and leaned its neck down to look at the gash in its arm.

"You'll regret that!" it snarled and looked back to the spot where Draish had been. He then looked down to see that the vampire was right under him. Draish cracked his knuckles and grinned full-fanged. The large beast was slow to react and was caught in the face with a fist. He didn't have to jump very high considering that the dragon only stood about twelve feet tall. Another punch and this time he retaliated with a tail lash. Again, Draish caught its tail, and with a great pull caused the lizard to lose balance.

"I have no regrets..." said Draish and the dragon crashed to the ground. His boot came down on his scaly neck. The dragon lashed his tail and wings wildly.

"Tell your master...I will not die so easily this time..." Draish told him through clenched teeth.

The dragon gasped from Draish's powerful control of him.

"I have no master...I am the Dragon Lord..." Smoke started billowing from its nostrils.

The white-haired man jumped back and let the beast go. The dragon scrambled to its feet and flew up. He knew that his defeat was imminent at this point. His opponent was reborn more powerful than before, and this the dragon could share with his comrades. At least next time, he'd know what to expect. The black lizard flew away angrily, still coughing up smoke.

Draish watched him leave the vicinity before walking casually back over to the two others. The Swordsman had turned the carriage back onto its wheels and was adjusting the horses' tack. Malphina was leaning against the carriage side, staring off into the dark fields.

"How do you fare, Cyan?" Draish asked the Mystic Swordsman.

He just nodded back.

After the men had a few words, Draish went back over to the Princess. He brushed off his leather pants and ran his hand through his white locks of hair before speaking with her.

"Are you alright?" he asked her.

She turned her head to him and looked annoyed. "I'd of rather taken my chances with the fire-breathing dragon..." she mumbled.

"Why not just take your chances with me," he smiled roguishly.

She had no response for him but to think about how this vampire was fiercer and more determined than the man her other lives had seen. That was almost effortless how he took on the dragon. She noticed that he dressed like a noble, but he was un-kept. He had on the blue suircoat and under it, his shirt was unbuttoned to show off his chest. He wore shoulder guards and a long dark cape covering his back.

"I see, you wish not to speak with me." He looked down. "Then I guess we should get you home."

He then had her attention. "Home?" she questioned.

"What's left of it..." he responded.

Her eyes narrowed. "What do you mean?"

"Cyan here got you out just in time... they were coming for you. You should be thankful that the Swordsman got you first."

"Well, I'm not because I was forced to resurrect you..."

"You wear my on patience, woman. I must tell you that you are the first human that I cannot control."

"Oh, lucky me..." she sighed.

Cyan then walked over to them, his armour was dented and clanking more than it should have been. "We should get going, sir," he said to Draish.

The silver-haired man just nodded in response and opened the carriage's steel door for the Princess to enter. She reluctantly went inside and he followed. Shortly, the horses started moving. Draish decided to sit on the bench across from Malphina. He used a flame from nowhere to re-light the lamp hanging inside. He could see without it, but he wanted her to see him in hopes of getting his influence through her walls of defense.

"Why are you acting in this way?" he wondered. "Are you not at all curious of your predicament?"

Her response was a nose in the air.

"You know," he said, "You are kindred with the former necromancer, Zaira. We were lovers once."

"I am not her… you creep…stop staring at me!"

"Maybe I can sway your unwillingness, another time…" he said then, crossing his legs and leaning back. He closed his eyes, pretending that he lost interest in her.

A short time later, the Swordsman, Cyan, called out, "The castle is in view!"

A moment later Draish responded, "I'm sure we'll be greeted by the blasphemous hunters…" His voice lowered as he added, "You get to see what they did to your home, Princess."

She could not see it in the shadows, but knew he had that smirk on his face.

"I hope that dragon rips you to shreds…" she told him.

He leaned over and relaxed his arms on his knees. "Why must you do this? It was the other vampires who destroyed your father's kingdom. I had to be summoned to defend you, understand?"

She kept quiet and just re-positioned the restricting dress.

"You could have prevented conflict if you had only cooperated with us," he told her, his grey eyes reflected in the dark cab.

"You know you deserve everything that is coming to you…" she said.

"What are you saying?"

"I will destroy you."

"Will you, woman… you are in no place to say such things."

"You are a betrayer. How can you tell me you're here to defend me…?"

"I can be very convincing."

"These weeks I have known you, you have proven just how wicked you are."

"So, that makes you a saint…" His words made him smile for some reason.

"After all we have been through, you say, how could you have done that?" her voice quivered.

"What are you speaking of?"

"You damn well know, you monster…"

"I must kill to survive…"

"Then just kill me…" she sighed.

"But I'm just getting to know you."

"Then, as I said before, I will kill you. If

I awoke you, I can put you back to sleep."

"Is that so, Princess…if you had only minded your words, maybe, just maybe, I would not be thinking of hurting you now…"

"Are *you* threatening Me?" She liked to act superior to him.

"You seemed surprised. What if we started over—made a compromise."

"I think not!"

"There is no reasoning with you. I thought you were a Princess, not a charlatan."

"Where's your honour, your respect for royalty?" she crossed her arms over her chest.

"In the grave…with my dignity. I care not for human hierarchies."

"Doesn't give you the excuse to look at me that way."

"I'd dismiss my honour, if it means that I can have you."

Malphina realized what he was doing and stopped amusing him with responses.

After he realized that she found no enjoyment from his attempts, he conflicted with himself rather not to take action. His determination took no rest as her resistance did not sway.

Malphina huddled in the corner on the seat trying to avoid any arguments.

She would only wished that dragon

was around so she wouldn't be center stage for Draish's performance. He got up and stepped over to her, leaning as he walked from the low carriage ceiling. To her dismay, he then sat down next to her, again and too close for comfort.

"Mind your space…" She looked at him.

"You're not so innocent, Princess, and I want just to prove that," he said, sitting back in the seat. He reached to grab her hand, but she yanked it away. His eyes were now blue, she noticed as he stared at her. *I will not give in…* she said to herself.

His hypnotic charm failed to abduct her own will power; he could not break into her thoughts. This angered him, but it was out of her control.

"It is really not like me to want someone so unwilling, but you even smell like her…"

"You smell of death…" she grimaced. Which were just words, as she couldn't smell anything over the pungent odor of perfume or cologne.

He sat up and turned to her, putting his arms of either side of her, and leaned his head in. His breaths were short and cold on her face, causing her to shiver. His lips were like ice as he pushed them to hers. The Princess resisted; protesting until she felt his tongue.

She pushed against his chest, urging him back. He chuckled at her, still remaining close. She was insulted, and then spat on his nose.

"How expected was that…" he used his sleeve to wipe it off. "I thought you would have been more creative."

"I don't see how you were ever trusted, even by this Zaira person."

"Don't speak of trust when your thoughts are deceiving you."

"You need to back off!"

"Saying that only intrigues me more."

He then put a hand behind her head and forced her toward him. He manipulated his hold on her so she would kiss him. He stopped to look at her and her hand came up and slapped across his face. She took no hesitation to slap him again and again. This time her hand was stopped by his hold on her wrist.

"I really shouldn't be wasting my strength on you…"

He used his hold on her hand to push her on her back. Forcing her to awkwardly lie on the bench seat, he lightly put himself on her. Her hands pressed to his chest muscles and she pushed, and then realized he was heavier than he appeared. His knee pushed down on her legs, becoming entangled in her skirt. His leg pushed between hers as he straddled her outer leg, his left leg on the floor.

The seats weren't meant to be laid upon. His hand forced down her left arm to position himself on her, on the seat. Using his other hand he softly touched her face, letting his nails gently scrape her skin. She closed her eyes, not able to face him anymore. His hand went to her neck and he unlaced her dress collar.

She became tense now as he began unlacing her gown. She took in a deep breath and suddenly made a move. How he was sitting made it vulnerable for her to bring her knee up forcefully into his groin. Her actions made him wince back and off her.

"That would have hurt more if I wasn't aroused by you doing so."

She took the moment to stand away from him. She didn't recall Draish being so dominating, but then, in this life, this woman was more demanding than Myiako would ever be. She couldn't help but to give into the spirit of Malphina. She had to do what Malphina did in order not to disrupt the past. Myiako might have welcomed the Draish of her time at consummating, but this wasn't the will of the Princess.

"We choose our own actions, why are you acting like this?" Malphina wondered.

"I have been in solitude for decades…I

am a vampire, but still a man with all the desires of the flesh."

"You're going to have to do more than that to win my affection. A lady wishes to be courted and respected. No matter who you are," she told him.

"Are you saying that I have never met a lady before you...? I know what women want." He sat back up and reached out to her.

"Don't touch me again!"

"Why do you deny yourself pleasure? You know that I could not harm you, Princess."

"Apparently you don't know that the definition of harm, it lies further than being material."

"I am really not that complex...as you like to think..." He tried to grab her again.

"Try it again and I'll make sure that my heel meets its target this time," she said, as she raised a heeled boot.

The carriage came to a sudden stop with an uneasy silence. Draish sniffed the air.

"What do you smell? Your demise?" She avoided eye contact.

{"What is it, Cyan?" Draish connected with him, mentally conversing. "I think you know already," Cyan responded.}

"Shit, I know I shouldn't have let one get

away…"

Draish then said aloud. "Damn heretics…more unholy vampire hunters," said Draish with a sneer, having no idea what to do after just being exhausted from fighting with the dragon.

{XIII}: Reaching the Count

She woke up from the fine beams of light escaping through dungeon bars.

It *was* Myiako, wearing her 'modern' clothes. Her hooded cloak was draped over her as she lay awkwardly on the dirt floor. Around her ankle was a steel cuff secured with a pin and mounted to a thick chain. It became apparent to her that she was captive in a dark, dank prison cell. Getting back to this reality took her a few minutes; and she then remembered. She was relieved to feel that her neck remained free of puncture wounds, as did her wrist. Myiako appeared to be unharmed, just confined. She could see from the dim light leaking inside through the aging building.

It can't be right, she thought. *Why was Draish such a tyrant in Princess Malphina's time? Why am I now relying on him to save me, if I was shown how he can be to me…or her.*

"The guardians…" she said. "Will come for me!" she then said louder. Her voice was rough and she coughed. It must have been all the screaming she at the creatures that kidnapped her.

Someone or thing was there.

The rock woman spoke with her shrill voice, "Oh, we hope they do come for you, which is the intention, to use you as bait—"

"Let me outta here, do you know who you're messing with!"

The creature laughed at her. "I am sooo afraid."

"I am the reincarnation of the necromancer, and you are just a minion of a vampire!" Myiako grabbed the cell bars in protest.

The dirt in front of the cell door became disturbed as the rock figure rose up.

"It's not a lie," said the lady minion. "But that still won't save the vampire guardian, you accurs'ed Draish Jau-Ri."

"I see, too weak to take him on all by yourself," replied Myiako. "I am just a human and I don't fear him."

"No! I would kill you if I could...but you can't be killed so easily."

"What are you saying?" demanded Myi.

"Why am I even talking with you…? I have already said too much," said the rock woman, noticing that her master was approaching.

"Just vhat were you talking about, Vondella?" The shadow of a man approached. Myiako noticed his accent was not local and different from Draish's.

"Nothing, master…I was just going…" the rock minion, Vondella responded.

"Who are you? Where are you?" asked Myiako of the mysterious man.

A menagerie of shadows collected in front of her inside the cell, and she stepped away. A dark figure assembled from the darkness, shrouded in a black cape.

"Let me properly intro-duce myself," he said to her. His cape unfurled to reveal his form. "I am de *Count Vladimir Dra'cul*." He wasn't vain enough to consider himself king as the others thought of him.

He was very pale with dark features and a long face. His chin was pointed and his lips thin. His brows were thick and eyes had golden iris. Though very old, he didn't appear but middle-aged, and still handsome. His armour was something else: custom fit leather chestpiece with spiked shoulder pads. His inner lining of his cape was purple to contrast all the black leather. His hair was shoulder length and a slick black to compliment the dark aura he possessed.

Myiako was speechless for a moment, but not afraid.

"So are you the cause of all this hatred?"

"It's a bit rash to blame me for the all the vorlds problems, my de-ar."

He stepped toward her into the light, to her astonishment.

"The sun!" she sighed.

"I've been able to valk in the light for quite some time now," he told her. "Literally — centuries ago."

He stood in front of her and she crossed her arms.

"They vill get here soon, with de dragon, I presume." The dark vampire would talk, not waiting for a response.

"A dragon..." Myiako was reminded of her dream.

"Yes, It vas simply your brother, as de dra-gon lord of time..." he said. "But you knew that deep in your heart." He brushed his cape back. "I vill kill him again, no one can stop me this time." His voice grew louder.

She could see it in his eyes; it was truly ancient and most likely knowledgeable. There was no way of trusting him, because with such age becomes such madness.

"I'm mad you say..." the Count could hear her thoughts, almost directly.

"The price of life eternal comes with a heavy burden. Ever-living, never-dying; if lunacy was the only problem of mine..." His voice was deep and echoed.

"I only vish to kill Jau-Ri, you vill only suffer minor injuries in the process. Not to vorry, my dear."

"You don't know me at all, really?" he said to her.

"What do ya mean?" she asked, looking down.

"In due time, you vill learn. As of right now you are pathetic."

"That's not nice," she said, raising her voice.

"Stay here a while longer…I still don't trust you." He looked her over again.

The Count Dracula used his ability to vanish back into the shadows of their surroundings and Myiako was left to ponder her fate, there in the dungeon.

Meanwhile…

Draish Jau-Ri searched the dark cave that was within the mountain. He found a wooden chest that was locked with a shackle. He pulled it away from the wall to open it. *Could this box contain what he was looking for?* He grasped the thick bolt lock with one hand and applied pressure. It didn't take long for the lock to give and crumble before him. He took hold of both sides of the chest lid and pulled up. Dust filled the air, but after it settled the contents were seen. There in the chest was a sword, tarnished badly. Under it was some cloth and iron of armoured clothing.

"I cannot believe this," he said to himself. "After all these years, the spell preserved them…"

He took out the sword and looked it over. After all these years he could still admire the cold steel of this blade. He then put it down beside him and continued searching in the box. He took out a long dark cape that had attached shoulder and neck guard. The cape was long and showed missing fabric and tears as he unfurled it and shook it off. He then put the cape around his back and placed the shoulder pads firmly on his shoulders. After attaching the neck latches, he leaned over to take another piece from the chest, the iron chest plate, and held it in front of him. It was cracked from the hold that penetrated it through both front and back pieces.

Draish expressed his emotions in a strange chuckle as he looked at the damaged amour, and then suddenly threw and slammed the iron armour against the wall and reached back into the crate. Big leather-studded boots and leg guarders were obtained from his findings and he placed them on the ground.

Draish then pushed down on the big lid and sat on the closed chest. He covered his legs and feet in the protective gear, and then picked the tarnished sword back up.

"Some things cannot be stolen," he quietly said as he attempted to polish the sword with the edge of the cape. After some time, he then slowly stood up and held the sword out.

Just then, Slayn appeared in the doorway.

"What are you so psyched about; it is still day you know," he said to Draish. "Looks like you found some armour, huh?"

"It is *my* armour, in fact." Draish glanced at Slayn with an uneasy expression.

"You're looking pale even for a vampire. You should rest before night fall," Slayn suggested.

"You do not say..." Draish put the sword at his side and sat back down. "One question..."

"That is?" asked Slayn.

"How did you become the Dragon Lord? I am entertained to hear another explanation than corruption..."

"Some of us may be even more insightful than you, Draish Jauri," he reminded the vampire in his own defense.
"Don't let your mind play tricks on you, do not be deceived..."

"Your words..." said Draish with a small smile. "...are just...just how they should be."

"I guess that means you trust me," said Slayn, probably relieved. "I cannot serve the darkness as a minion would, for I am very much alive."

"So, the oracle wished to enlighten me again..." Draish told him with no amusement.

"I'd mind you to be gone from my sight, before my hunger gets the best of me and you really become my servant..." Draish growled really for no direct reason.

Slayn then turned to leave without any question, and was careful to watch his back.

The sword dropped from Draish's hand and clanked to the ground. He looked at it with a narrowed brow, and then clenching his fist tightly as tears filled his eyes.

"How many...how many times...must we do this...How many must die at my hands? How can I lift my curse? When can I be with her?" He spoke under deep breaths.

The tears that filled his eyes were probably the first in ages. The drops were darkened like stained tears of an animal and streaked down his face.

"It is all because of him..." His fists were now so tight that his nails dug into flesh. The drips of blood collected in a small pool to either side of him. He knelt down on one knee and pressed his hands together.

*The smeared blood…*Draish began, "Va lumi deraneen la biunde' un dante'…Nadi raus supierous dur-ve, Enguran ve! Nadi ilu secani la gurun va-mae! Cruorem-rau-la-ull! Blood is the life…Pryvante de dante', Dayan de lumi'…provoke the darkness, awaken the light. Pryvante de dante', Dayan de lumi'… provoke the dark, wake up the light…."

Incantations always gave off a certain energy, which inoculated through the air.

附◆അ

Dracula had stumbled while walking through the halls, back in his mansion. His rock minion was quick to assist him. "Don't you patronize me," he told her as he straightened his posture.

"Did you feel that?" she wondered.

"Of course I did, fool…but I do not want to believe its source…"

The dark hallways of Castle Dra'cul were filled with hidden eavesdroppers to Dracula's dismay. "Go away, you worthless minions!" he told them. "Go feast on the flesh of mortals if you must!" He then laughed.

"There is no way that *he* is strong enough… there will never be an end to Count Vlad Dra'cul," he said sternly. His words echoed…

{XIV}: In The Forest Depths

The sky was barely illuminated with the diminishing glow of the setting sun. The orange sphere was sliced in half by the horizon of thick trees. In the distance, the smoke of controlled fires could be seen from out of the center of the forest. Lastly, the dark silhouette of a great castle was only seen beyond the forest and valley.

Slayn and Torru watched the sun disappear as they prepared the horses for a ride.

"Myiako..." Torru said.

"Don't worry, friend, they cannot harm my sister, Myi. She's tough, you know."

"Get real, Slayn, they are devils...she might be dead already..."

"What of it?"

"How dare you!" Torru challenged.

"There is something you should know," Slayn told him, "Myiako is the human representative of the necromancer, and..."

"And??" Torru wasn't convinced.

"She is her own ressurector."

"That makes no sense."

"Does any of this..." Slayn's face now almost eerie, covered by the shadows.

They did not necessarily hear anything, but it was apparent *he* was coming. The air thickened with his presence during the night. As if a different, more vamperic aura surrounded him. Then, Draish came from the cave hallway, not making any noise or footsteps as he walked on the ceramic floors.

He wore the armour he found in full, broken pieces and all. This was the attire of his former kingdom that he was once so proud to have had. The cracked chest plate decorated in the faded wolf crest, miraculously kept in wearable condition by the enchanted box over the centuries. *Some things will forever be remained undiscovered...*he thought.

The two men uncomfortably exchanged looks with Draish.

"Uneasy towards me?" Draish spoke. "I am not the one to fear...not this life time, anyway."

"What's that suppose to mean?" asked Torru.

"Let's just get going," said Slayn.

"This won't be easy, blood will be shed."

Torru turned to see Draish suddenly beside him.

"What the hell?" Torru jumped.

The tension broke when Draish exploded with laughter.

"So, you think I need to be more cheerful, heh." Draish then mounted the horse that Torru had saddled.

Torru watched in disbelief. "You!"

"Well, get the other horse ready...we're waiting." Draish laughed at him.

"I won't forget this..." Torru mumbled.

"Ah, come on, the extra work is good for you." Slayn's comment didn't help Torru rein the horse.

Draish took the lead down the path away from the mountains.

"We shall stop at the village in the woods," Draish told the others when they caught up.

"The what?" asked Torru.

"Then we shall, take a flight," Slayn said.

"Village in the woods, what, now you can fly?" Torru asked.

"Like most dragons can, why wouldn't I be able to?"

Torru just shook his head. "Why don't I get to change into anything like a dragon... all I get is armour."

"You're supposed to be the human hero in the legend." Slayn smiled.

"So, why will we stop in this village?" Torru changed thoughts.

"A real meal for starting..." Draish

murmured.

"We just might learn a thing or two from the locals," Slayn responded.

The three men rode forward, hooves kicking up the dirt path. Conversation arose as they neared the forest.

"So, why do you think this village is almost hidden here in the woods?" asked Torru.

"It is the Farie Forest," replied Draish.

"I'm sure the name has changed over the years," said Slayn.

"You don't think my castle is still called just that, what it was…not like the Count D, the bastard." Draish sounded uneasy.

"What?" Slayn wondered if Draish was just talking to himself again.

"Saying D, you mean Dracula?" asked Torru.

"Yes, the ancients would use a single initial to represent their names in scriptures… and sometimes to mark their kills…"

"I knew that," boasted Slayn.

"You know nothing of it, mortal." Draish told him. "I guess it's time I tell you two about vampires."

"Didn't we do this already?" Torru shook his head.

"Why is it important for a vampire

master to have minions?" Draish questioned them.

"To capture whining, nagging sisters for them?" Slayn joked.

"Ha-ha, that is beside the point," Draish responded. "The older a vampire is, the more powerful, right?"

"Ok, what's your point," said Slayn.

"My *point* is about power." Draish seemed excited. "Minions can be used to gain different types of powers, meaning the more minions under a master's control, the stronger he will be."

"I get it," said Torru, "But then why don't you just create an army of minions?"

"I'm surprised, Torru," replied Draish.

"Now, if I did that I wouldn't be any better than all the other blood-gluttonous vampires of history…those who corrupt mankind into eternal darkness through mischievous acts of violence." He then looked down.

"Umm, so what are you gonna do? I mean do you have a plan, Draish?" Torru looked at him.

The talking ceased to a moment of silence.

"What makes Dracula so different from you? You are both master vampires…" Torru asked a daring question.

Draish smiled. "We are not different at all, and we are perfect rivals in that." He brushed back his hair. "I have to tell you… my memories prove the horrendous acts that I have done…but I did never stray from the cause. I always liberated those in need. Doing so, one must collapse and recreate…I am the equal opponent to the oppressor, Vladimir Dra'cul."

"You can say quite a mouthful, but actions speak louder than words," Slayn said.

"What, are you saying that I am lying?" Draish turned to him.

"I am saying that you're a killer, Draish, whatever humanity that was once in you is long gone, which would be a common factor for any immortal."

"Strong allegation…what makes you feel that way about me?"

"I've seen it in your eyes, and I know Torru can back me up on this."

"Don't bring me into this," said Torru quickly.

"It is indeed a fact, you have seen and recalled many things…you can remember your own deaths…can you not?" Slayn said to Draish.

"Maybe I can clearly, maybe it is all blurry in the spiral of ages, and maybe there is only one thing that I am certain of…" Draish said, in his vague way.

"Just don't repeat the mistakes of the past, is all I'm asking," Slayn commented.

By this time, the forest was right in front of them. The horses slowed down, as it was hard to see without nocturnal eyes. Naturally, this gave Draish the advantage over most.

"There is a narrow path up ahead, about twenty feet away," he told them.

It was overgrown with foliage so they had to walk in a line, following Draish's horse. After a while, Torru broke the silence.

"You sure were just not going in a circle, this tree looks familiar."

"Quiet!" Draish growled, and then suddenly stopped. The other horses jolted to a halt.

They all looked up after Draish, noticing a sudden change in air pressure.

Lightning flashed over the tree tops, followed by a boom of thunder, making the horses and Torru uneasy. Rain started pouring down on them, the trees giving minimal cover.

"Great…thanks…thanks alot…" Draish said, talking to the sky. "Just keep moving, halfway there…"

A young vampire would have been slowed or even wounded by the rain, but it seemed to have no effect on Draish, not any more than a hindrance.

"It wasn't cloudy at all when we entered the forest, I don't get it!" yelled Slayn over the rain.

"Someone is making this happen, don't you see!" Draish called back to them.

Quickly, the ground began to soften and the horse's hooves began to stick. They were forced to get off their mounts and lead the horses through the mud.

The restricted path opened to a small grassy clearing in the woods.

"Stop here!" Draish told them.

"I'd like to get to that town now, if you don't mind." Torru was drenched.

"But you see…we have company!" Draish stepped away from the horses.

"Come out and play, minion wench," Draish said, as he stretched out his arms.

"Hahahahhahaha, you should know by now, Draish, that I am one to watch for," she responded, startling the others.

Then, from seemingly nowhere, four other minion monsters appeared and advanced an attack on them.

"Dammit! I had only expected three of you ugly bastards. I guess one more won't mess up my odds." Draish psyched up, and then pushed up against the constant downpour and levitated his body to draw the creature's attention upwards.

"So the first to die will be the one that is causing this confounded rain!"

Slayn sighed and struggled to salvage his clothes before he morphed.

"HAHAHA, it is not us, that is doing so!" shouted the rock woman, Vondella, with a hearty laugh. "But it sure gave us an advantage for attack." Her voice came from a different direction each time she spoke.

The serpent-like creature attacked Torru before he could even change into the Mystic Swordsman. The scaly tail lashed him, interrupting his transformation.

It was a giant beetle creature that attacked Slayn, but unlike Torru, he was quick enough to be a dragon at the time.

Draish indulged himself in taking on the two at once: the bat-like creature and the ghoulish werewolf monster.

Torru got in a good swing with his sword as the serpent reared back. With a rage of emotion, he started gaining his Swordsman's armour, the change ending with the helmet covering his face. He was ready for the next attack. They took turns fending off blows of steel to scale. Torru even impressed himself to remain uninjured for so long in a fight.

Slayn quickly moved around, dodging the thrust of the insect's mandible pinchers, playing the defense. He flapped his wings to jump up and drop-kick the bug.

It moved from the attack and grabbed the dragon's tail. Slayn growled out and smoke filled his snout, he spouted out flames from his breath. The beetle minion was roasted and backed off Slayn to run around on fire.

Draish had made the move to attack the bat monster first, off the ground. He flew up, but was tackled by the man-bat. Long fangs snapped at Draish's face as he held it back with his left hand around its neck. He drew a tarnished sword from under his cape. The bat saw it and immediately dropped altitude. Draish dropped down with the blade hurling at the man-bat, now grounded. He was too slow though, and the bat was airborne again after Draish had landed his attack.

He quickly turned for a sword block from another attack. The wolf man had seen his opportunity to get the vampire but had cut his hand on the blade and backed off. Draish came at him and impaled the creature before he could react. He screamed in agony as Draish ran him through to the hilt of the sword. Even though the werewolf was much larger than he, Draish was able to pick him up with the sword and throw him upwards into the air, sword and all. The wolf minion collided with the bat in mid-air and they came crashing down. The sword ended up impaling them both.

"What the Hell??" Vondella's voice was near Draish. She noticed that the sword was glowing. It was obviously a magic sword technique that he allowed him to pass through two minions at once. They got up and the wolf pulled out the sword and threw it at Draish. The sword stopped in front of him and he grabbed it up with a smile.

"Going again, dog-boy?"

The werewolf lunged at Draish, bleeding and snarling teeth covered in drool and blood.

Draish held the sword straight forward and a glow surrounded him, the energy stopped the rain around them, and the wolf just collapsed right before Draish's feet.

Draish then disappeared or moved quickly, ending up right beside the man-bat monster. He swung his sword at its neck, but it was blocked by its claw wing. Draish continued to glow and applied force, finally slicing through its wing. The creature called out in pain. Draish went for a kill blow with the blade, but was attacked by the other.

The werewolf clenched him with powerful arms and attempted to crush his body. Draish dropped his sword and gasped. His glowing aura faded and his neck went limp in the creature's arms. Draish then opened his eyes again, which were now glowing red, and he gained back up energy apparently as a last resort.

"...veo aveni mortary-filla'us!" Draish growled to make his offensive change.

The blood poured from the wolf-beast's mouth as the spikes came out his back. Draish then pulled away, revealing the jagged bone spikes that had grown from his back to skew his enemy. He turned around to the dying beast that was still standing.

"Heheheheh..." The bone spikes then subsided into his back, only leaving rips in his clothes.

"How..." gasped the wolf minion as he fell down.

The bat creature retreated, badly wounded, but Draish quickly regained his sword and faced no more enemies. But then, strangely enough, he ran the sword into the muddy ground before him. A scream was then heard and the rock woman rose up with the sword embedded into her forehead.

"Impossible, I am undetectable!" she screamed.

Draish pulled the sword from her. She was soggy from the rain and had a hard time making a solid form. He then plunged the sword into her form, completely cutting the minion in half. She remained, dissipated into the earth.

"C'est la vie, madam le Vondella…"

In The Castle…

"WHAT IS THIS? Assusiss-enato!" his voice echoed. "Besides just killing her, he mocks ME…" Dracula took a seat and gasped, grasping his chest as if in sudden pain.

"This proves Draish has learned a thing or two…you can't send a minion to do a vampire's job…" The death of his minions didn't quite sadden him, but became a searing pain.

It only appeared briefly, as if he was talking to himself, but then it came apparent that the eyes of many other minions gazed upon their master. It was seldom that they saw him this way, weakened by the re-death of one of his higher minions.

"Vat are you all staring at!" he shouted at them. "The guardians will die. I vill not let Draish get a second chance…"

{XV}: No Release, No Entry

She looked up at the visible stars through the slim window. Myiako found herself peering at the dark void of nighttime as she awoke in the prison cell. The waning moon was low on the horizon and all within the castle walls were quiet—too quiet.

She observed her surroundings: medieval dungeon and rusty cell bars. Even if she was able to break the old lock and get out, she doubted if she would get far in Dracula's Castle. *I know they will come for me…because I am the reason for all this.*

Myiako had to consider that it was she who had wanted to go to the tomb and search for treasure. They had questioned her motives, but she insisted that they must go to the old tomb in the mountains. It was she that had read the encrypted words, which awoke the ancient one, Draish Jau-Ri. She had caused this story to unfold, dragging her friends into it. Even though she was a puppet for the fates as well, she felt responsible for unleashing yet another vampire into her modern world. Myiako would soon loose sanity in her thoughts if someone didn't speak to her soon.

She stood up and straightened her pants then walked to the bars and grasped them tightly. She then knelt down, eye level with the lock on the cage door. The rusty metal lock had a skeletal face molded into it, with the mouth as the key hole.

"What a strange lock," she quietly spoke, still staring at it.

"Why you'RE sTraNge!" Myiako jumped back to hear the lock talk in a weird voice. "WHats Tha prOblem, NEveR yoU sEEn a DEADbolt oF tHe mAgiK VaRIety?

Myi was silent as she stared with her jaw dropped.

"I Am EncHAnTed, as ManY IteMs Are…"

"Huh?"

"Do I hAve To RePeat MySelf??"

"No, it just I've never seen an enchanted thing before you," she told it.

"SOO gLAd I can Be The fIRst," it chuckled.

"Now that we established that, can you please open, Mr. Lock?"

"OH sUre, Since YOU, asked so NicELY," it responded

Then it just started laughing. "HEHEHEhehheheEHE, you REAlly thougT I'D open for YOU, hahaahaHAhHHAHa!"

"Shut up already, it was worth a try…"

"No, nONe, No reLEaSe for You!"

Myiako sat down back on the floor, and sighed.

"Who am I kidding, I am talking to a lock…a stupid magical skeleton lock… I don't even believe myself."

Her quarrels with the inanimate animate were as useless as her gun right now. She sat alone in the silence to wait for her fate.

Meanwhile….

In the damp thicket of the forest, the rain ceased as the minions were either dead or gone. The three travelers regained their horses after recovering from the minion attack.

"So how do you know that she is dead?" Torru asked. "I mean, for sure."

Draish then threw a leather satchel at him that contained something heavy.

Torru caught it and looked inside. "Oh my god!" he quickly threw down the bag.

"What, what was it?" said Slayn.

Draish smiled. "Why don't you see for yourself?"

Slayn transformed back into his human self and went toward the satchel.

He opened it to reveal a human head, a woman's head. He covered it back up.

"It seems to be the head of Vondella,

but now fleshy…and smelly," Slayn stated.

"Ha, it seems that there was a second in the rock manifestation where she became vulnerable. I could smell the flesh that she still could be," Draish told them. "Keep the head it assures that she stays dead."

"You keep it." Slayn tossed the bag back at Draish.

"Heh, you know what this means, do you?" Draish asked, not wanting an answer. "He is now weakened…" He paused. "I fear the worse now though…"

His words got their attention. "There is another master vampire in the works here… that werewolf wasn't of Dra'cul's making…"

"The Ancients will meet when the fight for redemption has come…" Slayn quoted. "It makes you question where your loyalty lies."

Draish just shook his head at him discerningly.

"I don't get it. After what you just did," Torru said. "Do you even need our help?"

"Yes, I do; considering that I don't even know what I can do." Draish smiled.

"What do you mean?" asked Slayn.

"Spikes from my back…that was new to me." Draish straightened his posture.

They continued on horseback, the two following Draish as before. Travel at night would be rather difficult without his eyes to guide the way.

"Why do you think those minions are so damn ugly?" Torru turned to Slayn.

"I'd think it's how Dracula makes them, right, Draish?" Slayn said.

"Yes, the blood of the dead will alter them accordingly…it is only obvious that the minion would take after their master. Being stuck with you two gloats says the wrong thing about me," Draish responded, turning back to look at them. "My minions would be more attractive." He smiled, fangs showing.

"I don't care what you think of me." Torru got defensive and crossed his arms.

A time of silence ensued, broken only by the sound of horses sloshing along the muddy path.

"We are close now!" Draish called back to them. "I hope the elves want to be friendly…"

"What? Elves in Farie Village? I thought it was just a name," Slayn exclaimed.

"Human minds are feeble, so naturally, you couldn't see the true faces for the people who live in this region," Draish commented.

"Are you saying they are all disguised as humans, but are really elves??" Torru asked.

"Yes, and they might attack us..." Draish told them.

"Why? Another fight..." Torru

complained.

"They might due to the hatred of me as an undead, or they may sense the evil in you, as mankind," Draish said facing straight onward.

"They are here," Draish whispered suddenly. The horses stopped and began to stomp frantically.

In the light of the stars, they could see people coming out from behind trees and gathering to block the path forward. The group seemed to be made up of regular-looking people of various ages.

To Torru and Slayn they looked as townspeople of the late 1800s, dressed casually. But if you could see through Draish's eyes, things might pan out differently. These weren't human people at all. Some had elongated ears, some had tails, and some had wings. And one couldn't forget their radiating auras. Vampires could see a normal level of energy off of anything living thing, but these people had vast amounts radiating into Draish's eyes. Supernatural power wasn't enough to see the truth behind the townspeople, it was the vampire's age that gave him the ability to see them for what they really were.

"GO back!"

"Not welcome here!"

They spoke particularly to Draish. "Go

away vampire!"

"Your kind is not welcome here; every deal with a vampire is a deal with death."

"Did not your elders speak of me? I am indeed a vampire, but not one to trifle with."

"Do not try that trickery with us, we know of your kind. You can't go any further," he was told.

"If you do not know who I am, then I have no business here anyways..." Draish looked the crowd over.

Slayn dismounted his horse and stepped forward. "To make introduction for the master, Draish Jau-Ri, recently resurrected by the necromancer herself."

Whispers and comments flew through the crowd.

"No, it's just a legend it can't be," commented a man.

"How do we know it is really him!" someone else called out.

"It could be true; those two don't look like minions at all."

"We cannot take any chances after what happened earlier."

They continued bickering amongst themselves, leaving the three to wait them out.

Moments later Draish wondered if they were done yet. "Umm, beg your pardon...you seem to have a problem with us so we will just pass through, now."

They looked up to him. "Yes, indeed you can pass…but you must stop in the village," they proclaimed a different tone.

"Yes, if indeed you are "un de La Lucios" we must let you pass. There is something you must see…"

Now the mob of people became a welcoming mass and lit the way to the village nearby. The three travelers followed the group, Slayn led his horse and the others dismounted once at the town gates.

"Come meet us at the café," they now urged the three newcomers.

{XVI}: Prisoner Of Light And Dark

The light of dusk was still illuminating the room. Shadows cast through the large wooden window shutters onto her face. Myiako batted open her eyes to come focused on the elegant room. She was lying awkwardly on a canopy bed. When she sat up, she noticed the dress. Before she wondered how she got here, she realized this was the "dream world" she had come accustomed to recently.

She sat on the edge of the bed and put her bare feet on the cold floor. She saw a pair of ladies boots placed on the floor next to the nightstand. She decided the next step was to put them on.

After she laced up the leather boots, she didn't know what to do. She lay back on the bed and looked up. Her reflection peered back at her from the mirror hung from the bed canopy. This wasn't her reflection though, but that of Malphina. She now could feel normal as this other person, with dark hair and make-up. The tight, purple velvet dress was cut low on the chest and trimmed with a frilly collar. The bottom of the skirt had the same trim, and would be restricting if the slit up the side didn't go so high up her thigh.

Myiako felt embarrassed in this getup, and Malphina would feel improper. *Why is there a mirror up there…why do I ask…?*

She slowly stood up. "Let's see what act I will perform today."

She could sense him. *He's about to come through the door, now.*

In that instant, the door slowly creaked open before he came through it.

The vampire Draish was dressed oddly, but extravagantly. He looked almost healthy. His hair was very long and pulled back. She could find him handsome, but was thrown off by the spikes on his shoulder paldrons and long cape. His chest armour was tight fitted leather and was cut to a low v-shape on his chest. *He actually had large chest muscles this time.* His leather pants were even clean, and not ripped. Boots were shiny and polished. Though that smell did follow him, perhaps of musky fur and dried flowers. Then the necklace caught her eye, the green stone seemed to glow.

She then realized they had been staring at each other for some time.

"I...I...don't know what to say…" she stammered.

"You don't have to; it is about time that

I do the talking," Draish said as he stepped toward her. His eyes drifting to her breast.

"What do you want with me?"

"Haven't you asked enough questions?" he said and smirked. He made no attempt at indulging her in a legitimate reply.

"You…you take me in and dress me how you wish, like I am yours to control, like you own me….you have no sense, no sense at all," Malphina argued.

"Is that so?" He shook his head. "Well, if that's what you think, you are entitled to your own opinion, even though it's wrong."

"Just leave me alone…" she told him. "If it wasn't for you, I'd, I'd…." she stopped with emotion.

"Leave then, who am I to stand in your way," he said to her surprise. "But it's not a very safe place without me around, Princess."

"You had the door locked. I couldn't leave during the day!"

"Then leave at night if thou are so determined."

"I cannot…I know I won't make it far, without you just following me…"

"Is it that you think I'll follow you, or is it that you need me?" He took a step toward her.

"I do *not!*"

"Just admit it, that's why you stayed…"

He was suddenly right next to her. "You need me."

She turned her head away from him. "I am the one who resurrected you. You need me! So back off…don't you forget I have that power over you."

"Inconsiderate woman! I offer you protection from all the horrors of the demons who lurk the night and this insubordination is what I get?"

"You smell like a mule…" she said with hatred.

"You're the jackass." He shook his head.

She wondered if he had actually just made a joke.

"So, what now…if I am stuck here," she wondered.

"First mistake is asking what I want to do, but I know how unconvincing you can be," he replied not forgetting about how she stabbed him with a silver blade the day before.

"You are incomprehensible…"

"What else do you have to say about me, you seem to know me so well…"

"You need to change your attitude, be more respectful."

"I only return the given respect, and you, my dear?"

"I hate how you are always creeping

me out."

"But this is fate, you and I."

"Yes, like *that*, stop that!"

"I will grow on you, like scar, your hate will fade in time." He took her arm at the wrist.

"Let go," she said, but did not try to pull away.

He pulled her close and put a finger over her lips, gliding it down her chin and neck to her shoulder, his fingernail scraped down the arm he held. His expression then hardened and he clenched her wrist.

He then used his long nail to cut into her arm, not too deep, but enough to let the blood drip. His eyes widened at the sight of the oxidizing blood.

"Some wounds are deeper than others, these are the ones that will never heal," he said, then leaning over to clean the blood off her arm. His lips were cold and she felt his lips and tongue on the cut. He had quivered at the taste, and finished cleaning it off her. He then dropped her arm and tried to regain focus.

She noticed he had stopped the pain and bleeding on the fresh, jagged cut as it started to heal.

He embraced her; which wasn't returned, she still being ever in confusion. She looked up at his lips, painted blood red. She wondered how this Zaira could ever love this beast.

"Ok, enough. Can you go now?" She broke the tension she felt.

He backed off. "Could we start over?"

"Ummm, what are you saying?" She crossed her arms.

"Please, my lady forgive me…I will leave you be."

Then, oddly, he turned and began to leave the room.

"Don't lock me in!" she told him.

He didn't say anything else and was gone.

The door was left open.

She crept slowly to it and looked out.

"Here I go."

⊰◆⊱

Myiako alerted her attention and stood up. She went over to the cell bars after hearing footsteps nearby. "Draish" was the name that escaped her lips.

"Hardly…that fool." A woman's voice had answered her from the darkness.

"Who is there?" Myi nervously asked.

The footsteps of clicking heals neared her, right outside the cage.

The shadows flickered in the dungeon, and then the dark collected into a shape. The shadow made a shapely form of a woman wearing a puffy dress.

Myiako tried to make out what she looked like from her iron prison. The figure stepped closer. Myi looked over the strange woman and took in the pale skin and red hair. It was the Countess.

"What is wrong? You look like you've seen a ghost." The Countess's deep feminine voice gave Myi chills. She stepped forward, her long black gown dragging behind as she walked.

"Why…you are Scarlet." Myiako was astonished.

"Indeed, I too, know of you, though we have never met," the Countess told her. "Ironic how close you were this whole time… but now we finally have you."

"What do you want with me? My friends will come soon," Myi told her.

"You think that he will come for you, do you? That is what we are counting on. Take his time, he sure does…" Scarlet looked down through the bars at Myiako with her burgundy eyes.

Myi looked away, averting her eyes to the vampire's frilly dress.

"You didn't think that I was still alive,

after all these years, did you child?"

Myiako looked down.

"Maybe Jau-Ri didn't tell you that he was never strong enough to defeat me. Now all hope is lost for you and your light vampire. With me by Dracula's side, we are unstoppable."

"Why are you keeping me here alive? If you want me dead so bad, do it."

"Our fight is with him, you were just an unfortunate who resurrected him…"

"So, let me out of the cage."

"I suppose you are right, child, it is a bit medieval to keep you down here."

"Really, this isn't a trick?"

"Come, I'll give you a proper room."

Myi was hesitant at the generosity the countess vampire had offered and she stepped back as Scarlet approached the cage lock.

"Release your latch upon this door, until I ask of the seal once more…" she spoke to the skeleton lock.

"AnYtHiNg fOr The CoUNtessss…" the lock's weird voice said. The latch un-clicked and the iron door swung open.

Scarlet waited for the girl's cautious exit from her cage.

"Come now, child, I won't harm you… now…" She smiled and looked down at the trembling young woman. The vivacious way that the blood coarsed through her veins excited Scarlet.

"Don't worry about me. It is *time* that will be the end of you…"

Myiako, hesitant to follow the Countess, began to wonder. "What do you mean, time?"

"It is the passing of the ages, my child, you will see well enough soon," the Countess responded, but it made no sense to Myiako.

She then followed along behind Scarlet, careful not to step on her long dress. They went up the twisted staircase, passing flaming torches on the walls, until they were almost to the main interior of the castle.

{XVII}: Exception To Darkness

Laughter could be heard within the forest village. The people in the tavern had started early that night. A crowd surrounded the three adventurers as they told them about the fight with the minions earlier. Slayn and Torru were both clean and shaven, and finally got a decent meal. An attractive blonde elfin woman was seated next to Draish on the bench.

"Was it really that easy for you?" she asked them, particularly looking at Draish.

"Not to brag or anything…" The vampire paused a moment. "But the routines became simple…his minions don't seem to be that smart."

Torru was talking loudly to a group about being the new Mystic Swordsman, while Slayn sat back and amusingly drank the offered ale.

"Should we really be wasting time again?" Draish stood up and looked at Torru.

The elf girl eagerly responded, "You won't be able to make it to the castle by dawn, you know."

"Someone's been messing with the

time..." Slayn looked at Draish.

"You're saying we depend on the time...that she does as well." He looked down. his hair falling onto his face. "Chronos-rau anon..." he muttered.

"There is nothing to do but wait," Slayn said, then sitting back to drink.

"I think it's a good time to show them then," an old lady said standing beside the blonde. "Yes, that's great, they should see what was recovered..."

"What?"

"Come over here, boys," she said and motioned them over to the far wall. Slayn and Torru followed. Then, she stood in front of the dark wall and chanted, "Spirit Fira, grant us light on these old walls. Dear spirit, show us the hidden mysteries."

With her words, the wall lit up as if a torch flame was struck upon them. The light revealed an ancient stone mural, preserved on the wall. The stone was cracked and the images warped with time, yet there it remained.

"My family discovered this many years ago...I believe this is yours, Draish," the young elf said. Draish remained standing away from the group by the wall, but she had his attention.

"We seemed to have recovered all the pieces, but the ending is missing."

"Not missing, never finished…" replied Draish with a sorrowful tone.

"Hey!" blurted Torru. "Isn't this the legend?"

"Yeah," said Slayn. "It is the story of the past guardians that we resemble today." Torru was startled to see Draish suddenly beside him, now touching the stone of the mural as his thoughts flowed. *It seemed like it was yesterday…now that I see this…it starts with Dracula destroying my human life…the lady necromancer gave me un-life…then it shows the dawning of the time of the dragon and guardian swordsman…why a dragon I'll never know…and why would I need a dragon to help me? This was the time of that dark dragon named Raus-Lonnel.*

"The rise of evil attracts the only one who seemed to be chosen by fate to even cause a threat to such an evil…" Draish then quietly said.

The elf girl looked at him, seeing the look of mourning on his pale face. She knew that the stone had brought back bad memories. This tablet had been in his manor when it was burnt to the ground.

The woman stepped near to Draish and put her hand on his chin, taking his gaze from the painting. He then looked into her eyes and found innocence in the glassy blue sea of them as he tried to reach her thoughts. She put down her hand and blinked several times.

"I have such a burden to bear. Do you dare to see what I have seen?" He looked at her.

"I am not as young as you might think, vampire," she told him. "This century I will reach seven hundred years old, come back to me when you obtain the experience..."

"I guess you're right, but I do need your help," he said, as she watched his lips through the hair covering his face.

Meanwhile, the others had been explaining the story of the legend to the crowd.

"I grew up thinking this was just a fictional story about vampires and the necromancer. It was quite graphic for a kid to read," Torru replied, and then noticed a pretty, but chubby, woman starting at him. He blushed.

"Real life isn't pretty..." someone replied to him.

"All folklore isn't fake or we wouldn't be here!" a louder elf man commented, and a few of them laughed.

Slayn nudged Torru.

"I think we should stay here until the vampire can travel again."

"Thanks for referring to me as if I were an animal..." Draish peered over to Slayn.

"You do smell like one..." Torru

commented.

"You know...I...could just...ummm... kill you all." Draish gave them a toothy smile.

"You could get a bath here," the blonde said as she started to blush from telling him that.

"Ahh..." He hesitated, looking at her with obvious thoughts in mind. "Past experiences lead me to say No to that..." He smiled, not wanting listeners to know what he meant.

She took his hand and they went to sit back down at the tables and benches where Slayn and Torru had already proceeded. By this time, the crowd had depleted from the bar and a handful of citizens remained.

"So, why is the light vampire affected by the sun?" someone asked.

"It's just another shitty consequence that hast been bestowed upon my being, to be of light, and yet I must restrain my lust in eternal darkness." Draish became poetic after taking a dark liquor given to him. He took another gulp.

"You're speaking in 16th century dialect again." Slayn smiled at Draish.

"Maybe because I lived then...what's wrong with that...at least I know different dialects...coming from you "cognitive" countrymen." Draish had a cocky personality when he wasn't being shy or awkward. "I could tell you: Bonjoir Mademoiselle. Est-ce que vous en voulez touché dem Mah?"

The elf girl giggled. "Hehehehe, vous etes tellement tord!"

"What he say?" wondered Torru.

"Nothing important..." said the elfin lass.

"Ahh, you don't think so?" Draish looked at her.

"I never knew Draish would be such a linguist..." Torru looked confused.

"So, how long have you been here... this town?" Slayn asked.

A barmaid leaned over to Slayn. "Oh... just a couple hundred years." She smiled at him with a full set of teeth.

"You don't look that old, that's for sure." Slayn then realized that he said that staring at her cleavage.

She stood straight again. "Could I get you anything else tonight, gentlemen." The busty bar maiden put her hand on Slayn's shoulder.

Slayn exchanged glances with Torru, then to Draish. The vampire smiled at him.

"Don't you..." started Slayn.

"What? There's nothing wrong with wanting to bury your face in her chest." He grinned, full fanged.

They all laughed while Slayn turned red.

"You have no right to enter my thoughts…" He looked embarrassed.

"But it's too easy when you're drunk." Draish then look a drink from a bottle.

"Well, on that note, I think it's time for sleep." Slayn got up to leave the table.

"You can come to my house." The woman took Slayn's arm and they left the tavern side-by-side.

"Well, that takes care of his problem," Draish joked. "Maybe he won't be so uptight now."

"How'd you get humor?" Torru looked at him.

"Hey, I'm not completely dead here. Besides that was funny."

"So, where can I sleep?" Torru felt left out.

He caught eyes again with the plump, corseted woman. She gave him a classic "Yoo-hoo" by waving.

"You do have a thing for brunets," Draish told Torru from his thoughts.

Torru stared at Draish for a moment, and then the bearded man got up to talk to the woman.

The blonde elf was left with Draish and she watched him gulp from a bottle for longer than he should have. He put the bottle firmly down and licked his lips. "You stare at me so, in fascination almost…have you not seen a vampire before?"

"You are not like the blood-hungry demons that I have seen. How does the wine taste as a vampire?" she asked and brushed back her hair.

"It is not as sweet as the tissue of life…" he said, leaning toward her, "…that beats in one's veins." His eyes were seductive.

"What is it that you seek, Draish? It is more than just revenge…"

"I am not obligated to tell you my intentions, be that I don't even know your name."

"I am Lyhlia. I make a simple living delivering mail and messages with birds I raise," she told him, then bowed her head.

He looked up from leaning. "The messenger… Lyhlia, then…what do you want to know about me?"

{XVIII}: Walking In The Dark

Myiako nervously walked with Scarlet through the dark castle. She was wary of what was to come. Was the vampiress being sincere? She was about to find out. Her heels clicked and echoed as they entered the marble hallway. Myiako was unnerved by the sudden sharp noise breaking the previous utter silence.

"Here will be your room." Scarlet had stopped in front of a door. She then looked at the knob and it turned slowly, allowing the door to open soundlessly.

"Maybe you can find something decent to wear in the wardrobe," Scarlet said, looking her over. Myi's shorts and t-shirt were informal to Scarlet and would be considered disrespectful in Dracula's presence.

Scarlet then walked away, leaving Myiako alone in the dark hall. The vampire's footsteps faded quickly. Myi looked around, thinking she saw something down the corridor. Gasping, she went into the room and shut the door, no lock.

The room was elegantly decorated: silk covering the bed and rosewood end tables. The beauty of the oaken wardrobe was hardly seen in the dark. She fumbled around and found an oil lamp. She was thankful for the matches in her pocket to light the lamp. Now she was alone in the nice room with light, and could relax.

The room reminded her of her dreams of the past. The reason why was becoming clearer as she thought.

I have to live in Malphina's life as well as the present…but I began to see the past for a purpose. This is how I find out what is going on, this is how I know him.

Too awake to sleep, she just began to daydream. She tried to remember what Malphina knew.

The details of the palace became quite clear and familiar. Malphina was used to walking these halls in her long strange gowns. The dress Myi- Malphina found herself in was blue and lacey, tight in the waist. *Appropriate attire,* she thought, and then noticed that she walked beside Draish. Her eyes glanced to the low-cut leather armour on his chest.

"Wh — where are we going?" she asked.

"Just showing you around the town… as you suggested," he responded giving her a raised eyebrow.

"Oh yes, of course." She picked up her skirt to keep it from dragging.

They walked and she looked down at

the passing ground. "The floor is the same pattern…" she whispered.

"As what?" Draish wanted to know why the marble was so fascinating to her.

"Nothing."

"Is something on your mind, Princess?"

"Besides that fact that I can't leave here, none of your business."

"Hey, I've kept my distance."

"Yeah, today…thus far…"

They continued walking and she looked around. The courtyard came up at the end of stone corridors, then opening to the village pathways. The garden was green and lush in the moonlight as they passed on the cobblestone walkway. The village shops came into view. Malphina was relieved to be around other people.

"How come there are so many people?" she wondered.

"Are they bothering you? I can tell them to leave," he was quick to respond.

"*No*, not at all. It is just, where did they come from?"

"Actually…" he hesitated, "they migrated here after the destruction of…"

"My parent's kingdom?"

"Aaa…yes," he said. "Don't you look at me that way; I wasn't even alive when that happened."

He turned back to notice a cat was following them.

"But if the Swordsman wouldn't of have taken me…"

"You'd be a vampire's slave…" he stopped before saying more.

"Some difference…" she sighed.

"Remember, I am on your side."

"Well, start acting like it, Draish!"

She grew annoyed with his vagueness and stomped away into the crowd of villagers.

"I'll think of something to win this one over…" He looked down to the black cat now at his feet, as if it listened. He then went the direction opposite of Malphina's.

She enjoyed her freedom to wander around town, which was lively at night. She looked behind herself often to try to catch him following her, but never saw him. She didn't need money there, everyone knew who she was and gave her food and jewels."

The bracelet…" she muttered as she looked at the silver clasp.

Myiako snapped to again. The candle-lit room came in focus. She recalled the large chain.

"Where have I seen that…"

She reached into her pocket and rustled

around, and then pulled out the same bracelet seen in her vision. It was the gold and silver band that she took from the tomb, and Draish had let her keep it. Now she knew its origin, from Malphina in the past.

"Why would she give him that?"

Indeed, it was a masculine piece of jewelry, but she wondered why the Princess would soften up to Draish. It was with him. *What did he do?* She wanted to go back into the dream state so as to watch her soap opera of the past. He gave her the bracelet that Malphina gave him. *What did Malphina do, for Draish not to care in this life...?*

Focus, focus...

The renaissance village came into view, then seen through Malphina's green eyes. She now sat on a bench to rest her feet. An hour had passed, maybe, and he still wasn't stalking her. Malphina realized she was thinking about him too much, as if she wanted him to be watching her. Then a cat approached her and she reached to pet it.

"Me-ow," it said with voice.

"Umm, you just say meow?"

"So, you can hearr me..." the black cat had a male voice.

"Should I be talking to a cat?" She

questioned her sanity.

The cat jumped up on the bench next to her and flicked his tail.

"He wishes to meet you in a half-hour," said the cat.

"And if I don't go?" *I'm officially losing it!*

"I'm sure the master will be angry."

"What do you know?"

"I know what happens when vampires get mad...me-ow."

She looked at the bracelet, still in her hand. She knew she had to go.

"I have no choice."

She knew that you couldn't hide from a vampire once it had your scent.

"Follow me," said the cat and it jumped down.

She got up and started following the black cat, feeling foolish. Down the stone path to dirt in the back of town, maybe where storage would have been. An incline went to a gate and that was where the cat went. She stopped before the hill though, staring at the torches on either side of the gate.

"Go on now...me-ow."

"How do I know it's safe?"

"Nothing here is safe..." The cat then ran away.

She took a step forward. The gate began to creak open. She stopped to watch it.

"I don't know if I can bear your hesitation any longer," Draish's voice called to her from the shadows.

"What do you want?"

"Come join me."

She sighed then walked up the stone incline, past the gate. There were torches lit that stood from the ground, dimly lighting the way. She proceeded through a stone archway where she then felt Draish nearby. She did not see him, but instead her eyes focused on the table.

A dinner for two was set up eloquently as a pleasant gesture for Malphina. With candles reflecting off the wine glasses and the silk tablecloth, she felt as if she was indoors for a moment. Then the realization overcame and she became wary again, and cautious of him.

"I do not believe that you are just trying to be nice to me." She looked around to try and see him. "I know what you've been trying to get at…"

A chair was pulled from the table and she flinched.

"Please sit," he said.

Reluctantly, she did so and scooted the chair up to the table. She then looked to see him standing a few yards away in front of her.

To her amazement, he was dressed like a nobleman…not an eccentric vampire.

The royal blue doublet had a tall collar and broad shoulders. He had actually buttoned it up, no longer showing off his bare pectorals. His pants were clean, but he still wore what Malphina noted as the pirate boots (with the big cuffs). He then returned her stare. His hair was tied back and she no longer could avoid his gray eyes reflecting the flame light.

"I am guessing that you like what is in front of you." He stepped closer.

"Oh…umm.." She looked down at the empty platter.

"I have a suggestion that would require a different kind of hunger." He was then sitting at the table across from her.

"This would make you immortal, Princess…" he leaned toward her. "I wish to make you a vampire."

She was shocked. "For a change, I thought you were trying to be nice! Get away from me!" She stood and proceeded toward the gate.

"Maybe my powers of persuasion seem to overlook you." He appeared in front of her again, blocking the path. "I don't think that you understand, Malphina. Become a vampire with me and your choices wouldn't be so limited."

"You're crazy!"

"You must die to stay truly alive! Rule

the night, become a vampire!" His smile was now more insane than kind. "Drink the dead's blood and feast on the pathetic souls, you will be invincible by my side!" He then reached out to her. "Come now, this can only be done by your will. I do not have the power to force you to do things, if you haven't figured that out."

"No! I don't want to die!"

"But you won't…

Meanwhile…

As the daylight continued, Slayn and Torru were fast asleep within the limits of the forest village. Draish, on the other hand, would be found still awake in the darkest, deepest part of the town's storage basement; coincidently, next to the wine. He sat on the floor in the dark with emptied wine bottles around him. He started taking off armour pieces and piled it beside him, and then began to unbutton his shirt, but stopped to look around.

"Who is it that I fascinate so?" he said.

The elf girl, Lyhlia, stepped toward him in the darkness, she being as capable of seeing through that murk as he.

"Could I sit with you?" She looked down at him, and thought his white hair was, ironically, not much of camouflage at night.

"You think it a good idea?" He looked at her.

"What do I have to lose…I'm not afraid of you," she responded.

"Well, if you're so sure about me, by all means." He motioned a welcome with his arms to her. She then sat on the ground to be level with him.

Lyhlia stared at him for a moment then asked, "What do you expect to do, Draish? To make this legend end?"

"Abrupt aren't we? Who says my story will ever end?"

"You are destined to save the world from Dracula…only you can destroy him," she told him.

"You think so…" he said solemnly.

"I will help you anyway that I can," she said in the tone that he liked. "Even immortals must die. Nothing is forever."

"Then you're not really immortal…" he said back.

"You're immortal, but not a god, Draish. Just like you, Dracula is only a vampire."

"If that's what you think, I can't change your mind then." He was insincere.

"You just need to make a plan," Lyhlia suggested.

"Maybe I already have one. Don't you

underestimate me?"

"I didn't."

"There is something you could further accommodate me with, if you insist," he leaned closer to her.

"You are off base from what I had in mind," she reared back. "You have no desire to defeat count Dracula, do you?"

"Ha, it is not for an elf to assume my desires and needs!" It was obvious now that Draish was drunk, but not incoherent.

She then took it on her own to move closer to him. "I am well aware of what you can do. I have studied vampires and even you over time. You cannot resist the heart that beats in me, yet you seem to stray from the facts…" Her voice was quiet.

"You…you are too pure for my taste," he whispered. "It would be like a novice drinking velnis aquenous, holy water."

"Do you really think that purity still exist in this corrupting world?" She stared into his eyes.

"What are you saying? I didn't think you were a virgin," he smiled confidently.

"That is not what I meant, just drink my blood!" She extended her arm to him.

"You don't tempt me!" He grabbed her arm and started tightening his grasp. "You are too pure for a vampire to drink from. Why is it you think that your elf race has existed so long?"

His hold was painfully tight.

"You...don't understand," she gasped.

Then he came close to her face to breathe her in.

"I get it," he said. "There is indeed unjust in your bloodline..." He sniffed her again. "You are only half-elf!" he said and released her arm.

"Yes, and being that my blood would serve a vampire great power." She rolled up her sleeve and held up her wrist to him, showing the finger imprints he had inflicted on her.

"Why must you do this to yourself?" he said, shocking her with his integrity. "My further actions may be involuntary...do you understand that I am starting to lose control?"

"Then I can't be held responsible for my actions either." She smiled. "Drink, you may."

"I want it from the neck..." He then grabbed her shirt collar and pulled her close, ripping her shirt as he did so. "Its been centuries since a girl offered herself to me," he whispered in her ear.

{XIX}: Burden Is Mortality

Myiako woke from her sleep state repeating: "I don't want to die." She was in the castle room with the big wardrobe.

There was a knock on the door and Myi jumped.

"It is time to join us, dear mortal girl," said Scarlet, reminding Myi of her current state.

"Why should I?"

"You know by now that you don't have a choice. Now, just find a suitable dress and proceed right and down the hallway," the countess told her. "You listening, child?"

"Yes…"

She then got up to look through the dresser. After a few minutes of rummaging, she became discouraged. "This isn't medieval times anymore," she sighed. "I guess this will have to do."

Scarlet stood at the bottom of the stairs now accompanied by Dracula. He was wearing a black and red three-piece suit with his long cape. They waited for Myiako to join them, which she did. The vampires were glad to see that she had donned a beautiful blue gown, with long sleeves and a satin kirtle with a silver inlay near her feet. The dress was a perfect fit; coincidence, or did they somehow know?

"The dress…" Myiako looked down.

"Yes, it's simply lovely on you," commented Scarlet.

They knew it would fit Myiako, because it was *hers*, left there over centuries, somehow in pristine condition…

"What is it?" she wondered.

Dracula motioned for her to come down the stairs. "Apologies my dear, but mortals shan't be trusted." He smiled at her.

"Come this way." He gently took her hand, causing Scarlet to gasp.

They walked to the adjacent room across the marble floors. It was dark, but as they entered the candelabras luminated. The room had large Doric pillars supporting the ceiling beams from the gray marble floors. In the room's center was a long rectangular table with a divine banquet spread out in front of them.

Myiako stared in awe, almost drooling. Dracula was now beside the table and he pulled out a chair. The scene reminded her of her daydream and she stood still.

"Come now and sit. This is food you'll enjoy, of that I am sure," Scarlet said, as she came up behind, urging Myiako forward.

Like nothing more than a vampire trying to resist warm flesh, she had to consume some of these delicacies. She went for the wine vat first to quench her thirst, then to a chicken leg. After she was well into gorging, she noticed that the vampires took a seat at either end of the table. Myiako became uncomfortable and stopped chewing, cheeks stuffed. She turned to the red-haired woman then to the dark-haired man.

"I could use some privacy here," she said with a mouth full of food. After no response from either elder, she began smacking again. With a hard swallow she stopped. "Why do I feel like I am the main course?"

"That is impossible at this time and that is why we must tell you of your powers," Scarlet said.

"Powers?" wondered Myi.

"Yes, indeed," the Count replied.

"Don't get us wrong, we'd eat you if we could, but you are the Lady of Necromancy." Scarlet smiled, showing fangs.

"So I can resurrect vampires, big deal," Myiako sighed.

"It is a 'big deal'. You see that ability of yours is quite troublesome," Dracula said, crossing his arms.

"Then why are you being so nice to me?"

"Hospitality is in a vampire's nature, if you haven't noticed," he told her. "That is how you distinguish the nobles from the minions."

Myiako rolled her eyes. *Not from what I've seen…*

"So…what do you want with me?" she asked them.

"To compromise…for now," replied Dracula.

He exchanged glances with Scarlet and looked at Myiako.

Myi shook her head. "No…I don't like the looks of this."

Scarlet grinned. "It is not that awful really, you're just the bait to lure that pathetic excuse of a vampire to us."

"If I must sacrifice you in the process, let it be so," the Count told her.

Myiako looked at him and his eyes returned the notion that made her not believe him.

"Why did you kill her, long ago?" she confronted him.

"You have no idea, so I vish not to harm you. This vill make things complicated, you see."

"You didn't answer." She had noticed the waver in his tone, as if he was fearful of something.

"You vill find out soon enough. And

you vill see. Draish Jau-Ri is to realize that he has no purpose."

"Are you saying that vampires don't have a purpose anymore?"

The countess chuckled. "We thin out the herd."

"No," said Dracula, "it is him that is useless and bothersome. He vill always strive to kill me for what I have done."

"You admit to killing the princess, Zaira then." Myi stared at Dracula.

He sighed. "Vhat is said now: Curiosity killed the cat. You should really stop asking questions on things you know nothing of."

"I didn't ask to be stuck in this situation. If you despise Draish so much couldn't you have just destroyed his remains one of the times he was dead?"

"It's hard to destroy something that is being protected by a force greater than your own. I am intrigued and annoyed by my predicament."

"You're not telling me something important."

"She's a mind reader now, hahahaa," the Countess commented.

Dracula avoided Myiako and motioned for Scarlet to get up. The vampires got up from the table leaving Myiako alone in the large room.

What are they up to?

In the hallway, Dracula spoke with the Countess.

"You, cannot say anything, you old fool. You'll ruin what took life times to achieve," Scarlet told him.

"I don't know how much more of this I can take…just to taste her blood…she is beyond immortal." He seemed shaken up.

"And you'll never get to if you tell her now. If she only knew her power to resurrect vampires gives her a power over us. Her blood would be divine. But we must wait for the right time." She took his hand.

"Since when are you the voice of reason," he said and smiled at her.

{XX}: As New As The Moon

His pale eyes awoke to the pleasant darkness of the basement where he had slept.

"The dawn of night, I must go to her," he said, sitting up suddenly. He looked to find his shirt next to him and put it on. His hair was easily seen in the dark, but not so well with anything else. A vampire's eyes could reflect the light as a cats would and he saw where his things were in utter darkness. After standing up, buttoning his pants, and stretching, he started putting back on his broken armour.

The elf girl then returned holding a lamp. She threw a large sack at him and he caught it, forcefully. "What is this?"

"Its new armour, well it's old, but in good condition. New to you, anyway. Elfin-issued, but it suits you well," she said.

"You sure it fits?" He looked into the bag.

"Well...it's leather studded, so you can tear it to fit if needed. And I got you some new boots...here." She threw him the other items that were in her hand.

"You could have just set it down," he

said.

"Aww, what's the fun in that, besides you need to hurry. Time is not on your side."

"Don't you think I know that?" he said, as he took items from the bag. "Whose are these?"

"Well, I asked the museum for them. For all I know they could have been yours," she smiled.

He responded with a smirk as he shoved on the boots. "The irony is amusing, you know that, Lyhlia."

He looked at her watching him as he fitted on the breastplate and latched the paldrons to his shoulders and the gauntlets to his arms. After trying to single-handedly put on the leggings, he looked back at her. "Lend a hand?"

She stepped off the stairs and knelt down to his feet. She took the leather cuisse from his hand and pushed it against his femur. He watched her reach around his thigh to connect the clasp in the back. She did this slowly to his other leg and looked up to him. After securing the greaves to his calves, she stood.

He breathed in deeply. "…I don't know if I'll be able to come back to you… even if I live." Draish looked into her eyes as he spoke. "I'm sorry I must go to her."

"You do what you must, my lord, you can always depend on me," she assured him, taking his cold hand.

He kissed her hand and backed away.

He then put on the belt and satchels and flung the black cloak over his shoulders. The cape trailed with prestige behind him as he ascended the stairs. His dark brows lowered over his pale eyes and he left her standing down there with a devious smirk on his lips.

Slayn and Torru were back in the tavern, but this time for food. They were joined by other people, and to Draish's surprise, they both still had their lady companions seated next to them. This very mundane scene continued as just that until the vampire entered the room. Heads couldn't help but turn to look at the silvered-haired man as he walked past them. Besides the different attire, Draish seemed confident as he approached his traveling partners.

He put a hand on Torru's shoulder, then said to Slayn, "Tonight is the night, let us begin."

Slayn and Torru exchanged glances, wondering if the vampire was being sincere with the friendly gesture.

Torru sighed. "Too bad I still don't

know how to use this sword…"

"I'm sure you'll do fine. I only discovered I was the dragon after we found Draish last week." Slayn stood up.

Draish looked down, causing hair to fall in front of his eyes. "I never had any time…but if I had a "de chornos ava'nt" on my side, then what." He looked at Slayn, referring to the Time Lord that he is, now.

"What do you think I can do?" Slayn pondered on his true potential as a god.

"It's what I know you're capable of… to simply pause the clock." Draish smiled. "That would enable us to train." He looked at Torru's sword.

"Any hints on how I am to "pause" time?"

"Umm…" Draish became useless for that one.

"Just try something," Torru suggested. Everyone in the room stepped back from them in caution.

Slayn looked around. "Let's take this outside…"

They walked outside and onward to the nearby field where no citizens were this late."

"This is a good place to try…well, something."

"However you change into the dragon form, is how you can perform magic," Draish told him.

"What do you mean?" Slayn responded. "To become the Dragon Lord I must be protecting something."

"Appropriate abilities can be summoned at the right times. This would be a good time…"

Draish didn't know how to explain and scratched his head. He thought for a moment.

"Alright, I think I got it now…to turn into a wolf I want to be the wolf, I can feel its spirit," he said as he started glowing and morphing into the white-gray wolf. He now sat on his canine feet before them.

"It was the want to become, thus the need to use your powers," the wolf told them. Draish then changed back into a man, sitting on his knees.

"Did that make any sense to you two?" he said at their dumbfounded stares.

"I cannot use the energy of the Dragon Lord, if he is not needed. It is not my own personal gain to use him," Slayn told Draish.

"That's a good point, but don't you see that he is yours to use." Draish stood back up. "The Dragon Lord chose you, Slayn—use it."

"Ok, stand back…I will become the

dragon." Slayn held out his arms.

Nothing happened.

"Stop trying so hard," Draish commented.

Slayn relaxed, but concentrated. Then the golden glow surrounded him. Torru held up his hand opposing the light and Draish stepped back.

Slayn could feel the power growing and it looked to be almost painful. The surge of energy went through his body and he grew into the small dragon with blonde hair. His clothes were reduced to a loincloth for the beast and he looked around confused.

"Crap, I lost my clothes...I didn't before."

"You weren't concentrating enough to morph them as well." Draish then laughed at him. "But it looks like this is a good start."

"Just stay like that, Slayn, and attack Torru," Draish told him.

"What?"

"This will be good sword training to fend off dragon claws." The vampire smiled. "What are you waiting for?"

Slayn hesitated but then swung a talon at Torru, who just held up his sword.

"Hold on now!" Torru backed away.

"Come on!" Draish encouraged Slayn. The dragon swung again, this time coming in contact with the Mystic Sword. Torru's feet dug into the dirt as he was pushed back by the force of the blow.

"Why you…"

The Swordsmen's power grew. Another thrust. Now Torru began to gain his magic armour.

"Keep going, you can't let the dragon win!" Draish taunted Torru.

Their energy now electrified the air. A clash of talons and steel sparks. Slayn came at Torru with a tail lash and he was knocked down. The dragon lunged upon the man, who pushed back with the sword. The energy waves were able to make the spectator, Draish, lose his footing for a moment. The strength of the two pushed visible sound waves outward and all movement slowed. Slayn then stepped down and looked around. Besides the three caught in the blast, everyone and everything within sight seemed to stop completely. Complete stillness.

"Hahaha, you did it!" Draish brushed dirt from his hair.

Torru stood back up, using the sword to right himself.

"Time has stopped, but we are moving, but how?" Slayn was confused.

"Keep focused! Don't lose it!" Draish snapped at him. "Keep training , now that you have the time." Draish was un-doubtfully amused by this as he urged the friends to fight. "Figure out the physics behind pausing time later...attack him again!"

The dragon looked around and then focused back on the Swordsman. Once again, their auras glowed as they approached each other. Slayn flapped his wings and jumped into the air. Torru looked up and blocked with the sword as the dragon came down on him. The force blew him back and his armour clanked. Torru then swung the sword around from the ground and thrust upward. It came in contact with Slayn's chin and knocked down the beast.

They could feel the change when the motion of time reanimated around them. Torru ran up to Slayn, who was human again. "Oh shit! Are you ok?"

Slayn lay motionless in his tattered clothes as Torru looked down to him. He opened his eyes and spoke "That hurt...you asshole."

"I thought it killed you there for a second," Torru said, relieved.

"He'll be fine." Draish laughed. "That was a good start." He clapped his hands at them. "We'll continue after Slayn gets some clothes."

"Why, so the dragon outgrows them...

it's pointless."

"You must learn more, then."

"Thanks for seeing if I was injured or not, Draish," Slayn replied sarcastically.

"I knew you were all right, I didn't smell any dragon blood." He smiled, as he always did when thinking about blood.

Slayn walked away slowly from fatigue and Torru was left with Draish.

"Now, try to hit me with the sword," the vampire told him.

"My pleasure!" The armour-clad man ran forward with sword readied.

"Take your time, don't be so tense," Draish said after moving out of the path of the attack. Then Torru swung upward and downward, the blade hitting the dirt.

"Too slow."

"Of course I am, you're a damn vampire!"

Torru kept swatting the sword around in the direction Draish was.

"This isn't funny." Torru grew tired and stopped swinging as Draish stepped closer.

"Giving up so soon? I knew that humans were lazy, but...you have always wanted to re-kill me."

Torru panted. "You're right."

"What was that?" Draish was then

actually caught off guard by the flying sword. It had come down on his upper leg, but was aimed for his chest. Draish clenched his teeth in searing pain. "You better back off," Draish warned, looking at Torru's expression and wondering if he would actually stab him again. "Don't make me mad, Torru…"

Torru stood down and backed away. "You asked for it."

Draish was sitting now, holding his leg. "Curse that Mystic blade…"

"Silvers still affect you?" Torru asked, looking down to him.

"That blade is purified by priests. Blessed by four high clergymen already from last time I was alive. It seems like more now…"

"I thought religious things like that didn't affect you."

"Maybe I'm evil after all." Draish sighed.

"You asked me to hit you…"

"I didn't think you could."

"Don't underestimate me, Draish, I am the most powerful human after all."

"Boasting, that's a good sign from you, I guess." Draish then stood back up to show his leg had healed already.

"See, I don't need practice," commented Torru, as he then made the change back into his normal clothes from the heavy blue and silver armour.

"What do you think that was?" said Draish with a smile.

"Not even a warm-up," Torru bluffed.

A few moments later, Slayn came back in new clothes…again. Draish was eager for him to stop time for them again and so persisted he try again.

Slayn shook his head and concentrated. "De ma chronos era dron."

To their surprise it worked. Slayn's newfound spell enabled them to maintain active while anything outside the vicinity was simply paused…well, not so simply.

"That is incredible!" Torru exclaimed. "Never seen anything like it; and I've seen a LOT lately."

"He is truly the golden-god," Draish said softly for the fact he just did that without being a dragon.

"Now…you must change and morph your clothing with the transmutation." The vampire looked at Slayn, who didn't seem amused.

"I am so glad you're concerned…but I don't see how to do that…what if I just can't, I am not a vampire…"

"You just paused time itself, a feat not even the king of vampires can imitate. I have a feeling that you are capable enough." Draish grinned enough to show fangs.

"What do I do then, if time is paused by a spell and I can change into a dragon by will, then I must use a willful spell to change into the Dragon Lord?"

"Hmm..." Draish scratched his head. "Just use the power to blend yourself into the form, instead of growing out of your body, grow into it," he tried to explain.

Slayn looked up into the dark sky as to seek some guidance from the stars. The golden yellow glow accumulated around his human body. He didn't start to change right away as before, this method took longer, but he did it. The energies swirled around Slayn and his clothes now began to melt into the radiant scales of the beast as his body gained mass and size. Instead of ripping out of his clothes, he now could simply change back after the dragon left him. The 12-foot tall reptile stood before them.

Draish clapped his hands followed by Torru, and then applause from the spectators who were caught in the time dome. Draish laughed and said, "Next time clear the area before pausing time."

"I don't even know the radius of it." Slayn's dragon voice was much deeper and louder than that of his human form.

"That's another thing to work on

then," Draish told him. "Now, time for more fighting." The vampire cracked his knuckles. "Look, Torru, he's even grown larger than before."

"You got to be kidding," said Torru, who was exhausted from the previous sword swinging.

"You must keep up your stamina, or you will be killed," Draish told them.

"Can't we keep our energy for the real battles?" Torru liked to dispute.

"You aren't ready, yet…neither of you…nor am I." Draish wasn't afraid to announce the truth. "If you had all the time in the world to prepare yourself, what would you do?"

"En guarde!" Torru exclaimed, charging for Draish.

"Ha-ha! That's the spirit!" Draish was too fast for the mortal man to hit him straight on. Another swing and Torru got his sword stuck into the wet dirt again.

Draish came at Torru with his claws and Slayn rose up to defend. A wing flap and a tail lash sent the vampire flying back. Draish regained his footing with a smile on his face. Slayn breathed in deep, smoke came from his nostrils and a belch of flame came out his toothy snout. The vampire put up his arm to cover his face and the fire was reflected by his bracers. The scaly tail came at Draish again, but this time he grabbed onto it, stopping the dragon's attack. Draish pulled on the tail and Slayn roared. He moved the dragon around and swung him. Slayn flapped his wings and became airborne to avoid another attack. Draish looked up to him, but didn't fail to notice Torru charging him.

The sword just missed the vampire as it always seemed to, but this time was stopped with a clash of steel. Draish had used his iron blades that were his fingers to defend. He felt as if his transformation wasn't as effective as the Mystic Sword and backed off of Torru before the pressure grew too great. Slayn had already swooped down behind Draish and grabbed the white-haired man by the shoulders with his large front talons. They struggled as the Swordsman came at Draish with the sword out to impale him. Torru stopped, leaving the blade just a few inches from his torso.

"Give me a reason not to run you through," he said to Draish. The glance was returned and the vampire was anything but afraid. "Va al ire begi-guruns." Draish muttered before vanishing. He was behind Torru now and knocked off his helmet. Torru stumbled and Draish laughed. "I guess that is enough playing with you guys," he said and stretched his arms outward.

Slayn spoke to the skies, "Deyan chronos evat'an…"

A strange sensation came over their bodies, and then the scenery began to animate once again. The trees blew once again in the wind, and the nocturnal sounds reached their ears.

Slayn sunk back into his human self, this time remaining in his new shirt and pants. Torru sheathed the sword and his armour faded away back into his hooded cloak and pants.

"Never thought I'd have to *not* make up for lost time," Slayn joked.

"Yes, but before time does pass, we must leave." Draish started walking away from them. He seemed kind of irritated or embarrassed.

A crowd then gathered as the three headed for the village gates. The spectators, tavern dwellers, and other elves, all came outside to give the travelers farewell. Draish turned to face the crowd, which silenced upon looking at him in the glow of the street lamps.

"The support that your village has shown will be of great aide in our upcoming battle," his voice boomed over them. "I fret that we don't have much time. We must leave you now. Again, thank you." Draish took the side of his cape and bowed before them. Then he turned and walked away with no further words. Slayn and Torru were obviously surprised by the vampire's fair speaking voice and simply said "goodbye" and waved to the people. The woman that Slayn had been with came running up to him, bosom bouncing. "Please come back to us," she said, embracing him.

Torru said his goodbyes to the other lady, as she tried to persuade him to stay, while the other townspeople waved and said "Fare thee well!" "Good luck." "So long guardians! May the gods look down on thee!"

Draish turned just long enough to make eye contact with Lyhlia, who was at the front of the crowd. She mouthed the words: "See you soon." He nodded and smiled.

They left the village, heading north to where the land became barren and rocky. They all had the feeling that Myiako was endangered even more now. It felt as if something was about to happen, something that can be stopped.

"Walking will not do tonight, it seems." Draish broke the silence after about ten minutes of walking away from the town. "We must fly."

"I can't fly..." Torru sighed.

"Must you always have to state the

obvious…?" Draish shook his head.

"I believe I'm your transportation," Slayn said to Torru.

Slayn then took a moment to step back and slowly form into the golden Dragon Lord. He sat down on his muscular haunches.

"Hurry up and mount your friend, I'll go on ahead," Draish chuckled as he turned into the bat with the white hair.

"Did you really have to use the word, mount…?" Slayn peered at Draish, who then flapped away. "Besides, I did enough mounting last night." Slayn and Torru shared a laugh.

Torru secured his sword on his back straps, grabbed onto Slayn's scaly back, then positioning himself on the dragon's shoulders before Slayn started moving. Slayn then flapped his large wings and lifted from the ground. The continuous push of air and an altitude was gained above the tree tops. It was dark and they had already lost sight of Draish.

"What are you waiting for, go!" ordered Torru.

"I can't see anything, I'm not a bat… "Slayn sighed.

"Just go, I mean it's not like you're going to run into another dragon or anything else for that matter."

They took off into the direction that the

bat flew. At first, Slayn struggled to keep the man on his back, but then got used to the extra weight.

"I can't see a damn thing!" growled Slayn.

"Isn't it odd?" Draish startled them; they had not noticed that he was now flying next to them. "That there is no moon." The bat swerved in front of the dragon. "It was half waning last night…"

"Maybe it just isn't in sight yet…" Torru said with some hope.

Slayn caught a current and glided upward. "We'd be able to see it from this height."

"Something is not right…" Draish commented.

"I thought you were a master vampire, but you seem to draw a lot of conclusions," Slayn told him.

"What did you expect?"

"You can change people into minions, morph your own body effortlessly, use magic aimlessly… should I go on?"

"I guess you could go on, but I am not in full control of making minions, I have transformation limitations, and magik takes too much energy to use all the time…I am immortal, but not omnipotent."

"So what are we going to do?" Torru

questioned.

"What we must do..." Draish responded.

The chilled air fluttered under the dragon's wings and the bat flapped to keep pace, as they glided toward the dark outline of the castle.

{XXI}: Plans Are Imminent

Meanwhile... ...

At the base of the shadowy stairs was the elegant castle manor parlor. The Count D and his partner Scarlet were seated in the dim light.

"I don't understand why we are being so nice to that girl..." said the woman, "when we have plans to kill her."

"Don't you know that et iz bad to stress the prey before de feast?" he responded without changing his calm expression. "Her time iz coming...once ve have her tied in restraints, he'll be plenty mad. This should spark the fire in that vampire I've been vaiting for."

"Jau-Ri would never agree to side with us...not in another 300 years..." she said sitting forward. "Remember how I had him in the past?"

"Amnesia was a blessing to the damned. It is almost a shame that ve must kill them all again..." Dracula looked down as he spoke.

"We have his only weakness, and she is cooperating nicely," Scarlet confirmed.

"That was a burden I quickly came to refuse. A powerful being such as vampire should not have to bow down to the likes of the ressurector. Yet, ironically, one of our own dares to keep challenging my power." He stood up. "He vill surely find that it iz not I that makes evil happen; I am just here to glorify it." He stopped his speech.

"I am well aware of your power, my Lord Dracula, but you cannot underestimate the power of the opposing vampire." She looked up to him.

He turned to her with a smile. "You vould say that, on the grounds that Draish Jau-Ri killed you those many years ago."

She put her hand on her forehead. "Don't remind me..."

"Do you understand...vhat's in the future for you, Scarlet, my dear?"

"Let us go over it one more time, I don't want to attack too sudden—" she told him, but was cut off.

"If you vish, I am just ready to drink her blood..." His glance was serious.

The Count Dracula was said to be over 1000 years old at this point. He had never been killed such as Draish had. He did not have the option of the ressurector to revive him, as the ancient vampire could restore himself like no other. Within these years of knowledge, he had grown weary of everything, even blood seem to lose its flavor. Dracula believed that through sacrificial onslaught, he could finally gain the mortal power of release...

Myiako wandered around the long corridors with oil lamp in hand. She had no clue as to what was to become of her. No recollection of what her ancestor, Malphina, had done in the clutches of a vampire. She wondered if the princess died young or lived to be queen, and she wondered if they shared a fate. It was difficult for her to keep quiet as she walked in the satin dress, as it rustled along the floors.

She decided there was no use in getting away from there, so had settled on just looking around. She walked back down the hall toward the room where she had dressed. She took a doorknob in hand and turned... no use, the door wouldn't open. She went from door to door down the corridor, checking for unlocked doors. Finally, a handle clicked, but the door failed to open. She pressed against it and shook the knob. The door came open, suddenly, and she stumbled into the adjacent room.

Her lamp's flame quickly lit the dark room. She looked around to see stacked up furniture covered in cobwebs and undisturbed dust. There were some crates in the corner, and she held the light up to get a better view. Nothing seemed to catch her interest until she went over to a dresser against the left wall. This is where she chose to place the lantern on top of the cabinet. She looked down to see a painting leaning on the drawers. She picked up the framed canvas and held it near the light source. (The faded organic paints could have been as old as what we would know as the roman era.) The image focused in the lamp light, and reflected like a mirror in her eyes.

"What the…" *This is much too old to be a painting of me, and her hair is too light…this isn't Malphina. But, I look just like her.*

She noticed that the woman wore the same colour satin dress that she had chosen to wear.

"I guess it runs in the family…this must be my ancestor, this is Zaira."

Saying that name gave her chills, as if she were being watched by something ghostly.

A new series of questions were soon to arrive in her mind. *Why does Dracula have this here? What does this mean for me? What does this mean?*

"What's with my family tree and vampires?" she then said out load.

"Oh, but I believe you know everything…" Dracula's voice failed to startle her this time. "So feeble you block such things from your mind…"

She hurried to regain the lamp to see him better.

"Do I know then…" she walked to the doorway to meet him face to face. "You didn't want to kill Malphina, but you did, didn't you! And what of Zaira?" she confronted.

"As a young vampire, I learned fast…I learned that there were few to challenge me from having undocumented power. I offered the meek the charity of siding with me or the malice of opposition," he said, then turning his back on her, moved toward the hall. "Now come vith me and let us avait the arrival of our guest." He smiled, looking back at her dumbfounded expression.

She found confusion around every corner. Myiako as a treasure hunter had come across many puzzles and riddles, but the enigma of how she fit into this scenario baffled her mind. She was hesitant to follow Dracula as anyone would be, but she did what she was told. She thought of his words and realized he hadn't been that candid with her before. Maybe the sight of Zaira's painting sparked a bit of humanity in is soul, perhaps not. At this point she wondered if she had fallen victim of a vamperic trance, in the way that she systematically followed the master vampire's lead.

He doesn't want to kill me, but he has to, but at a certain time…why? What is with my bloodline? Zaira, Malphina, then myself…Dracula wants us all dead…

"What makes you so sure of yourself?" Myiako asked him after the long silence.

He turned to face her and his eyes reflected purple as he looked into hers. Myiako swallowed in discomfort.

"He iz not ready for this…Not ready to fight me," he finally responded, then quickly turned to continue down the hallway.

She could only assume that he was speaking of Draish, who had bad luck with fighting other master vampires in the past. She followed the Count to the right corridor where her fate awaited.

Meanwhile…

The bat flew and soared in front of the dragon. Slayn now had trouble keeping up with the vampire bat and became irritated with his flying patterns.

"Would you fly straight?!" Slayn gave a demand more than a question.

Draish just looked at them, and then zoomed forward, out of sight. The truth was that the vampire wished to find anything to do to entertain his wondering mind.

How does Myiako see me? Does she know I need her as much as the others? I should have been this patient in the past. I never have enough time, but I cannot rush things.

He might have these thoughts, but would he see that the descendants of the necromancer were the key and the flaw to his life and powers? Having too much time has proven him wrong in the past...

Torru leaned down to Slayn's ear and said, "What do you think is going to happen?"

The dragon took his eyes off the dark sky to respond, "If you are trying to say that you are scared, then you could have stayed in the town."

"Ha, me scared?" Torru only 'acted' tough.

"Draish is smarter than he leads on. He knows something we don't. I, too, wonder what he is up to," Slayn told him.

"Why are we involved?"

"Haven't you been listening... even if we were not guardians, there would still be the issue of saving Myi. But that is just it, this is too perfect. The four guardians are so simply united. Years past, they didn't know each other, nor were on the same side," Slayn explained to his narrow-minded friend.

"So you are saying it is certain that we

win this time?"

"Fate is on our side, my friend."

They looked ahead, the dark silhouette of the castle blocked out the blanket of stars in the horizon. They now saw the bat flying back to them.

"Tread warily; I do not know what he has planned for us. Just rely on the powers that inhabit you, this is instinct. You have powers you would never thought possible." Draish gave them a little motivation, as if he knew what they were thinking.

They kept in the air as they approached the castle. Draish turned back into human shape and continued levitating next to the dragon and rider. It seemed to take more energy to fly as human form than as a bat.

"If we were only given more time with these powers…" Torru replied.

"Why…just why would Dra'cul be so admirable as to give us that advantage. This leads me to believe that the dark ones are afraid of the bond the guardians make," Draish told them as he looked down.

"You are so trusting of us…This has always been your battle, since the beginning." Slayn looked at Draish.

"I don't care, I just want this tyranny to end, this sadness to dissipate," he spoke.

He wouldn't talk in that manner so earnestly looking anyone in the eyes...

"Did you not choose your fate? Were you not given the choice to be a vampire or not?" Slayn confronted.

"What of it do you know?" Draish lost focus of the castle to peer at Slayn.

"I know that you were asked to come back as an undead by the Lady Necromancy herself, and you agreed." Slayn didn't lie.

"Hmm let us see, what would you do? My love was killed by a vampire, I was accused of her murder, and then killed at age 26…oh, then in afterlife I found out that she… she is the necromancer. Not only that, but she gives me the opportunity to avenge our deaths." Draish said this with no emotion, as if he had said it too many times in his head.

"It is a tragic story indeed, but have you ever thought that you were tricked?" Slayn wondered. "Could the necromancer have taken on her form to get you to come back?"

"I suppose, but what would it all matter now, she's still dead….that bastard!" Draish said. "Vlad Dra'cul killed Zaira, right there… mocking me, knowing that I would come after him, one way or another. He must suffer… as I did…it is as simple as that," Draish said, then showed his fangs in a smile.

Draish lost altitude to land in front

of the castle gates on his boots. The dragon landed on all fours and Torru dismounted. They stood before large wooden gates, which were surrounded by torch fire. Slayn's scales gleamed in the firelight and he stood back. The gate doors started to creek open and stayed ajar. Draish took a deep breath and proceeded first. Torru drew his sword from his back and followed, and Slayn stepped through the doors lastly. They stood anxiously in the entryway as Draish walked further into the parlor.

They watched as the large wooden door began to creep shut behind them.

Draish looked around confidently in the dimly lit castle. He looked over to the closest chair as it shook when an orange cat jumped up on it.

"Well, hello." The cat looked at Draish.

"Don't tell me that you are reduced to a feline…Scarlet. Your idea of a parlor trick…" Draish smiled.

"The Countess Scarlet? But how, here and now?" Slayn whispered.

She licked her paw and chuckled.

"I began to wonder how and why the king himself was tossing his minions at us, but it all makes sense now, does it not," Draish replied. "Just how many of them were yours?"

A glow then surrounded the cat and she took human form. The long crossed legs sitting on the chair with a ruffled dress was Scarlet. "We just meet again and you wish to anger me so soon, Draish?"

"What did you expect, wench. Out of my way!"

"Ha-ha it is not that easy you see."

"I've had my quarrels with you and I have killed you, Scarlet. Do you want that upon yourself again?"

"Remember, I had killed you as well. I am not afraid of you or your minions, either."

"You have lived ages but yet you haven't been listening, have you..." Draish told her, making eye contact. "They are the guardians, not my minions..." Draish shook his head at her.

"I just could never understand why you keep them around if you are not using them to feed off of..." she said casually.

"That is why we could never get along...Now, get out of my way, fiend!" Draish said sternly. *Little did she know...*

"I'll do nothing of the sort." Scarlet then stood up and approached Draish. "You do look well," she told him "seems that you have been feeding as a vampire should."

"Ignorant aren't you," he said. "Remember that I can feed from your minions...their blood is indeed tainted, but I am able to purify it on intake." He smiled.

"You are bluffing…" she paused, and then stepped closer. She then snapped her fingers and three minions went to attack Slayn and Torru.

The wolf thing clawed at Torru before he was able to completely change form back into his armour. Draish reacted to help them, but she had grabbed him from behind; pining his arms behind his back with enormous strength, as if he was a mere child.

He watched Slayn get wounded, and Torru tossed around. Draish bared his fangs and tried to break free from her grasp. "Have you lost all honour!" he growled.

"It's a fair fight. You can't help everyone. Maybe one day you'll see that for yourself, Draish," she talked softly into his ear, which was intentional to his disliking.

She tightened her grasp right before she released his arms and threw him to the ground. He turned back to her and stood back up to exchange glances.

"Don't just stand there like a fool," she told him." Fight me!"

He shook his head with disconcertment of her feeble efforts to aggravate him.

Scarlet attacked Draish again and put her claws around his neck. He refused to struggle and didn't resist her stranglehold.

Her long nails dug into his flesh. As the blood trickled down, he noticed her grip loosen, and then she let him go and stepped back.

It took a moment before Draish realized that the dragon, Slayn, had just killed apparently one of *her* minions. The vamptress was in a weakened state suddenly, stunned like a bird flying into a window.

"That is enough!" This was Dracula's voice that boomed within the walls. They didn't see him until the shadows collected and formed his shape, standing on the stairs.

The two alive minions then ran to Dracula's side, not so much as to protect him, but to protect themselves. Torru and Slayn stood still despite their uneasy panting.

"Come to protect Scarlet?" Draish was the first to speak, as he wiped the dark blood from off his neck.

"Just trying to postpone the senseless killing iz all," he responded.

Draish looked back to the Countess. "He really took you in, did he? Is he the reason why you're alive?"

Scarlet sneered.

"You call yourself a master, when you're just his dog!" Draish laughed at her.

"Watch your tongue, boy," the count D told him.

"Or what? Are you going to kill me?"

Draish laughed, apparently losing his train of thought. He then lunged forward and grabbed Scarlet around the neck with his arm as to tempt the Count to fight him.

"What is this foolishness; you do not vant to fight me! You must understand something, Draish Jau-Ri, ve are just alike, you and I."

"That is a lie! We indeed both are vampires, but our powers vary greatly." The white-haired man stood his ground despite the energy that he felt emanating from the vampire lord.

"Now, I'll say this once, let her go," Dracula told him.

Draish hesitated. "I was just trying to have some fun with your woman. No idea what you've done with mine." He then pushed Scarlet toward the dark vampire.

"Why do you not enjoy your life as an immortal?" Dracula wondered. "I do not understand, you…you haven't lived as long as I. You have had the privilege of dying.

Draish wondered if the old vamp was getting senile. "You want me to kill you? Because by all means…" Draish raised an eyebrow.

"I am just trying to talk some sense into you iz all," he told him. "I guess you vill have to find out on your own."

"I came here not just to kill you, Dra'cul, but to save Myiako." Draish got back on course.

"Ha, you damn vell know that you cannot kill me, and as for her…that cannot be, she iz rightfully mine now," he told Draish, who didn't quite know what he meant by that.

"Just let her free…and…and I won't have to…" Draish paused.

"Won't have to die again?" Dracula smiled.

"No, so I won't have to…." his voice rose with anticipation, as he knew he was about to be attacked. He had jumped back in future sight of Dracula's attack. The vampire had hardly strained to launch an energy bolt at him. The magic missile then clashed with the marble floor. A loud boom echoed throughout the whole castle.

Draish landed in a crouch, just in time to jump away from another attack. This time, the Mystic Swordsman and the dragon advanced to protect Draish, but were intercepted by Scarlet.

"Don't you move!" she warned them with a toothy smile.

The next energy bolt was deflected by an invisible shield that guarded Draish.

"Stop being so abrupt…you're getting careless, Vlad." He stared at his adversary.

"Just testing you." Dracula smiled. He had remained virtually in the same position the whole time.

Draish growled then, transforming his right hand into steel claw fingers. He leapt for the dark vampire, but was only able to rip the black cape. The tattered silk fell to the ground, and the count had vanished. Draish looked around the vast candlelit parlor room, exchanging glances with Torru and Slayn.

Scarlet had vanished as well.

It was then Draish felt it rip into him, a purple glow surrounded him…what was this power? He fell to all fours and looked as if he was being devoured from within. Draish closed his eyes and focused. The dark aura then subsided into his body and he was able to stand again.

"It seems that your immobilizing spell failed to work, Dracula." He looked up to see the count standing a few feet in front of him. Dracula looked displeased for the first time in their conversation. Draish took another swat at him, but was fooled by the disappearing act again.

"Fight face to face!" Draish growled, annoyed. He spoke in the direction he assumed the count to be in.

Then out of the shadows, something jumped at him with fur and fangs. A black wolf, its back stood as tall as a man, tackled him to the ground.

"Does this face to face interaction satisfy you?" Dracula's voice was distorted through drooling fangs. The wolf's paws pinned Draish to the ground at both shoulders. "Besides this is how we first met."

Draish's hand had turned back to normal as he struggled; this was obviously Dracula's intention. With his body in this compromising position, Draish was unable to withhold any form but his own, thus making him vulnerable to the beast. This wasn't all though, the intense power that radiated from Dracula wasn't something the light vampire could tolerate. He could not harness it or even move at this point. The furry beast was draining him.

"Damn-you to hell!" Draish growled as he felt weighted down.

"HA! Something the matter, boy!" the wolf talked over him and its saliva dripped onto Draish's face.

"Think not for a second that this is over..." the man gasped from under the beast.

Slayn and Torru became nervous to see their leader become subdued so easily by Dracula, and they felt need to take the risk to help Draish.

"He's taking his power!" called out

Torru, his amour clanking as he ran toward the two vampires.

Scarlet had stopped him with a telekinesis maneuver, which halted him and Slayn and threw them backwards. She appeared overlooking the two guardians and screeched, "Give me a good reason not to feed on you!"

They looked at each other as if for an answer or maybe even motivation, but then their attention was diverted. Draish yelled out in pain, which was not something one would want to hear. It was a horrible sound... as if a wolfs' heart was being cut out, while still alive. This was not normal for him to flinch in agony or not good on their part. The dark aurora surrounded Dracula and covered Draish. He was exposed as the dark one attempted to rip his soul from him.

"There is no hope for you; I won't let you have Malphina," the wolf whispered loudly within his heavy breathing.

Slayn couldn't bear to see Draish suffer so and he picked up his scaly head and sneered at Scarlet. The dragon inhaled and exhaled an orange burst of flames, which engulfed the vamptress in a blazing inferno. She was caught by surprise and screamed as she caught on fire.

The dragon flew at the black wolf

beast, talons forward. Dracula would have been impaled if he hadn't moved within the last second.

"Your time is ending!" Slayn looked at the count wolfie, then to Draish, whom was stunned and lying in blood.

Dracula's laugh turned from a gargled growl to his normal chuckle. "I am done with him anyway," Dracula said, referring to Draish. "When you find her, you'll find me again…" The shadow of the vampire started to fade out.

"Wait!" Draish's voice was worn out, "Why did you call her…Malphina?" He knew that D heard him, but he left without responding.

Slayn and Torru had blended back into their mundane selves to preserve their energy and went to look down at Draish, who looked as if he was about to pass out. The vampire shook off the feeling of violation and thought of how he was to respond when that bastard tried that again. He could only explain the feeling as though his soul was being raped. *I cannot let it happen again. I don't know if I will survive…*

{XXII}: Reflections Always Know

He opened his eyes to the familiar surroundings of a stonewalled room. The platinum-haired man rolled over onto his back and looked above to see the dark blue material of his bed canopy.

"Awake, I see."

Draish flinched to hear a man next to him; the figure sat in the chair next to the bed. The scent…the man's familiar features (middle-aged, dark hair), then Draish noticed the Mystic Sword leaning against the bureau.

"Cyan?"

"You were sleeping longer than last time…"

"If you call sleep a constant dreaming in an endless perpetual motion, shifting back and forth…these alternate realities are my only memory of her…"

Draish sat up. His shirt was off, but his torso was covered in bandages that were stained from the seeping of blood. He moved over to sit on the edge of the bed and gazed down at his ripped leather pants and pale feet.

Cyan put down the book he was

holding, after using a ribbon to mark his page.

"I guess you would like to know what happened…" The Swordsman sighed with reluctance.

"What did you mean, by sleeping longer than last time?"

"She tried to kill you again; can you remember anything in your old age?"

"Ha, 300 years is merely a dent in time, old age…so, tell me what *she* did?"

Cyan looked at him for a moment, and then said, "Wooden stake, hit right below your heart, and a holy water shower…"

"What?!" Draish exclaimed. "Where would she find *velnis aquienus* around here?" The vampire always had trouble saying the human words: holy water.

"This princess Malphina has her ways about her." Cyan avoided eye contact, in doing so he told Draish what he really thought.

Draish scratched his matted hair. "Yeah…some way about her." He rubbed his eyes. His face was thin from lack of blood (his own blood and that of what he craved).

"She must know now that every time she weakens me, I must kill more to compliment my hunger." Draish sighed. "And in spite of her, I will make sure it's on those humans that she adores so much."

"Do as you wish, "Cyan said. "But I can

only protect you so much. Be wary because there might not be a next time."

"I know…she resurrected me, but that doesn't mean she has the right to kill me."

"She is bloody mad, Sir Draish, I hope one day you will see that."

"What? And I am not crazy myself?" He almost sounded disappointed.

"Do I have to answer this…?" Cyan sighed again. "Now that you are awake you no longer require my protection." He got up, taking his book, and then his sword. "Think of how much farther along we would be without her interference."

"Don't you speak ill of the Princess… my…my belov'ed!"

"Open your eyes, Draish, this is a different woman from Zaira…as I am a different Mystic Swordsman. We mortals don't live forever…" Cyan tried to make a point before he left Draish to his thoughts.

Draish sat there for a moment before seeking his shoes on the floor. An oil lamp lit the right corner of the room, burning brightly into his eyes and causing him to squint. He then scooted toward the edge of the mattress. His chest was bandaged around and restricted his movement. He then tried to stand, but hesitated. When he stood up the pain shot through him. Thus were the ever-so-familiar, but devastating, pains of being impaled. Why did he not know what she had been plotting, plotting against him. Why should he protect her anymore? It was obvious that Malphina cared not for him, or for what the vampire had to offer her in eternity…

He took a deep calming breath before pulling on his boots. He took a short look at that stiff leather chest plate before averting his attention to the wardrobe, beside the far side of the bed. Draish found a white button shirt and a blue doublet that fitted him well. He would have looked nice if he would have put on pants that weren't torn, but he decided not. He also decided to leave his cape where it hung, strung over the chair in the corner.

Draish stood in front of the mirror to look at himself. By doing this, it would prove that he was not the wicked one…would other vampires yearn to see their reflection? This was his way of reassurance of who the damned are. He stared into his own pale gray eyes before reciting, "Va ilullumite' la de Ocitar…"

The glass of the mirror became opaque and rippled like a droplet colliding with undisturbed water. Then the mirror revealed her. Malphina was sitting alone in a decorated castle bedroom. Her dress hung off the bed as she laid back on it….The image faded, not lasting too long. This wasn't meant to eavesdrop, but was rather for reassurance for him. He found spying unnecessary, but confrontation was essential. Draish made a mental note of her whereabouts and which room she was in.

The white-haired man left the room, knowing that he could not go unnoticed as he'd like to be occasionally. The wooden door slammed behind him. He made it halfway down the corridor before being intercepted by a man, whose chain mail under his tunic proved him to be a guard or bowmen.

"Lord Jauri, glad to see you well again." He didn't wait for Draish to make a comment, before continuing, "The lady is secured in her room." He paused.

"I know where she is, who do you think I am?"

The man lowered his head, and muttered, "Very well, Sir." Then the man went past Draish down the hallway, in the opposite direction.

Draish continued down the hall to where four guards stood in front of her room.

"What is with the high security?" Draish smiled at them.

"She is a threat to you, Sir," one man said. "Aren't you still wounded?" the other man's sincerity sounded bitter.

"Don't you patronize me. I think that I

can handle her," Draish sneered at him.

The four of them still stood blocking the door. Draish became curious as to them implying that they were guarding her from him, not what they had speculated to him.

"Shouldn't you check on the whereabouts of the dragon's advancing forces? You have been out for days, Sir."

"Stop stalling and move!" the vampire ordered and the four armoured men stepped aside. He turned back to them before entering the room to admonish them. "Perhaps you have forgotten how short your feeble lives are...shouldn't be taken for granted..." His words were not a warning but a threat.

He entered the room to see her quickly sit up and look at him with hatred.

"You recovered much faster from that than I would have thought," she told him, sounding anything but concerned.

He closed the door, after hearing the people comment outside.

"You are so trusting, so soon." She looked at him. "I'll do it again!"

"You can't kill me..." he told her. "You speak like you do not know what I am."

She stood up and crossed her arms to face him. "You're an abomination," She huffed.

"And, you are not wearing the dress

that I favor," he quickly replied.

"Thanks…and you wonder why I want you dead."

"Why do you hate me so?"

"Give me a reason not to."

"Destiny?" His expression changed.

"Ha!" she smirked. "If you cared anything about me, you would leave me alone."

"If you knew about the past, you would care about us," he said and looked down.

She showed no emotion and stood with her nose in the air. "I should have never trusted you…"

"This is for the greater good…you don't have to enjoy it, but we need to work together," Draish pleaded to her.

"What does a vampire have to do with 'good'? You are unholy," she began to become angry.

"And just what makes you holier than thou, Princess?"

"I've had family killed recently! By vampires and ghouls and minions — whatever! How can I trust you?" She clenched her fist, and then looked for something to throw. The hand mirror on the bed was the perfect thing. She gasped it by the handle as he stepped toward her, but just to let her smash it down on his head. The glass broke and shards fell to the ground. Draish shook his hair and glass shards and blood trickled down.

Somehow, she knew that he wouldn't react in anger anymore, like breaking the spirit of stallion, he didn't fight back. She couldn't face him and looked to the glass on the floor. She saw the sad expression of his reflection and the sense of intrigue came over her again.

"Fighting aimlessly is for mortals, fighting with cause is of the ancients," he said, for himself more than for her. "What is your cause?"

"What does that mean? So, does this mean you realized which side I am on?" she said to him.

"What do you mean by that?" He looked up at her.

"The Dragon is of chaos, but the Swordsman is helping you...what of me?" she said. "Just which side I have taken? Who states what's right or wrong?" She peered at him.

Apparently, this wasn't the confused Princess he had encountered just a few months prior, but a more devious, no, diabolical Queen... It would be impossible to think that she would have gotten this far on her own.

"Whose side am I on?"

Draish paused. "Well, that is for you to decide."

"Since when do I have a choice?"

"You are making your choice by still refusing to cooperate with me."

"You have crossed the line too many times, Draish! You lost my respect, and you damn well know why."

"Always such a sweet talker, Princess. On the fact that I have saved your life…one, two times now, I'd say we should make a truce."

"You shouldn't be alive," she told him.

"Nor should you. What you have been through is not something to take light of…"

"I will have my kingdom back," she said strongly.

"It always has been yours, my dear."

"Then why do I feel like a prisoner? This has to stop."

"But weren't you a prisoner before? You see…you could not leave the castle grounds unless you were scheduled to…hmm…what was that, no visitors after dark." Draish smiled. "That sounds a little like confinement to me."

"Shut your mouth! You could never keep silent for one minute could you."

"It's just something about you that brings out the bastard in me, if you want to know." His smile looked more like a sneer on his pale lips, as they stared at each other.

Could that be it? The necromancer and

the vampire are on different levels. Having a history as lovers, their future exhibited annoyance that could be the demise of them both. Needless to say, it was the decimation of those that the guardians wished to protect. Malphina and Draish would have to come to terms, or he would die trying. Or they would be killed while arguing with each other....

{XXIII}: What's In A Friend?

He jerked up from lying down, and his eyes focused on the large parlor room. Draish sat up, and realized he was seated on the sofa just a few yards from where he had encountered Dracula earlier.

Slayn stopped pacing around and his concerns went back to his vampire friend. His sword clanking every step, Torru went over to see Draish as well.

"You were out for quite some time," Torru sounded concerned, maybe just because anything that could overpower Draish scared him.

"Don't say that…" Draish said as he cupped is face with his hands.

The bearded man looked confused. "It's weird how they have just left us alone like this in their castle. What are they planning?" He felt safe enough to take a seat now that Draish was awake.

"He wanted me to recover…" Draish then stood up. "There is something he wanted me to do. Not sure if it's a test or what, but *he* is tormenting me for a cause greater than any of us."

"But we are the cause." Slayn sighed. "If not for us, he wouldn't be here and now."

They watched Draish cringe in pain as he put his arm across his chest. His armour was cracked from the impact of the giant wolf. He was breathing deeply.

"You should sit back down," Slayn said.

"No…" muttered Draish. He reached to his side to unlatch the chest plate one fastener at a time. He slumped his body forward and the armour piece dropped to the floor. His shirt was blood-stained but still intact. After standing up straight, he rolled up his sleeves and brushed back his hair.

"Let's go," Draish told them.

"What? I don't think you're in any condition to take on Dracula again," Slayn said out of concern.

"Just a broken rib, I am more prepared than you think," Draish replied, as he approached Slayn. "Do you think this is a game?" Draish peered at Slayn, who didn't respond.

"I do not have a choice…" Draish's voice became solemn. "I need blood…"

"What?" Slayn backed away.

"You wouldn't!?" Torru broke in.

Draish looked at Torru. "No, not to you

again, but the dragon…"

"I…I don't think that's a good idea, Draish." Slayn took another step back.

"It's a wonderful idea, I need my strength, do I not…"

The vampire stepped toward Slayn, who ran out of backing up space. He heard Torru's sword being drawn from behind him.

"Get away from him!" Torru grunted.

Draish looked over his shoulder at the now fully armoured man, and then swung his arm back at Torru who was jolted back and slammed into the adjacent wall.

Draish looked back at Slayn, who now looked shocked. The hunger had taken over Draish, or maybe it was some influence of the dark energy that had been inside him, but the once calm vampire was becoming crazed for blood.

"Fight it, Draish!" Slayn pleaded. "Don't give in!" Slayn started changing form.

The vampire's breathing was heavier now. "I can't help it… it's just that you look like food right now."

Smoke started escaping the dragon's mouth. "Back off! I'm warning you!"

Draish was in frenzy, but he was still aware of what he was doing. Much like a wild dog, a friend can turn into a feast within seconds.

"I am sorry, but I need your blood." Draish then jumped at Slayn, who reacted with a burst of flames.

His hair was singed, but Draish ran through the fire wall anyway to jump onto the dragon's back. Slayn roared; flapping his wings and thrashing his tail. Draish grew claws to grip through his scales and fur. He made his fangs extend from out of his mouth in order to stab into the tough flesh. Slayn roared again, this time in pain not panic. A moment later, Draish climbed off the dragon, who then huddled down to turn back into a man.

Slayn then laid on his chest as the wound seeped blood into his cloak. Draish had taken a few steps away before collapsing onto the floor himself.

Torru ran to Slayn. "Are you alive, Slayn?!" There was no response. "Slayn!" Torru shook his friend.

"Stop it! That hurts," Slayn responded finally.

"Oh, thank god, you're ok!'

Slayn opened his eyes. "You don't think that I would be killed by this if you weren't? Now do you?"

"What was that about?" Torru wondered, then helping Slayn to his feet.

"I guess he was hungry?

They looked down at Draish. "What's his problem, now?" Torru asked.

"Looks like he's sleeping..." Slayn looked at Draish, who was passed out with his face smashed on the floor.

"I think we should leave him and go find Myiako ourselves," Torru suggested.

"We should stay together," Slayn replied. "We need his help."

"Even after that?"

"Forgive and forget..."

"But, Slayn, buddy...that just happened."

"Just a scratch..."

"Right..." Torru was uncertain. "Let's get going, into the castle corridors."

Slayn stood over the unconscious vampire.

"WAKE..." He drew his foot back. "UP!" His boot collided with Draish's stomach.

"What gives!" Draish woke up with his normal eye colour. "You could have just tapped me awake..." He got up to rub where he'd been kicked. He looked healthier; his skin back to white instead of gray and his hair looked longer. But Slayn cared not for his benefits.

"We have something to do here! No more of that shit, Draish, or I swear I'll put you back in your grave." Slayn looked him dead in the eye, before turning away.

"I am so scared." Draish sighed. "Maybe I should explain something to you," he said as he followed Slayn and Torru down the first hallway. "I am a vampire, and in that when I am wounded, then I require substance. Understand?"

"I'm listening…" Slayn huffed.

"I will then lose all and will train my senses on the first living thing that I see."

"What do you mean?" Torru wondered.

"It means that even people that I wish not to harm become just something to consume."

"But we are supposed to be your friends, have you no shame?" Slayn stated.

"Have you remorse for your food; the plants and animals that you consume?"

Slayn hesitated, then said, "No, I guess not."

"And why is that?" Draish asked.

"Because…we eat to survive." Slayn seemed understand now.

Draish seemed to know how to explain things to mortals for a better understanding of what he was, or was this just one of his talents of persuasion.

Meanwhile...

The tall stone walls formed a strange circular room, she guessed about 40 yards in diameter. Myiako was led to this tower room and made to sit on the stone table in the center of the room. She sat quietly, but nervously, as she clenched the blue material of her long skirt. The torch flames made it hot...and the room was lined with them. She almost wished it was dark, because the shadows messed with her eyes. The room was lightly furnished and unlike the elegant rest of the castle. Myiako shifted her weight on her seat before she realized that she wasn't alone anymore.

The Count quietly approached her. "My dear, they did come for vous, as I knew they vould...besides vhat are friends for?" He smiled. "But they vill soon find out they are valking into oblivion." He almost sounded excited.

She noticed Scarlet then, looming in the doorway. Why did she look different, besides that new purple puffy dress? Her attention diverted back to Dracula, who was now right next to her. She couldn't resist the empowerment of his dark eyes. This was not how she saw Malphina resist Draish... Dracula's gaze was much different. She was at his will.

"You were always so beautiful..." he told her. "Tis a shame your blood must spill." He was so calm.

"I've done nothing to you," Myiako said, with no expression change. He could not control her mind.

"You haven't, have you? You vill soon see that I have been vaiting idly for personification. My plan is perfect..." He smiled, and then let go his hold on her.

"Why bother?" Scarlet walked forward. "Don't waste your breath on these mortals."

Dracula looked annoyed at Scarlet. "Shouldn't you be somewhere?" he said, as though asking her to go.

The Countess stepped into the torchlight. "If I didn't know any better, I'd think that you were trying to get me killed," she told him.

Myiako now could see the blistered skin on the left side of her body. Her eyes began to grow deeper burgundy with her anger.

"I thought that you vanted to kill him, again," Dracula said to her, now turning away from Myiako to face Scarlet.

"Yes...but ...umm," Scarlet started, but then she looked at the girl. She wished to keep her dignity, so she stopped speaking. She peered down Myiako one last time before lifting her skirt off the floor to trot back out the door.

The vampires exchanged glances again, as to talk mentally. Myiako had been around them long enough now to noticed them doing this. Scarlet was getting fed up with Dracula's superiority…his dominance. You didn't have to read minds to see that one.

Dracula turned back to Myiako, who then became uncomfortable again.

"As you see, vomen keep their disobedience even in death." He smiled as if to joke.

She gave a nervous smile. *Where are you?* she thought.

The Count Dracula went on as if he thought his platitudes and lessons were entertaining her. Myiako didn't know what to think…*was he bluffing about killing her?* She could spend lifetimes trying to figure out the reasoning of the undead and not get very far.

Draish, where are you?

It struck him as they passed the decorative corridor; this is where she passed just hours before.

"You sure this is the right way?" Torru would always question him.

"I know it's her…I can smell her scent down this hall," said Draish as he quickened his pace. "She summons me."

Torru held his sword in readiness while he and Slayn followed.

The corridor was dark, too dark. After a few moments, Torru interjected, "Ummm… we can't see a damn thing."

"Oh…" Draish stopped walking. "I forget that you two are mortal sometimes… Your blood speaks different from human." Draish turned to face them as he spoke.

"Could you just light a torch or something?" replied Slayn.

"Yes, I suppose that I could do that something."

Draish put his arms out in front of him. The two others stepped back slowly. He faced his palms upward and spoke, "Lumanite' ar'a'tos shi' vous route." His hands started to glow with a blue light. He was concentrating the blue energy into a ball. They watched as the vampire took the light and moved his arms outward to his sides. The light was soothing, not blinding and it lit the path ahead.

"What was that?" wondered Torru.

Slayn looked around, his eyes focusing. "Where would a vampire learn to make light? I mean why would it be of purpose to you?"

Draish smiled. "It is not where I learned it, but when. And it is true that I only require a miniscule amount of light for my eyes to adjust…I still need light to see. Without light the world is blind."

He then turned to the right path and continued. The blue light orb guided them past a few more doors. There was a large double doorway on the end that was now visible.

Draish suddenly stopped and the two others almost ran into him.

"What?" whispered Torru.

"She's here…"

Torru and Slayn flinched to see Scarlet now standing a few yards in front to them.

"Well, well… you guys just won't give it up." She sighed. "You're a pathetic bunch."

"Stand aside, wench, for you pose no threat," Draish told her. "Your wounds haven't even healed."

"Are you sure? What if I'm just bluffing?"

"Don't be imprudent, I can smell your fear."

"Always talk down to your elders now? It wasn't always that way, Draish. I've seen you obedient in the past."

"Shut your mouth, woman! You can't be simple enough to think you can take on all three of us."

"No, that's why I plan to take you down one at a time." She put her hands on her hips.

Draish stepped forward and she

stepped back. Scarlet then vanished into the shadows despite the light.

"She's gone?" Slayn looked around.

Draish looked aggravated and clenched his right fist. "Cowardice becomes you, Countess! And here I thought we were going to have some fun!" he yelled to her, his voice echoing.

Slayn backed away from Draish and Torru drew his sword. Scarlet then reappeared right in front of Draish, and he gasped in surprise. She laughed. Draish raised an eyebrow at the sight of her twisted smile on her scarred face. She looked older than usual, her eyes were sunken in.

"You could have joined me," she spoke softly to him. "I'm sure you remember us...so long ago now."

"Not long enough to forget, unfortunately..." He looked uncomfortable.

As they stared into each other's eyes, they connected the past and images of a history as dilapidated as the castle they stood in. Scarlet would put the memory of lust into his head and he would fight with intentions of harm to her. They were mind speaking.

"You betrayed me!" she told him, breaking the silence.

"You had forsaken me a lifetime before that...you only get what you deserve," he responded through clenched teeth.

She crossed her arms and looked him over.

"Get out of my head, witch!" He knew he had to stop putting his guard down, but women always seemed to be his weakness.

"Give into me, Draish… isn't it easier just to do wrong," she smirked.

"Maybe for those without a conscience. I have always felt more than I should."

"What a pity!" she responded. "You with all these emotions and your human girlfriend captured. I can't imagine how you are feeling, I mean I really can't." She began to laugh. "Mortals will cause the death of you, Draish Jau-Ri."

"Enough! I'm done with you!" Draish lunged toward her to grab her, but she had already vanished again.

Draish's light spell dimmed as a black shroud filled the room, and then her hypnotic chanting filled the air. " Pryvante' la guruns-un-dante; adeen un chron'os-nalayl la kishul un begi a biu'nd va ohm…dur-mistui ruli 'till la vietor a tea' Pryvante' la guruns-un-dante; adeen un chron'os-nalayl la kishul un begi a biu'nd va ohm…dur-mistui ruli 'till la vietor a tea'!"

Her dark energy surrounded Slayn, not Draish.

"What's happening?!" Slayn called out. He began changing into his dragon form to fight off the energy. "Do something!" Slayn growled at Draish.

"There is nothing I can do…just let the darkness take you."

Slayn was confused and enraged as he tried to struggle free of the dark grasp.

Torru swung his sword at it, but was thrown back.

The dragon's limbs flailed and his tail thrashed about, and then, in one moment, he was gone. His roar echoed as if he was still there.

"NO! Slayn!" Torru called out. He looked to Draish. "What the hell?! Why didn't you do something?"

"I didn't think that she could do that…" Draish told him. "There was nothing I could do! It was a spell intended just for him…just for the dragon."

"Where did she take him?"

"I can't tell you where, only why she took him: to single out and fight."

"Let's go find Slayn and kill that bitch." Torru looked more desperate than brave.

"The magic she just used is unknown to me. I cannot tell if they are even in the castle anymore," he paused. "I cannot feel Slayn's essence nearby."

Torru then sheathed his sword and looked down the empty corridor, staring in the direction Slayn had vanished.

"We must continue to find Myiako then…" he said solemnly.

"My thoughts exactly."

They turned and headed toward the end of the hall, where the large double-doors stood out. The blue light that Draish summoned, awaited them there.

{XXIV}: Conduit de' Inferno

The golden scales of his wings engulfed him for protection. Slayn wasn't ready to look until the strange noise was gone. He propped back his wings to see Scarlet standing before him.

"What did you-!?" he growled, and then his large eyes glinted from side to side. "Where are they?"

The castle hallway was dark and empty.

A smile came across her red lips. "They are where I left them, and the question you should be asking is: 'Where are we?'."

Slayn slashed his tail around in aggravation. "Single me out, did you..." he began in angry anticipation. "It seems that you have paused time around us, ironic that I am this supposed Time Lord."

"You know nothing of your magic, little lizard," she mocked him.

"You could be right, but I think I know why you singled me out."

"I doubt that." She began to grow restless herself.

"You couldn't face him, you are scared of Draish," Slayn said, with a confident smirk. His teeth glared from the reflecting light source behind him.

"You are a fool!" she told him. "You should come and join us while you still have your life, mortal…"

"I am not about the destruction of all humans…"

"Nor am I, we need humans around. I just wish to have my way. Is that really too much to ask," She crossed her arms.

"We are not all your dogs! You can't train us," Slayn said, making the first move to advance, lunging at her and swatting with his claws. *A miss. Where did she go?*

Attacking from behind him, Scarlet shot something like an energy bolt at his back. It struck him and the dragon was pushed forward. It wasn't strong enough to inflict much damage, so he turned to face her again. She was too arrogant to realize that she was using too much energy for maintaining them in limbo. She couldn't use her full powers to fight him. Would Scarlet have a chance fighting the dragon without her strength?

His nostrils started smoking and flames began firing within his jaws. He let out a bellowing inferno of flames from his mouth. After the smoke cleared, to his dismay the attack did not touch her. Scarlet was again behind him.

Slayn as annoyed by her constant vanishing.

She expelled another energy bolt from her palm. He jumped to the side to dodge it and said, "You have to be faster than that."

She laughed. "Cocky, aren't we. Maybe some attitude from your vampire friend has worn off on you. I'll consider it a flaw."

Her hands started glowing the colour of her energy attacks, causing a better view of the burns on her face. She forced straight lightning from her hands, as if channeling the thunderous sky. There was no way around this for the dragon. He was shocked and singed in several places all over his scaly body. He fell down into a crouch.

"Creation is only caused by destruction…can you feel it?" She had let off the lightning and closed in on him.

"You bitch!" He thrashed his tail in front of him then at her.

"Is that the best insult you can muster? Your anger pleases me."

Another tail whip, but it fell short when she caught it in both hands. Somehow, she maintained her ground and pulled on his tail. She flung him to the right wall, smacking into the stone, then to the left, then to the ground when she let go. He gasped and spit out some blood before standing and walking backward. He realized that he couldn't escape when his back hit an invisible wall that cut the hallway short. He started to inhale and breathed out another firestorm. The hall was heated like a stove, but the vampire had been able to protect herself by a magic shield.

"I have already figured my way around that attack. You're going to have to be trickier than that to hit a master vampire," Scarlet told him as she stood her ground.

"Some master you are, nothing but an apprentice to Dracula," he told her.

"Is that what you think?" She smiled. "You claim to have a god's power, yet you know nothing of the truth."

He heeded no hesitation and lunged at her, grabbing her right arm in his jaws. He figured that he was able to wound her earlier because it caught her off guard, and it worked again. She had been using her right arm the most therefore it had to be her strongest.

She yowled in pain, wishing that she hadn't hesitated to move. Her blood dripped out through his knife-like teeth as he continued to clench down.

"Nege'a dera al vas!" Scarlet told Slayn in Mortary, causing steam to rise off her arm and into his mouth.

The dragon freed her arm and flailed his head in pain. Her blood that dripped from his tongue looked as if it was burning him. He backed away and couched down with his hands over his snout.

"Fighting fire with fire is a cliché that I've always loathed, but in this case…" She smiled.

The dragon's golden luster began to reside and his aura started to fade.

She could sense that he has lost a lot of energy and commented, "How does the blood of ancient evil taste? It is a taste I have yet to know.

She stood over him, her right arm mangled, hung limp. She raised her left arm and morphed it into large finger blades. Slayn looked up at her and a glint shined in his eyes.

"You…thought…it…was…over…" he gasped.

Scarlet was forced backwards by the intense light that started to surround Slayn. He started growing from eight foot to eighteen. His angular head hit the ceiling and he bent his neck down.

Scarlet stepped back further with her mouth open in awe, her metal hand was now used to guard her eyes from the light.

"Useless is your power," Slayn said. "Mine is divine. You are now fated to witness the true essence of time!" His voice echoed around the astonished woman.

She sneered and then flew at the dragons' head with her clawed arm.

He stopped her in mid air by opening his mouth and drawing energy from the air around. A blue liquid ball formed in front of his head.

"Guruns un venili aquenu's!" The dragon spoke the undead language to launch the water-based attack.

The big ball had knocked her to the floor in a tidal wave, the wake crashing against the invisible corridor barrier in front of him.

Scarlet's screams filled the room as the water melted pieces of her dress and burned into her skin, except for the arm which had been shielded in metal.

"You…you summoned holy water!" She was confused and in pain.

He just responded with a laugh as he watched the water subside.

The Countess fell to her chest, gasping for breath.

"You're suffering shouldn't be so entertaining, but it is."

She then got oddly quiet. Slayn paused.

She dug into the wooden floor panels with her nails, now using her wounded arm as well. A chuckle quickly turned into an insane laughter. She looked up at him with wet stringy hair stuck to her pale face.

"Shit…" muttered Slayn.

Scarlet's aura emitted a dark purple light, cracking with lightening. Shockwaves of bolts radiated off her, conducting on the water pools on the ground around Slayn's feet. He was electrocuted and began shrinking to normal size. He then fell with his head hitting the floor.

She let off the attack and stood over him yet again. His scales began to fade and he began changing. She watched him turn into the skinny blonde man that he was. His clothes torn and his body bruised. She was no sight herself with melted clothes, scarred face and ripped up arm. She was dry though, her hair in fact frizzed out from the static charge.

"Flesh is a lot easier to bite than scales," she smiled as she knelt down to Slayn, who was barely conscious.

Draish's wolf-like growl suddenly filled the room, echoing up the stairs. He stopped walking and clenched both his fist and teeth.

"What is it?" Torru looked at him.

Draish sat down on a step and started breathing heavily. He hadn't done a lot of fighting today but his shirt was ripped and armour cracked. He looked different from his healthy handsome self, appearing weak and tired all of a sudden.

Torru took off his helmet and leaned down to Draish. The white-haired vampire turned to the Mystic Swordsman and just shook his head.

"What?" Torru wondered again.

"She…she overcame the dragon…" Torru's expression filled with concern. "You mean Slayn?"

"I…I don't feel his life force anymore… they were here the whole time." Draish told him.

Torru gasped in disbelief. "He's dead?"

Draish nodded.

No, I don't believe you!" exclaimed Torru.

{XXV}: Past Discrepancies

Malphina sat at a large table with a plate of food in front of her. She looked around with common confusion. *I guess I'm Malphina again,* she thought, looking down at the uncomfortable dress.

"Surely you must be hungry, my lady." Draish's voice came up from behind her.

She was sitting still, observing the weird purple dress, then turned her head to the floor beside her where his big boots appeared. She then slowly moved her eyes up his leather pants, armoured legs, waist tunic, that chest armour with the wolf crest, then finally meeting with his pale gray eyes. He had a questioning expression on his face.

"Oh, I am hungry…but…" she stopped.

"What's wrong now?" he said, shifting his weight on the other leg.

"It's umm; that you always watch me eat…it's weird…okay?" Malphina told him as the volume returned to her voice.

"Fine, I'll leave. You can eat alone."

"No, wait," she said, and then took a gulp of water from the silver inlayed cup before standing up to face him. "I was just wondering…what type of person Zaira was."

His expression softened. "Za…Zaira?"

"Did she know of her powers in her human life? Or why wasn't she immune to death—because she was the necromancer, correct?"

"Ummmm," he said thoughtfully, "I can't answer something I don't know myself."

"If this vampire, Vladimir Dracula, was so brazen as to kill her, where is he now? If he is so powerful, why are you here?"

"I don't know…and what's with all these questions?" he asked. "I do not understand you…one day you won't talk with me and the next you have everything to say."

"I am just remembering more is all. Besides," she paused and stepped closer to him, "you do want me talking with you more, don't you, Lord Draish?" Her voice softened as she put her hands on his armoured chest.

He looked surprised and spoke in a hushed voice, "Maybe I just gained pleasure in the way you resisted me." He smirked, and then asked, "What's this diversion you're giving me?" He couldn't help but to glance at the exposed part of her chest and neck.

She gingerly shoved him back. "You men are really all the same, alive or un-alive…" She smiled.

"What can I say…I'm used to a challenge," he told her as he stepped back close. He reached his arm around her back and pushed her in to him. He leaned down to meet his lips with hers. He kissed her lightly, and then deeper upon finding that she didn't reject him.

After a few intimate moments, she got uncomfortable from being crushed by the armour and getting pricked by his spiked paldrons. She pulled away. He took hold of her cut hand. She pulled her hand back and clasped it with her other.

"Your lips are so warm, yet your hands are so cold…" she told him.

"Is that so bad?" he looked into her eyes.

She began to wonder if this was her will or if it a spell or something that he had influenced on her.

"How can I trust you?" she asked as a daily routine of a question.

"How can you not?"

"You just can't expect things to go your way."

"And why not, you seem to think that you can get your way, Princess."

"Maybe it is my destiny to be with you, but that doesn't mean you don't have to earn my companionship."

"Is this really necessary to discuss every day?" He sighed. "Moreover, what was up with that kiss?"

"It is crucial to find where I'm at every day that I am here," she said, taking his icy hand.

"What is that supposed to mean?" he wondered. "And what do you mean by remembering more?"

"Just be quiet and come with me," she said and led him out of the room.

"Do you even know where you're going?"

"Did I not just tell you to be quiet?"

He shook his head as she stopped to look around as they met a fork in the hallways.

The dwellers of the castle always looked content with their daily lives, even though the humans lived amongst monsters that used to be humans and were now a vampire's minions.

"I've been here a few months now, right? I'm sure I can find my way."

He noticed that she sounded unsure today, questioning herself. She released his hand and he looked at her, not quite sure what to say.

"Umm, this way," she then said, as she took the path of one of the halls.

Draish didn't proceed immediately, instead just watched her quicken her pace and draw further away.

She knew he was still following her. She also realized he had now lost confidence in her as he wondered of her plans with him.

She passed some of the royal armoured guards, who were standing around talking to one another. They had stopped to watch her walk by. She had just ignored their wide-eyed gazes, but Draish did not. The men failed to notice Draish was now standing right behind the six of them.

"I suggest you remind yourselves who the lord of the castle is, gentlemen," Draish said calmly, but still startled them. As he past the group, his eyes kept with them but his head did not turn from her direction, looking ahead.

The guards just exchanged dumbfounded expressions. "Sorry, Sir."

"I will not tolerate such insolence, again," he growled this time.

Malphina had stopped to look back. "Draish will you leave them alone and come on!"

Draish sighed and continued walking, still peering at the men before he turned back to her.

A few minutes later down yet another hall, she stopped in front of a set of doors.

"Surely, you don't wish to go in there

with me?" He looked at her.

She pushed open the doors to a large room, a bedroom. She walked inside the dark room and took a flint stone from a tabletop to light a lamp. The light projected shadows of the nightstand and canopy bed. It was his room.

"And I thought I'd be the one to bring you to my chambers…and forcefully," he said to her.

She smiled. "Just dig yourself a deeper grave." She then went back to shut the doors. "Why is it that you don't sleep in a coffin?" she wondered.

"This whole keep is a tomb of sorts, is it not?"

"It's not that bad," she said, then came to stand close to him.

"I hope you don't have any tricks in store for me, Malphina. I don't think that I can forgive you again."

She reached her arms around him to unlatch his chest plate. As it was unbuckled, it fell to the floor.

"You can't do anything but forgive me," she whispered. Then she rubbed her hand on his shirt, up his chest and searched for the latch for his shoulder armour and cape. She avoided the spikes and tossed the armour to the ground. She then started to massage his muscular shoulders.

"Wait, hold on." He took hold of her hands.

Their eyes met. Hers were like green emeralds flickering in the dim light. His eyes were now a deep blue with his look of amazement of her. As if he was seeing a creature that had long passed, he didn't quite know what to make of her.

She embraced him first and his arms reached for her back. She pressed her ear to his chest to hear that his heart was beating fast. He couldn't resist but to smell her hair, then to her neck.

She put her fingertips into his back.

"You should stop…" he was urged to say, holding back. He showed his growing fangs by a lip raise and picked her up to be cradled in his arms. She was carried over to be sat down on the large bed. The sheets were satin and a darker purple than her dress. Malphina pulled the hair clip from her hair to let her amber locks fall down over her face and shoulders. She sat the clip on the nightstand, and then he took a seat next to her.

Draish became almost shocked when she pushed him down onto the bed and then crawled on top of him.

"So…are you going to tell me what you did with Malphina?" he smiled.

"What? You don't like this side of me?"

"I didn't say that…I'm just wondering what has gotten into you."

"Nothing yet," she said with heavy innuendo before leaning to kiss his lips. She went down to his neck, and then dug her nails into his chest. He grunted and leaned his head to a rest on a pillow. She began to rub his body while his breathing hastened as she got lower.

Her other hand reached into her boot at the concealed object.

She started to unbuckle his belt and go into his pants, but then stopped.

"…I had more faith in you, Draish," Malphina lifted her head.

"Hey! What's that supposed to mean?" He had thought the comment degrading to his manhood.

"I just didn't think that you would do it again," she replied as she slowly raised a dagger behind her back.

"You can't be serious, now…?" he wondered.

She then swiftly brought the knife down at him, aiming for his throat.

He had moved much too fast for her to get a direct stab, but it caught his shoulder. The slash cut through his shirt and burned his skin.

"You have got to be mocking me…" he

complained, now standing beside the bed and fastening his pants back.

"That's four times, Draish…my darling." She laughed. "Four times you let me take your guard."

"How in the hell do you manage to find silver in my castle!" he growled as he noticed that the wound was not healing.

"If you think that everyone here is faithful to a vampire, you are delusional," Malphina told him, now turning to him, gripping the dagger with point down. "For someone who claims to have lived for centuries, you sure are ignorant."

"Shut-up!" he growled. "I have never known someone to be so disobedient and treacherous as you." He began to raise his hand to hit her, but stopped.

"I'm wondering now who the dark one is…" he told her, and then vanished.

She stood up and looked around. "Hide, vampire…I'll find you." She pointed the knife in his unseen direction.

"I don't know what you want out of me, woman," his voice spoke from the shadows. "But if you think I've been rash with you, you will not even recognize me now."

"I will drive this dagger through your heart when you sleep before you get the chance to show me your true colours." She was sure of herself and she stepped toward his voice.

"I wouldn't say such things..." he said, then appeared behind her and grabbed her arm, "...if you can't keep a promise." He clenched her arm until she dropped the dagger. It clanked to the ground and he pushed her to the side, back onto the bed.

"I wasn't planning on hurting you, my dear. That is the truth. I only wanted to give you want you wanted," he looked down to her, now seeing the hint of fear in her eyes.

Suddenly, he was on top of her. He pinned down her arms with his. "Haven't I told you...how you bring out the worst in me?" His breath hit her face and she winced. He hovered over her face for a moment and began to smell her. His mouth went to her neck and she gasped when she felt his fangs penetrating. He was quick to pull away and a look of confusion. He let the blood drip from his mouth.

"What...is...this?" he gasped.

She began laughing. "You haven't done your research..." She smiled as he backed off her. "I do not fear you, Draish."

He spat out her blood. "I never wanted you to!" He stood back up, a few feet away from her.

She sat up and her neck began to heal.

He realized she was just putting up

a front before, she had powers that he was unaware of.

"Remember this for the future; you cannot take the blood of your resurrector, unless she lets you." She rubbed her neck.

He spat again, blood hitting the floor. "You're poison," he told her as he tightened his belt and straightened his shirt. *I've never been so sexually frustrated in all my life…*

She chuckled at his expression. He glanced to the door, someone was approaching.

"Lord Jauri!" a voice called though the door. "The enemy has decided to attack the fortress. What is your response?" the man asked.

"I'll be right out!" Draish responded. *And for god's sake, it's Jau-Ri.*

He looked back to Malphina. "We will finish this later…my lady," he told her in an arrogant manner and bowed. He then retrieved his armour and cape, still peering at her.

"Lucky for you that the enemy is careless enough to attack in our territory," he told her. "You think you're a prisoner here…" He clipped his chest plate back on and leveled his paldrons and cape.

"Don't abuse your powers. You think too much of yourself, Draish." She stood up and adjusted her dress. "I just wanted to tell you that."

"You really are unbelievable…" he said with no formality. "Nothing like the brilliance that was Zaira…" He quickly opened the door and left with a slam. In his haste, he caught a piece of his cape in it. The door reopened and he freed it with a look of embarrassment.

Malphina sat back down on the bed. "I think I got this one figured out."

{XXVI}: Close To Your Friends, Closer To Your Enemies

Myiako sat in the circular room, just staring blankly. Her eyes were glazed over as if in a trance. She noticed Dracula standing next to her and he leaned over to look at her in the eyes. She showed no expression.

"He failed you in the past…so vhat makes you think he von't do it again." The vampire's voice was low.

She batted her eyes until she focused on him. "Get away from me," she told him, then scooted back on the stone table that she was seated on. "What happened to your hospitality?"

"Have you not figured it out yet, my dear?" He stood up straight.

"What…that there is this 100-year loop-hole that gives you the right to take the blood of a vampire's necromancer? I think you're lying," she said confidently.

"Call my bluff then, but I will still destroy him if anything good comes from this."

"How does that not make me immortal

then, if you can't kill me?" She sat up straight.

"Why have you thought any differently...you can raise the dead...the necromancer can inhabit you as her vessel," he spoke out of his usual precise speaking patterns.

"But now you will find a way to kill me as you did to Zaira all those years ago." She was sad, but held her composure.

"How is your mind so jaded from the truth?" he asked. "What the truth is, is the flaw...and reality is only what you pretend it to be?"

"I'm not pretending. I'm living my life."

"In which you fail to realize something..."

"Maybe so, but I do understand what evil is, and that it starts with you." She crossed her arms.

"Such a mortal thought, good and evil. I never had claimed a side."

"Now you sound like Draish. How does that make you feel?"

"All vampires are kindred, et makes sense." He smiled and turned away from her.

The Count started walking in the direction of the door, his cape dragging behind him.

"To your knowledge, remember the

painting that you found en the crowded room in the mansion? It vasn't Zaira…but a woman who existed even before she did," he told her, before exiting the room.

A fourth woman who I look like…does this Lady Necron like to possess only people of my ancestors who resemble each other? she thought. *What kind of cruel joke is being played on me? I feel like my identity has been stolen.*

Meanwhile…

Draish and Torru were finally finished with the ascending staircase. They faced a curved hallway with stone walls.

Draish sniffed the air. "She's in there," he said, looking at the wooden doors ahead. He walked toward them.

"Didn't you say that at the last door?" Torru's eyes were red from holding back tears.

Just then, something came up behind Torru and knocked him in the head. He fell down a few steps of the staircase, armour clanking.

"But I am right here!" Scarlet had taken advantage of the knight not wearing his sallet and had knocked him unconscious. She advanced to Draish.

He shook his head. "Your face is burned, your clothes are torn… why would you wish to add more pain onto your suffering?" he asked as he effortlessly dodged her claw swipe.

She came at him again with pure rage, leaving herself open with each swing. He took one of the opportunities to grab her arm and pull her forward to make her lose footing and fall on her face.

"Pathetic," he said, as he watched her struggle to get back up.

"You were supposed to be weakened…" she complained.

"Was I…" he contemplated. "Why did you leave me to recover? Your battle tactics prove your inefficiency."

"You very well know that I cannot take all three of you on at once."

"Your efforts of separating us are fleeting."

"Ha…speak for yourself because the dragon can't anymore."

Torru started to come to and shook his head. "YOU…" he said, "Where's Slayn?" He stumbled to his feet, looking up at her.

"Stay back," Draish warned to Torru.

Scarlet started motioning her hands in a circle and energies gathered. The black light started radiating enough to now shadow the hall torches.

"Octisous la lumi de dante!" she called then, causing the black energy to explode with a gale force.

Draish put his arm over his face to shield it as the energy rushed him. He managed to maintain footing as he widened his stance, but was being pushed back, his boots scraping the floor. The wind tunnel of her power continued and started to cut his skin. The force shattered his forearm bracer and went through to slice his cheek.

Torru was stunned from the blast and was unable to do anything but watch helplessly.

Draish managed to push forward with his arms to hold out his hands. His palms faced toward her and he began pushing back.

"What!" she exclaimed, as she started losing her ground, thus being pushed back. He was using her attack against her. He had turned so that now her back faced the stairs and Torru could remain unscathed.

Scarlet gave all that she could, but he was reflecting her force.

"Grrrr…aaa…" he growled, as he tried to get her to lay off.

She couldn't keep it up and ceased the attack, falling to her knees, panting.

Draish smiled, his teeth white. "It appears that you kneel to me, Scarlet," he said and looked down to her as the blood on his face from the cut started to dissipate.

A black blur then swooped down from nowhere and tackled Draish to the ground.

"Vampires don't kneel to dogs!" Dracula now stood over Draish. He tried to bring his boot down on Draish's neck, but Draish was too quick and rolled out of the way. The younger vampire countered with a foot sweep, but Dracula jumped back.

Draish stood up and replied, "As I recall you were the one who was a dog in our last encounter."

Dracula stood in front of Scarlet as to block her, and she tried to stand.

Torru came at her with his blade, causing the dark one to sneer at him. This left a moment for Draish to charge at him. He drew the sword from under his cape where it had been concealed since the forest village.

Draish thrust the blade at Dracula. The attack was dodged and the sword was swung in the direction in which he moved. Dracula could move much faster than Draish and caught his arm in mid-swing. Dracula pulled on Draish's arm and a pop was heard. His shoulder had been dislocated and the thin sword dropped to the ground. Draish gasped, and then lifted his knee to kick Dracula away from him.

Draish turned to Torru who was keeping the female vampire at bay with the heavy sword. Without worry of fighting two, Draish could focus on one. Grabbing his limp arm with his left, he shoved his shoulder ligament back into position. His expression remained unchanged.

The King furled back his cape and gave a fang-full smile.

"Truly remarkable that you vould still have so much power after I took so much from you," came Dracula's crude compliment. "Now vill see how you stand up against your own energy."

The dark vampire was able to form spears of light and heaved them at Draish. He couldn't avoid the attacks and was impaled by one, two, three energy spears. Draish raised his chin and covered his face in his hands, but then Dracula noticed the muffled laugh. Blood started dripping from the javelin holes, but then started to return back into him. Draish then peered at him though his fingers as he still covered his face. That was just the boost Draish needed to call upon reinforcements. He dropped his arms and started howling as his wolf-self might.

Scarlet flew past Torru and tried to stop Draish's call, but she was pushed away by his now glowing aura. Draish grew quiet then and smiled at Dracula. "I decided to summon some more friends, sorry that you didn't invite them."

"Ha! Like I said: nothing but a dog. You cannot take me on alone. I see how wolves like you travel in packs."

"I had never said that I wanted this between us, Vlad. This was your doing; therefore, I must use all my necessary resources," Draish explained, then spreading his arms in welcome. "I never once thought I could even do this well fighting you."

A number of black circles shadowed on the space that surrounded Dracula. The shadows began to rise from the ground and take shape into three minions that looked more vamperic than monster. They took on the likeness of Draish with white hair and pale skin. There were two males and one female. One man had long hair to his waist and wore brown and black leather. He wielded a long sword. The other had short hair, messy on his pointed ears and wore ripped slacks and a white button shirt. His claws were dominant and he was barefoot, showing the long claws on his feet. The lady minion wore a black skirt and had a tight corset top that was covered in sheathed knives. Her hair was in many braids. They were individuals once, but now were to follow Draish's will, by way of blood.

Dracula looked them over. "I am impressed that you have minions at your disposal." It seemed he wanted to applaud Draish, rather than fight with them.

"I do get around," responded Draish.

The three went to attack in unison with their weapons. Dracula became transparent and vaporized into a smoke form.

Scarlet tried to run, but was intercepted by the Swordsman again.

"I will avenge Slayn." Torru told her, who was now standing back at the top of the stairs.

"Get out of my way!" Scarlet motioned her arm in a swipe and Torru was tossed up against the wall.

She again attempted to attack Draish, but was intercepted by the three minions. They stood in front of their master while it looked as if he was recovering.

Dra'cul's force could still be felt, but maybe he just liked to watch.

Draish had started to show exhaustion again and he sat on the floor in the middle of the three. He began to mediate or at least that is what it looked as if he was doing.

Knives went flying at Scarlet, just missing their target. Claws came at her from above and while she deflected that, she was stabbed in the torso with the sword. She screeched and backed away.

"Lord Dra'cul, do something," she

pleaded to him.

"Vhat could I do, Scarlet?" His voice boomed from no particular direction. "You have failed me like so many others. I can't keep protecting you from making foolish decisions."

"What?! What do you mean!" she growled.

"Sometimes you need to save yourself." His presence seemed to fade from the area. Dracula left her outnumbered. He grew weary of coming to her rescue, or maybe just wanted her dead.

She screamed and radiated that energy again. The three minions were tossed back behind Draish, who then stood back up.

"Ar'a'tos satori," said Draish, causing his look-a-likes to fade back to where they came from. He had just put his minions into play to try to impress Dracula. He couldn't risk them being harmed. Draish knew now that his powers reigned superior over hers. He was unscathed by her attack this time and walked toward her. Before she could react, he grabbed her by the neck.

"Kadama-dur-sancant," she muttered in Mortary.

"A disappearing act is useless now," he told her.

He clenched her neck tighter, now

lifting her off her feet. She gasped from the pressure.

"Just...tell me...then..." she struggled with her hands clawing at him. "How did you become so powerful?"

"How does a vampire gain their power?" he questioned her.

She either didn't respond or couldn't.

"We do so by using what we think we're better than. The weakest of creatures in numbers are the strongest. The weak make us stronger," he replied.

He lifted her up higher, and then used his other arm to grab her hand.

"By the blood we drink," he said softly then to bite into her wrist. He sank his teeth in deep, almost to take off a chunk of flesh. Her dark blood started dripping out. He closed his eyes as he lapped up her blood. He savored it. She grew weaker and limper in his grip. He loosened his hand from her neck, dropped her arm, and then dropped her to the ground, black blood dripping from his face.

"I remember what you did to me all those years ago... I would never take advantage of an enemy as such."

"Don't fool yourself of what I gave you. I could have killed you again, but I did not," she said weakly.

He went over to pick up his sword and stood over her. "You turned her against me. Malphina loathed me and for what reason, but you Scarlet…"

"Blame what or who you want, but it doesn't end here, Jau-Ri."

"It does for you…" He lifted the blade and brought it down into where her heart should be. The blade was twisted in her chest cavity.

"Fare thee well onto the afterlife," he whispered, as the life went from her eyes.

{XXVII}: One Immortal To Another

"What just happened?" Torru walked over to Draish, but then he stopped in his steps.

The expression on the vampire's face was less than inviting. His thick eyebrows were furrowed over his eyes, which were deep purple with anger. Torru had seen this rage in him before.

"Is she dead?" he asked then stepping over Scarlet's body.

"She was dead already," Draish was keeping a stern face.

"What should I do?" wondered Torru.

"Stay alive." Draish looked over the Swordsman's dented armour.

He then checked over himself and started taking off his broken arm bracer. His cape was torn, linen shirt was sweat-soaked to his pectoral muscles. He combed back his platinum hair with his hand, and then regained a confident posture.

Torru found it odd that he was sweating. "Ummm, one more question," said Torru, as he leaned on his sword. "Where did you get those other vampires of yours?"

A smile returned to Draish's lips. "Just a few friends that I gathered back in town."

"Yeah…that's what I thought." Torru was devastatingly reminded that Draish was indeed a killer of men and actually showed little compassion for human lives. Torru was glad that this vampire was on his side.

Draish turned his back toward the doors and said, "I think you should look for Slayn."

"But I thought you said he was dead."

"Perhaps he is, but don't you now know a couple of people who can raise the dead?" He peered over his shoulder at Torru as he took a step toward the door.

"Where are you going?"

"I'm sure that you know where. I must continue an audience with the King." He stopped to take a breath. "It ends here."

Draish heard the armour clank behind him, Torru still hanging around.

"I said go find your friend, and make sure *she* doesn't get up.

He then motioned the doors to open, but they just moved a little on their hinges. He then went up to the door and punched his hand through it right above the knob. He was able to reach his hand in to unlatch the door, and then opened it. He shook the splinters off his hand and the blood drew back into him almost as quickly as he was injured.

Myiako scooted back on the stone table, not knowing what had just entered the room in the darkness. He could see how she was shackled by wrist and ankle to long chains secured to the altar. She wore a dress that made her look more like Malphina, which made him cringe of the thought.

"Who's there?" she said in a small voice.

"Is that really you, Myiako?" he asked her.

She recognized his voice. "If that is really you…"

He walked closer to her. "I guess we meet again." He smiled.

"Is this another dream or illusion? Have you really come to get me out of this place?" She had learned so much about him from the life of Malphina, but he really new nothing of her.

"Well, I'm not here just to watch you sit there, so I guess I'm here to release you." He came over to the table and stood near her.

"How can I trust you any more than the other vampires?"

"I'm not sure what brought on this change of heart." He could see that she grew tired of this charade. "We barely got a chance to know each other. I can see if you don't trust me."

He took one of her hands and gasped the bracer. He pulled on the chain; it finally gave and the link bent.

"I cannot assure you that I am much different than Dracula. But I *can* tell you that I only wish you well. As I did for those before you. It is your choice rather to accept me or not." He reached for her other hand. "You are Myiako, right?"

"Yes, I'm Myiako."

Despite what she unveiled in his past, she could feel that he was being truthful. This Draish seemed calmer and more understanding than the ones in her dreams. Maybe he grew wiser with age, or maybe it was the fact that she was a different person, but she liked him. She could feel his devotion to her in her soul.

He broke the other chain adjoining her wrist. The cuffs were left around her hands. He looked them over as if to figure a way to get them off without causing her injury.

"He only put chains on you to anger me," he told her with a soft tone.

She took one of his hands and looked him in the eyes that were reflective in the darkness. "He watches, you know," she said.

"Yes, I know." He turned to face the over-looming shadow. "I don't understand why you have let me come this far."

The presence was that of Dracula, an unmistakable aura. He would make the air dense with an unearthly chill.

"So sorry to break up your little reunion." The King's voice echoed.

"No, you're not." Draish stood in front of Myi.

"Is it a reunion or confession?" Dracula now appeared a few yards away from Draish. His eyes glowed a hue of red in the darkness.

"Draish has nothing to confess. You're the one who is evil, you have something to hide!" Myiako stood up beside the table, next to Draish.

"Ha…don't you see, there is no evil. No black and white. Only the shades of gray," Dracula told her as he clasped something in his hand.

"Why the masquerade then, Dra'cul? Why always hiding in the shadows? Why kidnap Myiako and lure me here?" Draish took a step forward.

"Were you not an arms-man yourself, Jau-Ri? Could you not know that a fight iz best von on your home terrain?"

"This is a fight between us, you and I, alone. My hatred for you has been smoldering since I was human." Draish crossed his arms over his chest.

"Another flaw in you is that you vould fight me in anger."

"Well, why would we challenge each other for any other reason?"

"For her…" Dracula's eyes went to Myi.

Myiako sighed. "It is typical that you think that I am something to win."

"We are master vampires. I don't find it necessary that mortals are to be involved."

The one with white hair unclasped his arms to brush back his hair.

"You were the one to involve the mortals, boy," the dark-haired one put whatever he was holding into his belt satchel before continuing. "You teamed up vith your mortal guardians as you always have done. And you made humans into minions, as ve are supposed to do as masters. Really, to summarize: you've done vell."

"That's real supporting coming from you…" Draish's sarcasm taunted Dracula.

"Maybe if you asked her, you would know the truth." The Count was becoming tired of reasoning with Draish.

"Me?" asked Myiako.

Draish looked at Myi then back to Dracula. "She's only involved because she's my necromancer. Why else would she even be here?"

"I… I am the cause of all this," Myiako quickly said.

"No, my quarrel is with him," Draish told her.

"I think you should listen to what the lady has to say," The King of Undead replied, with a look of amusement.

"I'm not a mortal, Draish," she said, causing his pale-eyed glance to return to her. "I am not a vampire or minion either."

"It is true; she's a hard one to kill." Dracula now stood right next to Draish, but showed no aggression.

Draish stepped back and peered at him, being on edge.

"That is why I am still alive now," she replied, then sat down again, her feet still in shackles.

"So glad your memories are returning…" Dracula smiled.

"What are you saying? I am being tricked by the two of you." Draish stepped back from the stone altar.

"I realize now that I am the necromancer, and I always have been. I just forgot…"

"What you're saying is that you are not just my resurrector, but you are in fact Lady Necron…" He scratched his head. "Just how long have you been immortal?"

"I do not know. I barely just figured this out."

"Who are you?" Draish looked into her eyes.

"I am Myiako Oaiku, but…" She pulled up her dress sleeve. There was a scar, clean across her forearm. "I am also Malphina."

Draish examined the scar. "It cannot be true. You have a completely different energy than she did…"

"This is why we looked alike. I am her. I thought she was just my bloodline, but then I realized why I had all her memories." She paused a moment, and then continued, "I am Malphina."

{XXVIII}: Past Deceit Passes On

Dracula took a few steps to pace and looked down.

"Oh, my dear…you failed to mention something…" he spoke softly with his deep voice. "You are Zaira as well." He turned his head to look at their reactions.

She looked surprised and Draish looked doubtful.

"Nonsense!" Draish growled. "I saw you kill Zaira, I remember I was there."

"I have none of Zaira's memories," she lied. "I don't believe you either," she defended.

"Have I lied about anything thus far?" Dracula replied. "I am not the one pretending to be others…"

"You killed Zaira…" Draish repeated, and then walked up to Dracula to come eye to eye with him, Dra'cul only being slightly taller.

"Why vould you be mad at me? She is the one who has been lying to you for centuries."

"Your manipulation is erroneous. Her

body was burned in her funeral. This is not the same woman as Zaira," Draish sneered at him. "How could she even be Malphina? That woman hated me."

"Is that so? I don't think you vere around to even see that, before you vere killed yourself…"

"But I know." Draish looked ready to fight with the dark one. "Why didn't you just kill me then?"

"Ha… I bet you have been vondering that your whole life." Dracula smiled large enough to flash his fangs. "Where's the fun in that? If I had killed you vhen I had that chance to kill Zaira, we vould still be here now. It vouldn't have changed anything, and it vouldn't of made your death as agonizing. I needed you to experience that mortal pain." Dracula looked almost pleased. "By the way… how did it feel to be tortured as a man and now as a vampire?"

A rumbling growl came from Draish's throat. "Now you're just pissing me off…" His eyes started to darken as he tried to hold back his anguish.

"You only feel this hatred for me because you hate yourself," Dracula said, shaking his head.

"Don't believe him, Draish. He's trying to make you mad. He wants you to fight him."

Myiako broke in.

Draish turned to her. "I cannot believe you either. I still haven't accepted that you are Malphina." He sounded angry. "Do you remember what you put me through?" He wasn't waiting for her to answer and he diverted his attention back to the other.

"This conflict between us vas only created by her…by the Lady Necromancer," Dracula replied, his voice now sounding angered. "She made you this vampire of light simply to oppose me." He paused, lowering his voice again. "Our quarrels and opposition are due to our likeness. You know, you and I are just alike, Jau-Ri."

"You may be telling the truth, but you're leaving out precious details. So tell me…tell us… because the woman is oblivious to what she is as well," Draish demanded.

"I so vanted to watch her tell you.,," Dracula started, "But as you said…she is oblivious, delusional even."

They both turned to Myiako, who just looked scared. "I don't remember any of this!" she blurted. "You two seem to know me better than I do." Her voice was shaky, frightened of what she didn't want to know.

"What are you getting at?" Draish questioned the King.

Dracula sauntered over to Myiako and

took her hand. The look on Draish's face was perhaps of jealously, but he did not move nor say anything. She did not wince, but returned a look into Dracula's dark eyes.

"Don't you get it?" the dark one looked at Draish with her hand still in a soft grip. "This was the woman that made me a vampire, as well." His look was serious.

Myiako's jaw dropped while Draish's eyebrows rose in suspicion.

"You are Zaira," Dracula said, looking into her deep green eyes again. "I could never truly kill my necromancer. Only get a taste when the time was right."

"You're crazy…" Myi pulled her hand back.

"That may be true, but as I mentioned before, I do not lie," Dracula told her before going on to say, "I am only unholy because of my faith in a certain God, who betrayed me. He had forsaken me, and so I vowed by the order of the Dragon…A'vat de la Dra'cul; to get revenge."

He stepped away from the altar to face Draish. "You know how one might get another chance at life, after death."

"She didn't…" Draish refused to believe the truth after all these years.

"It's not true!" Myiako shouted, as tears filled her eyes.

"You get another chance for revenge…" Dracula continued. "Who else would have made me a master, but the necromancer herself?"

Myiako was crying, wondering how she could have been the one to unleash such a usurper unto the world.

"Why are you telling us this?" asked Draish, whose eyes returned to pale. "You could have just let her be with her blissful ignorance."

"That vould be very unlikely. Why vould I spare your feelings? Besides she vould figure it out as her dreams unraveled the truth of who she iz." Dracula spoke quickly, becoming irritated that he had to go into such detail for these two to follow.

Draish returned his eyes to her. "Is this true? Can you see the past in your dreams?"

"Only since your resurrection have I been having those dreams." She sniffled and went on. "I thought I was just viewing the past through Malphina's eyes. What was I suppose to think? I had no memories of Dracula… except…" she stopped.

"Go on," urged Draish, "What?"

"I don't remember," she said. "But I know Zaira…or umm… I would have never given a person like Dra'cul this power."

"Why is that?" Dracula had himself

wrapped up in his cape. "Is it because I enjoy spreading fear into the minds of impudent mortals? Does that make me evil?" He smiled.

"I can't say that makes you good," Draish replied, mockingly.

"If I am so, then so iz she…Zaira iz evil, and therefore Draish as vell."

"What is your proof that she's the same necromancer that created the light vampire, Draish, and also created the dark vampire, Dracula?" Myiako questioned.

"I wasn't always so bitter…" The dark vampire was suddenly seated on the table with his legs hanging off next to her. "I was under your power once…I was, my dear," he told her, then paused to comb his long fingers through her hair.

Draish became tense, but Myi really stayed calm.

Vlad went on, "And it was then I realized that I had to take my un-life into my own hands. No longer would the Lady have any power over me, if I took her blood. Evil no, independent yes. Something Draish Jau-Ri apparently could never accomplish, thus he has been bound to you."

Dracula reached into his belt satchel and pulled out a chain necklace. He dangled it in front of Myiako's eyes. It was a green stone pendant; almost identical to the one Draish wore.

"After I took blood from you I broke your spell over me." Dracula handed her the necklace. "Now I could never really die. I wanted to be as powerful as you. Ever-living and never-aging."

"Then why would you betray her, after she gave you another chance at life?" Draish said and shifted his weight.

"Because she vould continue to forget, playing the role of a mortal girl and not embrace the fact that she created a monster." His voice grew with intensity. "She made the decision that my uncontrollable bloodlust was wrong. She created the essence of evil by giving it a name." He loomed over her as if ready to strike.

"If I can't remember, then I deny it ever happening," she said, looking at the pendant in her hand.

Draish moved to her side and attempted to push Dracula away from her, but he had vanished. The dark aura had left the room, for the time being anyway.

The white-haired vampire hung his head down and looked to Myiako.

"I understand now…" he spoke quietly, "that is why I could not take your blood."

"You forgive me then?"

"Your deception is unforgivable, but

I don't understand…How could I have been so naive?" he questioned himself. "If the necromancer could reanimate the bodies of others, why not herself?"

"I…I just couldn't hold the memories of so many centuries, and so I forgot. I even forgot about you, and us," she told him, unsure of herself.

Draish held his head down, hair covering his face. "I really always knew you were Zaira, in the back of my mind, that's who Malphina and Myiako were to me. Why else would I have cared so much for them?"

"I'm sorry, Draish, for all I have put you through. I don't understand how Malphina thought so little of you. I had to take on different personas just to keep my sanity," she pleaded.

Draish continued to avoid eye contact with her. "I only loved you and you lied to me. I have been deceived for centuries. You have forgotten because, much like Dracula, you created another failure, another monster." He dropped to his knees and didn't raise his head. He couldn't face her. The memories of centuries had driven him mad, but she… she looked fine.

"I don't know if I can accept this…" he mumbled.

She had thought about the past, and

how all the innocent blood spilled by both Dracula and Draish was all her doing. She created Vlad Dra'cul to restore a balance, and then she lost him to the darkness and his own will. She created Draish Jau-Ri to oppose the dark vampires that were now the army that Dracula had built. It seemed to be a never-ending circle of betrayal and lies. Draish didn't have any room to complain about what she failed to remember, because he had holes in his memory as well. A single mind cannot function properly to live so long. How much knowledge, pain, deceit, love, and hate could the mind store? If it was infinite, it caused the immortals to block certain events that only stories and dreams could relive for them.

Zaira was the cause and solution to Draish's death. Did she feel it was necessary to bring him back as an undead because she had ultimately cut his human life short?

"What do you think of me, now?" Myiako wondered, as she wiped her eyes with her dress sleeve.

"I think you're quite foolish for an immortal." He turned his head from his fixated gaze of the floor. "We are to learn from our past mistakes, not pretend that they don't happen." He spoke almost in monotone, as if his fire was burning out. "That is what separates us from beast, from humans."

"I have never known you to lose your passion or even think of yourself as the fool for not figuring me out. You had plenty of opportunity," she told him.

"You played me like a harp. Plucking the strings to see if I would break." He shook his head. "I give up now. Isn't that what you wanted? What do I have left to live for if not you?"

"I had never lost faith in you, Draish. That is why I would always find you and bring you back to life. You were always mine."

"Then when does it end?"

"It doesn't have to end. Happiness is never lasting. I found this as a human, and as an immortal," she told him in a soothing voice, much like that of Zaira. "It would take years to get it, but a few moments of happiness are worth an eternity in sorrow."

She got off the stone table and knelt down to him as close as she could, still being tethered to the altar. She wondered why he left her still shackled by the ankles. She felt the trust was gone.

"I always felt an undying love for you, as infinite as the immortality I know we now share." His expression became less solemn.

"OH, come on!" Dracula's voice broke in. "By now, I was hoping you would have taken this chance, Jau-Ri. Her blood is up for the taking and you are sitting there sulking about your love for her." Dracula laughed. "You have and vill always be a lesser vampire than I. This woman is your master and you, her slave!"

Draish quickly got to his feet and looked around for Dracula.

"Let's get this over with!"

Myiako retreated to the other side of the stone table as Draish stepped away from her.

"Tell me, Vlad, were you in love with Zaira?"

Dracula sighed, "I bet you still have so many questions that only I can answer. Don't be so rash. Perhaps we should talk more." They could hear the sarcasm in his voice.

"Just one more question," Draish looked into the shadows, "Why did you let me kill Scarlet?"

"Oh, my dear sister-in-law? It was her time to go; she pestered me for too long," Dracula said, still unseen. "Unlike you, I do not require lackeys."

The doors to the room swung open and in walked Torru with his hands bound and his armour gone. He had a dazed look on his face and his head dripped blood from a cut. Draish flexed his muscles and clenched his fist.

"I thought the Swordsman here would

like to witness your death." Dracula appeared behind Torru as he walked further into the round room. "This iz how your compassion iz your downfall. How could you be a powerful ruler when you care so much about others?"

Draish realized it was a mistake to leave Torru alone, but he had been thinking about himself.

"Only call your other minions if you want them dead." Dracula smiled. "I require no help, and neither should you."

"Where is Slayn? What have you done with him, Vlad?" Myiako demanded.

Draish's expression changed to glance in her direction. He shook his head 'no' at her.

"WHAT?" she exclaimed. "You killed my brother?" She got up and tried to get to the Count, but was jolted back by the chains.

"Catching on quickly now, dear? But it was not I." The King smiled. "At least Scarlet was good for something."

"Unchain me, Draish, so that I can fight him!" She tugged at her restrictions.

"I don't know why you have been stalling the inevitable." Draish looked back at Dracula. "This world cannot handle the both of us, so I suggest you leave it." His eyebrows furrowed and his voice deepened.

"Don't you talk down to me, boy. I have been here before you, and I'll be here after." He spoke intensely, but failed to make a move.

"Darkness shades your vision; I have more power than you know of," Draish told him, perhaps in a bluff.

"Then the light blinds yours!" Dracula caused the doors to slam shut. "A pity that you didn't free her when you had the chance, she could have helped you, and you need all the help you can get."

"Fight me now, Dra'cul!" Draish provoked.

"Noo!" screamed Myiako. "This is all my fault! Leave them out of it. I'm the one you want," she pleaded.

"You are correct, but the suffering of your friends is a greater gift to me than your death."

Dracula walked over to the adjacent wall. "Haven't you had enough, Draish? You really want to experience again what I did to you earlier? Or did you like being violated? Such a masochist." He now stood in front of a gear contraption that hung on the stone wall.

"Oh...shit," Draish mumbled after realizing what Dracula was up to. But before he could react, the lever was already pulled. The gears turned with a horrible screech.

Draish lunged at Dracula, only to catch air. Once again, the dark one had vanished and the room began to rumble. They all looked up as stone particles fell down. The round ceiling was covered with a metal device that started moving. The roof was folding in. The first shutter opened causing the bright day's light to pour in. The switch that Dracula activated caused the roof to open. Draish ran to the doors, only to be pushed back by a force Dracula emitted.

"I call this the sun room. So many lesser vampires have met their demise here, and now you're next!" His voice echoed, followed by laughter.

"I might die here, but you're still a coward for not ending me by your own hands!" Draish's growl echoed.

As the other side of the roof opened, Draish weakened and fell to his knees.

"But…he was always steps ahead of me…killing me by what I live to protect…the light," Draish's words became gasp.

As the sun came down on him, his skin started burning and smoldering. He dropped to all fours and coughed up blood.

"Oh, the irony. This is too easy," Dracula commented to Myiako, as he put on some sunglasses.

The light vampire's face became vein-ridden and his eyes red in agony.

"Remember me…for next time, Zaira,"

he gasped as his voice lost strength.

"Noooo! How could you? That's not even a fair match," Myiako cried.

Myiako and Torru could do nothing but watch their comrade fall down to his face and cringe in pain. His skin smoldered.

"Draish!" she screamed and with her words, energy grew. Blue flames resonated from her body and shot off into streams. This caused the shackles to shatter off. She ran over to him and ripped off her dress to reveal her corset and petticoat. She draped it over him to shade him as she knelt down beside him. His face was disfigured, burned and his mouth opened. She held his head on her lap and cried.

"Take my blood!" she pleaded, as she exposed her neck to his face.

Dracula laughed. "Your fleeting efforts. You can't save him now. Just wait maybe two to three hundred years from now.

She felt a response. His eyes rolled back in front to see the flesh taunting him. He tensed up and butted his face into her neck and his hand went up her back. Myiako gasped at the sudden but expected pain of his teeth. Draish's grip on her back tightened as he drank.

Dracula looked surprised. He had wasted too much time and it had become the day that she became vulnerable to vampires.

For the first time in all his years, Draish was able to drink the blood of his creator and not have it rejected by his body.

Lord Dra'cul appeared next to them and tried to grab her away, but this time he was forced back by a force emitted from Draish. He tried to advance again, but was pushed back by a collecting energy. Myiako started to become uncomfortable and tried to pull away. Draish sat up as her neck was still in his mouth. She had to kick him for him to get off her, and then scurried away from him.

Draish let the blood drip from his mouth, and then slowly got to his feet. His legs were shaky and his knees wobbled before he was standing with normal posture. Myiako noticed how he looked different somehow in the sunlight. His skin had a flesh tone. His eyes were a deep blue, almost glowing and his stare went right through Dracula. Draish squinted, not being use to such a light, he tried to look up at the sky, but couldn't. His skin was healed from the burns and he was radiating a white light. He was blinding to look at, even Dracula covered his eyes.

Draish peered at Dracula with an intense look as the white light crackled around him. It was like he had been resurrected again, before he had even died…

{XXIX}: The Powers Of Masters

The sunlight no longer affected the vampire of light. He stood tall, muscles tensed. He looked like he was feeling better than ever. He grinned, his teeth stained with Myiako's blood.

Myiako was confused. She held her neck with pressure. He took a lot of blood, but his bite wasn't deep enough to cause permanent damage. *Why did the King let him do that? He could have pulled me away a lot sooner.* She wondered as she looked at Draish in a new light. Torru had run over to her to see if she was alright.

"Nau rau la termina un veo!" Draish said before rushing to Dracula. His tattered cape flew behind him as well as an energy tracer. Dracula still moved faster and was suddenly standing on the stone table in the center of the room.

"Now those are her true powers." Dracula looked at Myiako, then to Draish who came at him again.

"Why didn't you finish her off, Jau-Ri? She still holds a power over you!" He sounded displeased.

Draish tackled Dracula and they came crashing to the ground. The white-haired one was able to pin him down, pushing his shoulders into the ground. This time Draish was the one sneering like an animal over his opponent.

"Vos e n'étions jamais digne d'être une terra tutrice," Draish said, as if Myiako couldn't understand, for it was a human language this time. He went on, explaining to the dark one. "Ca c'est tiens! Vous n'aviez pas de choix mais ont Étreint les ténèbres. Differ vous, J'ai à l'exception d'immortelle puissance." He continued speaking differently from normal. His voice was strange, deep, and heavy in accent.

Draish started clenching Dracula's neck with both hands and Dracula used his power to raise the both of them up to standing and shoved Draish away. Draish flew back and slid on his heels to stop the momentum. He then focused the white energy in front of him to gather in his palms. He shot out a glowing stream of energy that had decimated the stone table in its path. Luckily, Dracula had dodged the attack. Draish looked at his hands in wonderment as to where such a power had come from. He had never been able to do an attack with such magnitude as that.

His glowing energy aura was gone, for now.

"Watch Out!" called Myiako, seeing Dracula's on-coming move.

He ducked down just in time to avoid the boot coming at his head. The dark-haired one then followed through with a punch and a claw swipe. Draish was able to out maneuver him until he was caught off guard by a strange black energy escaping from his adversary. The claws came at him, striking him in the chest. Draish jumped back even faster than he normally would move. Four large gashes caused blood to drip and seeped into his shirt. He then observed Dracula, who was gaining an aura himself. Red and black flames burned from his body, delineating his armour. Smoky swirls broke from the flames and the air grew thick. His energy dimmed the sun-filled room. Draish looked both shocked and curious.

"Whatever is the matter?" Dracula smiled. "Have you never seen this trick? Darkness is where the real power lies." His smile became more twisted than usual. The dark vampire went on to chant. "Al dante' begi-guruns, la fira's nau dajines, avens veo'r superiorus mortary!"

Black streams of fire swam from his body that gradually formed into small serpent-like dragons that were headed for Draish.

Draish jumped back to avoid the first

snake, and then punched the next one that reached up to snap at him. He levitated up to be out of reach, only to come face-to-face with three more of the fiery dragon things. Two creatures grabbed his arms and the other wrapped around his neck as snakes would to constrict their prey.

Dracula had full control over his powers and looked pleased with his decision. The energy pulled Draish back down to the ground. Dra'cul ran over to Draish, his armour clanking with each step, as Draish tried to free his arms from the serpent bonds.

"What now, boy? Can your heavenly powers save you?" Dracula teased his arms still aflame with magik fire. "A vampire of light…she should have known that such a contradiction vould never vork…"

Draish found a solution to his dilemma by changing into his bat façade and was freed from the restraints. The smoke dragons fell, but before hitting the ground, seeped back into Dracula. He looked irritated of Draish's clever escape.

"Changing form takes a lot of energy, and ve already fight in daylight…an amateur mistake."

The bat flew up and Dracula attempted to hit him with an energy bolt projected from his hand. With a raised wing, Draish maneuvered around it. Another shot and this time it came crashing into the wall. The room shook enough to cause Myiako to lose her balance. Another bolt was shot, again missing its target to hit another wall. Parts of the stone structure crumbled off.

Draish realized that Dracula would hold nothing back and might destroy the room. Myiako and Torru may have further harm done to them if this continued. He flapped backwards, and then flew at Dracula gradually changing back into his man form to come at him with a boot. Dracula vanished to teleport behind Draish and swipe his claws at him. Draish dodged and countered with a punch. The King was actually hit in the face with a fist. He shook it off and growled to counter with more swipes with his long white claws. The white-haired vampire was able to avoid his enemy's claw advances until being cut in the face. Bloody nail marks dripped from his cheek and Draish ground his teeth to take it in.

Dra'cul drew back his arm as to punch, but instead formed his arm into a blade. He now had a black metal sword where his forearm was, and he smiled to see his opponent back off. He took this time to strike before Draish could think of a tactic around it.

Draish managed to duck around the

first swing, but the second caught him. He had blocked the blade from coming down on his head with his arm, which cut through to sever his left hand. Draish growled in pain and held his bleeding wrist as his hand fell to the ground and dissipated into dust. Myiako screamed.

Dracula looked surprised. "…In spite your face…I'm impressed." He then thrust the sword forward and Draish fell back to avoid it. The arm-sword came down at his head again. This time the black blade became locked with Draish's steel claw hand. He somehow was able to regenerate his left hand by summoning the power to form the bladed fingers that he had fought with before. The dark vampire still had the high ground, but was almost caught off his guard. Draish had used his other hand to hurl a magic sphere at Dracula, who had avoided the pre-emptive attack by flying backwards. Dracula kept his distance not knowing what this glowing blue sphere was going to do. Draish didn't just throw the energy, but he was able to control its direction. He stood back up as he manipulated the sphere. It paused in front of Dracula, who had put his sword across his body for defense. The energy slowly started to grow, and then suddenly it exploded. The room was filled with a white light that dimmed the sun.

Myiako huddled with Torru, who covered her for protection. His restraints had been unwound by her previously during the fight.

"This power is like nothing I've seen him use…" Torru commented.

The immense light had faded for the other two to see Draish standing over Dracula. The dark one was on his back, his arm-blade back to normal.

"Ipso facto…" started Draish. "By the very fact of balancing the powers, gives you control," he replied, as his voice and accent returned to normal. He looked down to Dracula, baring his fangs. "You even said that there is no good or evil, just shades of gray." Draish held his steel hand out and was forcing Dracula to stay on the ground. "It was within those shades of gray that I could find equilibrium."

"Vous underestimate me, Draish," Dracula said. "I am 100 years older than you and have stayed alive this entire time. You really are a fool if you think you can rid the vorld of me." With that said, he leaned up on his elbows as he started to resist the force put on him. "No matter how much power you get, you vill always be my inferior, never my successor." His eyes started glowing red and the black and red flames ignited him.

Draish stepped back as the flames were projected toward him. He tried to push it away, but soon he too was engulfed in a dark energy. Even though Draish had felt what this assault can do before; there was no way for him to avoid it.

"Ha, ha, ha!" laughed Dracula. "You know you can't circumvent this move, nor can you absorb it."

Draish growled when he started losing his balance. His metal hand melted back into flesh and he put his palms to his forehead. The pain looked uncontrollable in his mind and he backed away. The black energy exuberated from Dracula to Draish while the dark one stood back up and Draish fell to his knees.

"Face it," began Dracula, "You are an inferior vampire because of the humanity that resides vithin you!"

"No…Dra'cul…" Draish was breathing heavy, but remained calm. "I am not going to die so soon…not this time…"

"Vhat iz it that you are rambling?" Dracula replied. "Conversing means nothing vhen you're on your knees before me."

"I overestimated you…" The white-haired vampire rubbed his head. "For being the great Vlad Dra'cul, you're taking your precious time in destroying me. I'm beginning to think that you're enabled." His fists were now clenched, much like his teeth as he fought the dark flames.

"Even the best of us enjoy tormenting our inferiors." The dark one smiled. "Now, how am I suppose to know your full potential if I let you die so soon?" His smile was twisted and his demeanor relaxed.

Draish tried his best to remain calm despite the black flames shrouding him.

Myiako watched, her eyes now filling up with tears. "What's going on?" she asked quietly to Torru.

"He has been drained by this spell before," Torru told her.

They had hopes that Draish still had power in him to break through the spell, because there was really nothing that they could do. What was the use of being guardians when they couldn't even protect their leader? Draish went from his knees down to sitting. He crossed his legs and started a deep concentration. He closed his eyes and his aura started to radiate again. The white energy started pushing at the dark, but this proved a difficult feat for Draish. Even though he had newly acquired immunities to the sunlight, prolonged exposure wasn't healthy for any vampire or undead alike. The inner light energy was summoned slowly, but surely and Dracula was angered again.

"Vhat are you doing?!" his voice boomed.

Draish then neutralized Dracula's power. The dark flames drew back into Dracula as did Draish's light. He rose back to his feet and did not hesitate to make his move. He charged at Dracula, who was too exhausted to vanish this time. His fist went into an uppercut into Dracula's chest plate, which cracked under pressure and through into his torso. The dark-haired one spat out blood onto Draish's arm as Draish buried his hand deeper into his chest. Dracula grabbed the impaling arm with both hands and smirked at Draish through his own blood on his teeth. He started pulling Draish toward him.

"You ruined my best armour," spit Dracula, with the arm halfway into his body. He laughed as his body started healing around the intruder.

Then from out of his body came those weird smoke serpents that wrapped around Draish's shoulder, and then his neck. Their mouths bit at his face as Draish tried to pull his arm away. Dracula put his claws around Draish's neck and the magik snake-sized dragons slithered down his arms and aided his strangle. As Draish started being choked, he raised his boot up under his stuck arm and pushed off of Dracula's chest until his arm was freed from his chest. It appeared as if Dracula's blood had injured his arm; it was like acid seeping though his shirtsleeve, melting to his flesh. Dracula kept a hold of Draish's neck and proceeded to lift him off his feet. Draish clawed at the strangling hands and gasped for air…

{XXX}: Banish Thee In The Name Of Light

His nails dug into Draish's neck as the magik snakes made it possible for him to have exponential strength. Draish grabbed Dracula's forearms and tried to loosen their grip. The serpents migrated onto his arms now and their powers were draining him.

"How much longer can you keep this up?" the King of Undead spoke through clenched teeth, as if he was asking this to himself. He then pushed harder to break the skin on his adversary's neck. Blood dripped down and the smoke-like snakes started feeding on it.

Myiako was crying again as Torru tried to comfort her. She knew she was not to interfere again, not wanting to disgrace Draish's pride even if it meant his death.

"If I get no response from you..." Dracula looked up at Draish. "I'll just end you here and now," he said, as if he wanted Draish to fight him longer, as if he wanted to see Draish make a comeback.

Dracula let one hand off and drew back his arm to form it into a sword again. It was jabbed through Draish's chest and out his back. He withdrew the blade just to stick him again. This time Myiako screamed, perhaps because Draish couldn't. The sword was withdrawn and the blade formed back into an arm.

Dra'cul let go of Draish's neck and let him fall onto the floor. His neck was punctured, and there were two holes in his chest where blood oozed out. A pool of red liquid formed around him.

"You must be joking..." Dracula looked down at the white-haired man, who was barely moving and lying on his side.

Draish was too weak to recover his wounds, and the snakes continued to feed off his energy as they trickled down from Dracula. The dark one looked more displeased than content. He looked down, still waiting for a response.

A heavy wind then picked up, and a gust blew in from the opened ceiling. Dra'cul's cape bellowed from the sudden wind. A loud clanking was heard. Dracula looked to see what it was; it being the sound of the gear mechanism of the roof operation device. He looked back down to Draish. He was gone, just leaving the partial body imprint in the puddle of blood. The roof shutter closed, leaving them in darkness. The wind had blown out the torchlights and Myiako and Torru couldn't see a thing.

Dracula looked around for Draish. His aura had resided back into his body and the serpents were gone.

"Vhat are you going to do, boy?" He looked from side to side. "You have lost your blood and I dare you to drink from one of your friends…"

Myiako couldn't see but Dracula made his position apparent. There was a silent pause until he spoke to the darkness again. "Give yourself up or face further humiliations, because this time I'll cut you limb from limb."

"All bark and no bite…" It was Draish, his voice in its usual tone. A location couldn't be acquired due to a strange echo.

"Don't you make me laugh, Jau-Ri. You know you can't keep hiding. The darkness can't save you as it does for me." Dracula went in the direction where he sensed Draish.

"Behind you," Draish told him. Dracula turned to see Draish a few yards away. Even though his clothes and armour were in ruins, there were no recent wounds on his body. Draish brushed back his hair from his eyes and smiled. "Now, you are starting to bore me," Draish said. "So, are you going to kill me or not?"

Dracula gave an un-amused laugh. "Vhat have I told you about talking down to me? I am actually royalty, unlike you, Sir Knight."

"I do not talk down to you as an elder, nor was I belittling you. Vlad Dra'cul, can you fathom that I am merely trying to confront you not as an enemy, but as a fellow vampire, as a peer that understands the demented reasoning that faces us each night," Draish explained.

Myi and Torru could hear them, but not see them as clearly as the vampires could see each other. *What is he up to? I know he's a strange one, but what's he doing?* Myiako thought.

"Have not ve been through this?" Dracula sighed. "I must admit you lasted longer than I vould have thought, but you are past the point of talking your way out of our predicament."

"You realize that I will always be back, no matter what you do to me," Draish told him.

"I know, and it pains me that you are as immortal as I, because you vere created in the same vay." Dracula looked at his bloody fingertips. "But for now, I can take your power to grow my own. I can rid myself of your pathetic attempts for another century or so..."

Draish shifted his weight to the other leg. "I'll give myself up if you let them go without doing any harm to them." He referred to Myi and Torru.

"Oh, how grotesquely touching. Your heroics are ephemeral when you make a deal with a devil. Who's to say that I vould keep that deal?" Dracula's aggravation began to rise again.

Myiako screamed as someone grabbed her. Torru was pushed aside and he stayed back. It was Draish who appeared behind her, not Dracula. He pulled her close to his chest when Dracula appeared right in front of them.

"You see..." started Draish. "I read it in your mind that you were about to grab her. You wanted her blood..."

"Nonsense! Vous can't read me!" Vlad protested.

"Is that what you think? I have had you inside me...in my mind. Do you really believe that I didn't take a part of you with me?" Draish countered, continuing to hold Myiako.

"You lost your chance with me lifetimes ago!" Myiako pulled back to peer at Dracula. She could only see the vampire's glowing eyes in the darkness.

"Why vould I want to be like Draish? Foolish girl!" Dracula sneered. "You are just a meek little child, but not to mention a cursed immortal with your necromancy jurisdiction. You might as well just give up, Zaira...or whomever you claim to be!" he growled at her, and then looked back to Draish whose eyes had been fixed on the drying blood on Myiako's neck. Dracula smiled to notice the look on Draish's face.

"You should just kill her before I do, then maybe ve can be the peers as you spoke of moments ago." Dracula tried his influence over Draish once again.

Myiako looked back to Draish. "No!" she told him. "You don't listen to him, you listen to me!" she ordered Draish, sounding as she did as Malphina. She turned her glance to Dracula. "And you step down!"

Dracula responded with a laugh and tried to grab her, but both Myi and Draish were no longer there. Myiako was standing on the other side of the room and Draish was standing guard in front of her.

"Finish this, Draish," she told him.

Draish raised his arms up and the torches on the walls lit back up, he wanted her to see what was happening. Or was it that she wanted him to do so?

Then the platinum-haired man stepped away from her and walked back toward the King. His tattered cape flowed behind him and his boot soles firmly lifted and went down with each step to echo within the walls.

"I know an old one such as you must be

weary of living…this is it, Vlad," Draish spoke confidently because of her reassurance. Draish looked less than formidable though, his shirt was ripped up, exposing his chest muscles, he had only one arm gauntlet, and his loin tunic and pants were stained with fresh blood soaked down to his boots.

Dracula turned to face him, his only discrepancy being the hand-size hole in his chest plate.

"You know…" Draish tilted his head as he spoke. "I'm beginning to think that you want me to kill you."

"Vhat do you place that kind of reasoning upon?" Dracula wondered.

"Then kill me, Dra'cul! Destroy these earth guardians that stand in your way. What are you waiting for?"

"It seems that you are the one so eager to die." Dracula shook his head.

"Maybe we should be all fervent to see death, so that this will end once and for all. We can leave this world to the humans not fearing us un-holy creatures." Draish smirked at Dracula.

The dark one charged at him to be locked hand to hand in a strength struggle as if a test of will. They pushed and were in a deadlock of sorts, palms and fingers locked.

"Feel the purity of my might. I have

sought atonement…have you?" Draish taunted.

Draish projected his aura and Dracula's hands started to smolder. He could no longer endure and he let go. Dracula slid back from force on his feet and looked at his hands. His hands were scorched, but he hid his pain.

"You vere lucky this time…" Dracula spoke through clenched teeth. "You had them all on your side…but…but you are one short." He smiled.

Draish didn't know how to respond. He had never got to this point before.

"You needed all the guardians to seal him away, Draish." Myiako broke in. "Without the Time Lord we cannot accomplish the banishing seal." She had a hint of hopelessness in her voice.

"What are you talking about?" Draish looked questioningly at her.

Dracula lunged at him, but was deflected by an invisible field of energy that surrounded the light one. Dracula then reared back and laughed. "I do not die…and maybe I vant to know vhat it feels like. There is nothing you can do for either of us."

A strange desperation came from Dracula. *Had he became insane from living and remembering everything?* Draish raised a brow at the thought.

Myiako...Zaira, on the other hand, had made herself forget lifetimes in order not to undertake the gravity of memories. While Draish was actually the youngest of the three, he had seen many eras of time, but had also slept in purgatory for centuries. Now it was time for Vlad Dra'cul to feel the solitude of sleep, but could this be achieved without all four of the light guardians?

Dracula came at Draish again and this time Draish grabbed his arm at the wrist and pushed the white energy to subdue him from struggling.

The light vampire then chanted, "Pryvante' guruns un-lumi ve la rau aven'g veo'n mortary...Dayan dur veo'r merunaus seca al dant!"

A bright blue light exploded out of Draish and blasted through Dracula. The light engulfed his body and poured out his mouth and eyes as if the light was drowning the dark vampire. The Count yelled in agony for the first time that they had heard,—a desperate sound that would even make the living's blood pump cold. He vanished in a flash of light with his scream still echoing. Their eyes squinted from the immense light, and then all three exchanged glances.

Dracula was gone. His presence was no more.

Draish fell to the ground in exhaustion, his chest heaved to catch his breath.

"Is it over?" wondered Torru.

"What just happened?" asked Myiako. "I thought you weren't able to banish him if all of us weren't here."

"This..." Draish panted. "Is only... temporary....I reduced him to nothing but energy...and when he reforms he will resent me more than ever." He was now laying on his back.

"We have time now..."

"Well..." Myiako said. "Let's get the hell outta here."

"I'm too tired to move..." Draish told them.

"Then we'll have to drag you." Myi smiled. "We could all use some sleep."

{XXXI}: Will Love Live On

The view was lovely from the castle top. The bluest sky met the lush green hillside. She leaned over a stone rampart to look over the side, down onto the moat below. Someone watched her from the balcony's doorway as her long blonde hair and green dress blew in the wind. She turned around to notice him.

"May I help you, Sir Knight?" Zaira asked.

"No, my lady," the young man bowed to her. "I just enjoy coming to this ledge as well." Draish smiled a human smile.

"Well, do not be shy, come on outside," she told him.

He stepped from the doorway to stand rather far from her at the ledge.

"For all my service to my lady…." he began, "I do not recall that we have ever met."

"I'm sure we have not," she said. "I would remember a face such as yours. So tell me, who might you be?"

He blushed and responded, "I am Sir Draish Jau-Ri, captain of the Calvary. Nice of you to have a word with me."

She just smiled at him and returned her

glance to the hills in the horizon.

"Why is it that you like coming out here?" she asked.

He hesitated, and then said, "To think, mostly. And this is the side of thine castle that faces the sunset." He paused not wanting to be too talkative.

"It's alright; I do a lot of thinking out here myself. Like if I am doing the right thing or not," she confessed.

He didn't know how to respond. "What does thou mean?" he then asked.

She turned her head again to face him. "You should always follow your heart."

"Why are you telling me this?"

"You must know, Sir Knight, that us meeting here was no mistake." She stepped toward him.

His jaw almost dropped and he remained speechless.

"Aren't you rather young to be a knight, and a captain no less?" She got closer to him.

"I guess so…I did not know there was an age requirement." He kept his hands on the rampart's surface.

"You remind me of someone…but I can't quite say who," Zaira told him.

He averted his eyes from her glance to focus on her necklace.

"That green stone…what is it? Malachite?" he asked her.

"I'm not sure," she responded. "I have always had it."

He looked away. "There is something ominous about it…" he said quietly.

"What? My necklace?" She grasped the stone.

"It is nothing…forgive me, my lady. I should go. I have over welcomed my stay." He looked down.

"You will see me again then, at this time tomorrow," she demanded more than asked him, as she flicked her hair to the side.

"Yes," he simply replied, then bowed very low to her.

Before he went back inside their eyes met again, and like a portrait, they would always remember every detail of one another.

Draish as a human was already unnaturally handsome, as he was always told so. He was tall and with broad shoulders, high cheekbones, long nose, a perfectly symmetrical face. His hair was always platinum and his skin flawless. Those immensely grey-blue eyes would dig into her soul.

Zaira was a living goddess among humans, at least to Draish she was. Her golden locks, unruly in the wind, the long dark lashes around her emerald eyes. Her lips were lush, long legs, and her physique shapely and pleasing.

They would never get past the physical attraction, no matter how much they had in common or not. From that day forth their relationship prospered. She could remember it like it was yesterday. That day at sunset, the first time they met, was the beginning of an eternity.

03◆80

She slept seated in a canvas chair. The bright setting of the sun pierced her eyes through the tent flap. She looked similar to Myiako and dressed much the same; tan cargo shorts and a white tee shirt. Her long brown hair was stuffed under a brimmed hat.

"Come look what we've found, miss." A young woman popped her head into the tent. She had braids and freckles and was dressed almost the same as Myiako. She then went back to the outside area.

Myiako got out of the low sitting chair and folded the tent door back to exit. She looked around the flat savannah landscape. The woman with the braids waved for her to come to where she was. The ground was littered with tools, hammers and pickaxes, buckets, and brushes.

"You were right about starting

excavation in this area," the woman told her, as Myiako walked up to the stringed off area she stood in, amongst the many stringed off squares at the archaeological site.

"We cannot seem to identify this one… it looks ancient," the woman added as she knelt down next to a laptop computer. On the screen were symbols of ancient pictographs and writings.

Myiako looked down to the part of the dusted artifact. It was a familiar-looking sarcophagus with an encrypted writing all over it.

Another woman and a man dressed in cargo shorts were busy dusting off the coffin and slowly breaking away the soil to further uncover it.

Myiako's eyes went wide. "It must be time again," she said softly.

"Excuse me, miss. What did you say?"

"You'll find out," Myiako reassured her. She then knelt down to the stone.

"I don't even remember what happened last time…" she said. *Do I want to remember?*

The young woman looked away from the computer screen to look at Myiako with a confused expression. "Are you ok, Dr. Oaiku?"

"I will be," she replied and smiled.

"Maybe you have had too much sun today," the woman told her.

"Perhaps we have all had too much sun in our lives." Myiako smiled strangely at her.

"Do not fear the events that will unfold today," she spoke loudly to those around her. "None of you fear!"

"What has gotten into the doctor?" She heard whispers from her peers.

Myiako reached for a crow bar and knelt back down to the half-buried crypt. She began frantically chipping away at the dirt that covered the opening. Once reaching the cleavage point of the coffin lid, she stuck the crow bar in.

The others watched in amazement, not wanting to interfere with the strange trance that their proprietor was in. Myiako, or whatever she went by now, opened the lid to the old sarcophagus. After the cloud of dust cleared, they all looked down at the skeleton. The skull had been misplaced and was intertwined with its rib cage. She leaned over to pick it up, and then dusted off the skull. They saw its teeth, fangs intact.

"My Lord…" Myiako exclaimed, "My Lord, Draish Jau-Ri!"

The other archeologists backed away with uncertainty.

She began chanting: 'Dur kadama al-la rula un-la null- ull ante'n ve Avat un lumi. Tea'- al-la-rula!"